SHEER
BLUE BLISS

LESLEY GLAISTER

BLOOMSBURY

To Joe, wishing you luck
and love on your adventures

First published 1999

This paperback edition published by Bloomsbury Publishing Plc 2003

Copyright © Lesley Glaister 1999

The moral right of the author has been asserted

Bloomsbury Publishing Plc, 38 Soho Square, London W1D 3HB

A CIP catalogue record for this book is available from the British Library

ISBN 0 7475 4420 4

10 9 8 7 6 5 4 3 2 1

Typeset by Hewer Text Ltd, Edinburgh
Printed in England by Clays Limited, St Ives plc

PART 1

LONDON

ONE

The effect of the elixir entering the bloodstream is swift.
The sensation is of lifting and lightening. Ordinary objects
may appear luminous with significance. Haloes are common.

Tony closes his eyes and squeezes, trying to imagine how it
would be. Sees a sprinkle of bursting lights or a spray like
thin petals. Opens his eyes. No significance in the ordinary
objects here, not a halo in sight, though he can see a glow of
sun on dusty leaves outside the window. Significance
though? Tried magic mushrooms only once, put off by
the taste and the weird slithery nauseous feelings they gave
him – followed by the shits. And anyway, he doesn't need
drugs, Tony, likes to stay in control. World strange enough
without, doesn't need artificial strange. But the elixirs, the
elixirs would be something different. If they exist he will have
them. That is his reason and his purpose.

He rises from his cushion on the floor, presses his forehead
against the window. Light on leaves and below on cars and
below that the road with its milk-cartons, fag packets, dog
turds. The community centre with its wire-mesh windows
throws a bulky shadow in which two Rastas in gaudy hats
are joking. A head thrown back, glint of gold tooth, spike of
laughter. Tony moves back, runs his finger thoughtfully
through the greasy oval his forehead has printed on the glass.

The day bellows out there, laughter and light and the sound of traffic. Now the regular tin-can clang of the town-hall clock. He counts to three. Afternoon full on. Needs some stuff to eat, some carbon monoxide in his lungs. Ha. Pulls on jeans and a shirt, white shirt, all buttons intact. *Clean*. Sniffs the cotton. Nothing like the smell of clean cotton. Won't have polyester or even a mix, though Donna always says that's easier. No, one hundred per cent pure cotton, white, and he pays for his shirts and sheets to be laundered. Likes starch, the smell of it, the feel of it in the creases of his elbows when he bends his arms. It's a specialist job, starching shirts and sheets, not done much now in these polyester days, not commonly done for your common person which Tony is, no way, not.

He likes tidiness, to be tidy – and clean. You know where you are if you're tidy, what's what. Now the bed, that's most important. He makes the bed each morning in a special way. Pillows beaten to aerate the feathers, sheet swept and swept with the side of his hand to rid it of any flakes of skin or hairs. Top sheet whipped through the air and allowed to float down, blinding, airy white. Sometimes as it settles he has to blink against the outline of a child waiting, breathless with the gasp of air the sheet brings down, for the cool weight of fresh cotton on his limbs. Hospital corners, blankets and a proper bedspread, deep green chenille. Doesn't believe in duvets. Tony likes the weight and tightness of the tucked-in blankets, likes the bed-making ritual, possibly the only male of his generation who prefers blankets to duvets. Likes that thought. Gets a charge from the flat tucked-in shape, the rectangle of white sheet turned down over the green. Loves squeezing alone into the tight, cold, starched place at night. Will not put a thing on the bed. Will absolutely not sit on the bed during the day. If it *was* sat on, if anyone, say, was to come in the flat and sit on the bed, he would have to strip it off and make it all over again. Not that he's obsessive, he's read about obsessive compulsive behaviour, it's not that. It's just that it would spoil the moment of going to bed for him. And that's harmless, isn't it?

Outside is warm, warmer than the flat, the tired stewed heat of the end of summer rising from the pavement, soaking out of brickwork. He wanders down the shrieking street. Bouquets of skinny chickens hang by their rubbery feet, eyes skimmed white, little heads loose. Raucous peppers, plantains, hairy root things, yams, sweet potatoes and everywhere teeth flashing, the blare of bright cloth, smiles, sharp blades of light on chrome, hooting, the overhead rumble of a train. Wet meat smell, spice, pig's foot in gutter, pineapple and reggae, reggae, reggae from speakers in the street, from shops, from open windows. God on a megaphone. *Beware, beware.*

Milk and bread are what he needs, jam, tobacco. Thinking about cooking – fish in coconut milk. Yes? Buys the stuff and a paper, too, and walks a bit, sits in front of the Ritzy, bench scratched and sprayed, watches for a minute the gentle bob of McDonald's boxes in the fountain. Lets his head drop back, stretching his throat tight in the sun so it's hard to swallow, sun hot on his Adam's apple. The weight of that head . . . awesome, the task of balancing it on the neck. Thinks of these things, Tony, he is a thinker. His long black hair hangs down behind him. He can feel the softness of it, each strand, beautiful hair when washed, they say every one of them when they get their hands on it, Apache hair, one said, once. Squirms at the memory of a girl with her hands in his hair, her voice in his ear, shocked at the strong stir in his groin.

Change the subject. Opens the *Standard*. What? The usual: murder, rape, corruption, pollution. A recipe for courgette tian – might be worth a try. Some beauty guff – Autumn Eyes. Huh. And then, turning the page his heart stops, actually stops then starts again stuttering like an old engine before it finds its rhythm. Because there *he* is, staring up at Tony. There he is: Patrick.

TWO

At first the sound of the engine is indistinguishable from the sigh of the sea. But it grows louder. Definitely an approaching car. Oh hell – and did she really say lunch? Connie stands behind the door, nails in her palms, listening to the grate and scutter of shingle, the slam of doors, the sudden voices. She cannot know how she will be with these.

The gate brays open and the voices come along the path. First a young woman's. 'What a completely brilliant place.'

'The air – what a blast, eh?' This a man. 'Wonder what's on the menu?'

'Don't you think of anything except your gut?'

'Light's just amazing.'

'Gonna knock?'

A ratatatat and Connie tries to smile before her hand reaches out. There's a sort of gargoyle stretch in her cheeks. Won't do. Then her hand goes to the door and a smile comes to her, a real one. Their eyes move down simultaneously. How tall did they think she'd be?

'How do you do.' A young man with shoulders, she does like shoulders, Connie, and a big warm handshake that makes her hand feel like twigs. 'Jason.' She stands back to let the pair of them in. A long time since there's been a man in her kitchen.

'Miss Benson,' the young woman says. What rosy cheeks!

'Connie, please.'

'I'm Lisa. I've been so looking forward to meeting you.'

'Nice of you to say.'

Connie, who has been dreading this invasion, finds it's actually rather nice to have company. All this young breath in her kitchen along with perfume and the snazzy smell of a new leather bag.

'Interesting place.' Jason has his eyes narrowed, as photographers do, judging, judging, her square red table and the sea-shells stuck on all the walls and the window frames. In a jug on the table are wild flowers Connie found this morning among the scrub of sandy soil: sea-pinks, thrift, feathery grasses and one harebell, blue as – itself.

'It's a prefab,' Connie says. 'Only meant to be temporary, after the war, you know. But look how it's stood up.' She stamps her foot and the room lurches. 'All the rest of them went to ruin years ago, years and years.' She tries to remember how many but it seems like for ever she's been alone behind the sand-dunes. Seems impossible that there ever were neighbours.

She catches Jason's eyes on the cooker. Nothing bubbling, no cooking smells. She feels ashamed remembering. You have to feed a man. She takes a bottle of whisky from the draining board and luckily there are three glasses.

'Drink?'

'Driving,' Jason eyes the bottle regretfully.

'Just a small one?'

'Go on then.' He grins. He is a looker all right. Connie glances at the fluff-haired Lisa and wonders if she fancies him, if there's anything going on. But no, there's not the chemistry there.

'Lisa? I expect you're both hungry?' Connie pours the drinks and twists her fingers together behind her back but they say yes, rather, the sea air and all. She opens the cupboard and reaches up. There are a few tins, some rice.

'You like rice?' She takes out a carton of rice and a bare silver tin. 'The snails eat the labels off,' she explains, sloshing it close to her ear. Something wet.

'What do you think?' she asks, tossing the tin to Lisa, who, though taken by surprise, catches it very niftily. There is a sideways glance between the two of them, a twitch. Well, Connie can play up to that. Eccentric? What else would she be?

'Beans?' Lisa hazards. 'Tomatoes? Peaches?'

'We'll take pot luck, shall we?' Connie reaches for the can opener. 'It won't be peaches,' she reassures them.

Connie cooks the rice while the whisky goes down well and fast. The tin turns out to contain spaghetti hoops which, mixed with rice and sardines, makes a surprisingly respectable concoction. She sags with relief when she tastes it, never mind the squashed-down grins on Jason and Lisa's faces. She hasn't entertained for some time. Anyone who knows her knows to bring their own provisions. These two had her rattled for a minute there, but all is well.

Connie doesn't bother much with food as a rule, lives on tea, tobacco, Fisherman's Friends, a sausage now and then if she can be bothered to cycle to the Spa shop in the village. Spirits she likes and salted things in packets, anything like that, nuts, crisps, Bombay Mix, all yellow with those crunchy neon peas.

'I'm really excited about your retrospective,' Lisa says. 'Does it feel odd . . . so much attention after all the years . . .' she tails off, maybe wondering if she's offended but she hasn't offended. Connie revelling in the chat and the whisky, watching Lisa's cheeks get redder and redder, like watching a fruit grow ripe and shiny tight. And talking of fruit, Connie has to wonder about Jason who, with the whisky in him, seems to have a suspicion of the homo about him, a touch of the camp in his gestures, the giggle with his fingers to his lips, the hyperbole and eyes frequently flung up to heaven. And that is fine with Connie who likes queers very much, far better at gossip – at least they always used to be.

Connie leaves the table to climb up the ladder to fetch her pipe from the studio. She pauses for a moment in the hot slick of syrupy light to look at Patrick. The carriers are coming for him tomorrow, to take and hang him in the NPG along with her other portraits but he, Patrick, will be the star of the show.

She picks up her pipe, tamps and lights it, listening to the two downstairs laughing. She sucks on the pipe, ivory-stemmed, carved-bone hands, angel-baby hands clutch the little bowl. A present from Patrick. Sweet cool smoke fills her mouth and dances in her eyes and Patrick winks.

It started as a joke, her pipe-smoking. She used to light his pipe for him sometimes, liked to suck where his lips had been. He bought her a pipe of her own and the joke became a habit. The throaty gurgle and the warming of the bone fingers can bring him closer to her now.

She goes down and they exclaim about the pipe which she rarely smokes at lunchtime or in public. With the whisky in her veins Connie doesn't care. She plays up to them, demonstrating a tap-dance that makes the window-glass rattle in its putty; saying scandalous things about the dead and gone, and telling them in a hot and breathy voice what a demon of a lover Patrick was right up to the very moment that he went.

'I haven't been naked since 1965,' she says and leaves them speechless. 'Since Patrick,' she explains.

'It's so romantic,' Lisa says after a pause. 'And is it true that you haven't painted again either . . . not for over thirty years . . .'

'Not since Patrick.'

Lisa shakes her head admiringly but Connie feels a pang, hearing it said like that by this fresh-faced girl. *Nothing* for over thirty years.

Jason unpacks his camera clutter, big white parasols and such, and Lisa offers to wash the dishes. 'Thank you, dear. You'll have to boil a kettle first.' Connie has to hide her smile at the falling face, poor girl hardly expected her to accept.

'OK,' Jason says. 'We better get on before the light goes.' He opens the door and stands back squinting round the kitchen through a wedge of sunny dust.

'I do like the shells.' Lisa strokes her finger over a dusty cockle shell stuck above the sink. 'Did you stick them all on yourself?'

'Not this room,' Connie says. 'Upstairs.'

'But . . .'

'Up the ladder.'

'Surely not a room up there – there can't be the roof-space.'

'You come and look.' Connie climbs the ladder again. 'Patrick did it. We were warned, not the structural strength and whatsit but here it is.' She stands in the room and Jason pokes his head up through the trap-door blinking in the blatant light that floods through the skylights.

'Amazing,' he says. 'I am amazed.'

'It's all right for me,' Connie says, 'but Patrick couldn't stand up in it. Used to crouch like a monkey, knuckles practically grazing the floor.'

'But what fun . . . and the little chair . . .' Jason looks at the child-sized yellow chintz armchair that sits in the middle of the floor. He pauses as Patrick's gaze snares his. 'And this is the portrait that all the fuss is about? Extraordinary. Lisa, you must come up and see *the* portrait.'

'In a mo,' Lisa calls through her dish-pan clatter.

Connie feels a tug inside her, a yank of memory. Remembering the love that was made in this room, light frank on naked skin. Oh there really is something about those eyes, only pigment on canvas, which she put there herself for God's sake, not quite brown, not quite hazel. They meet her own eyes. A little smirk? How Patrick would have loved these two. Such a palaver for a Sunday article about her home. As if anyone cares tuppence.

'What's it like?' Lisa calls.

'Fantastic.' Jason narrows his eyes again, looking round, searching for an angle. Jason and his camera, halved by the trap-door, bleached by the hot September light.

He backs down the ladder to get his equipment. Connie puts the kettle on again for tea. With her tongue she fidgets a bit of sardine out from under her plate and sits watching Lisa at the sink. The shape of her knickers shows through her thin white trousers, lovely little bottom, neat. How Patrick's fingers would have twitched.

Tomorrow a carrier will come for Patrick. And then she'll follow. The thought of returning to London after more than thirty years: of hotels and restaurants, of gallery chat, traffic, lipstick, teeth, suits, chatter, chatter, chatter . . . she has to close her eyes. And she must get round to dyeing her hair, the white stripe just will not do. Quite a buzz, Deborah said, Deborah the new agent. Someone somewhere unearthed Connie and to her surprise she feels like it, being unearthed. It's Patrick's portrait that will be the star of the show though, the unknown quantity. Her tongue buzzes against her plastic palate. Upstairs the floor creaks under Jason's feet like an obscure memory.

THREE

Tony blinks against the dazzle of newsprint in the sun. Poor grey speckled reproduction but it is Patrick all right, Patrick very different, beardless, young. *What?* The portrait painted by Constance Benson and never before seen. Although he looks so different, Tony recognises Patrick as if there's some sort of imprint on his heart. Not that he could ever have seen Patrick, who disappeared on the day of Tony's birth: 5th July 1965. But he has photographs, paintings – reproductions of – he has articles and Patrick's memoir, everything Patrick was ever known to write. In Patrick's memoir is a description, never completed, of the Seven Steps to Bliss. Which Tony wants and means to get. And will because Patrick has got inside him somehow, like a guiding spirit, that's it, guiding him on his quest for the elixirs. It's been a waiting game, since he stepped out of jail – price paid, slate clean – till now.

A retrospective exhibition of the work of Constance Benson opens this weekend at the National Portrait Gallery. Benson, controversial portraitist and lover of the late eccentric visionary Patrick Mount, will allow to be shown her last portrait of Mount which she has kept under wraps for the thirty years since his mysterious disappearance.

Careful not to crease the photograph. Tony folds the paper and walks home. Constance Benson, lover. He's surprised, more than surprised, jolted. Constance Benson alive and in London. Somehow he's supposed her dead, or faded anyway from the picture. Feelings fidget within him but he holds them down. It's good, Tony. Get to Benson and take the elixirs. Which she must have if anyone does. If not. No, not possible. Don't even think that, because then? No, think positive. Patrick is leading him and he only has to trust. So, this is it then, this is the start of it. He is on the trail.

He grins at himself in a window, cool customer with his long black hair, white shirt softened by the sun and his body heat, but still a stunning white. Puts his nose down to his shoulder and breathes the warmth of himself, the fizzy yeast smell of clean sweat and starch. Girls look at him as he walks, girls and boys. He exaggerates the swing of his skinny hips. Thirty, could pass for twenty-one easy, could fuck practically anyone on this street if he felt so inclined, anyone would. So magnetic, so charismatic. He has that special, indefinable something that nobody can deny.

Holds his breath entering the front door of the flats, steps over a pile of unclaimed post, legs it up the stairs the no man's land no one cares enough to clean, air dry and teeming with dust-mites, takes the stairs two or three at a time and is inside his door before he exhales. Leans back against it, safe. Donna's TV on next door. OK. Cool.

First, cut out portrait and article. Think later. Next drink milk from white mug. Next, roll fag. Light up, breathe in. Ah yes, smoke hot and clean. Queen Queen Nicotine.

And then the rap rap rap of Donna's knuckles, must have heard him on the stairs, the door's bang. Roll-up pinched in the corner of his mouth he opens the door.

'Well, I'm off.'

'Right.'

She stands as if waiting for something. What? Hair is pulled back from her sallow face so tightly that her eyes look slanted. The only bright thing about her is the flash of her red glass ear-rings. Looks dressed for a frigging funeral otherwise.

'So, aren't you going to say good luck?'

'Sure . . . good luck.'

'And you'll water my plants and that. Got the key?'

'Sure, oh yes, best of luck.' It comes back to him, something medical, gynaecological, some operation.

'Nervous as hell!' She laughs and holds out her hand to demonstrate the tremble.

'You'll be fine. Hey, look at this.' He steps back and picks up the cutting. 'Recognise anyone?'

She peers, frowns, shakes her head.

'It's him, Patrick.'

'Oh . . . great.' She smiles. Light through a glass ear-ring makes a floating red stain on the skin of her neck.

'You'll be fine. Don't worry.'

'Long as I feel better after. Come and see me?'

'Maybe.'

'Ha ha ha. See you, Tony.'

'See you.' He nearly calls good luck again, doesn't, shuts the door. Isn't it the surgeon who needs the luck, the steady hand? He goes to the window and watches her emerge below him in the street. She moves well, Donna. She's plain close up, nothing special, nothing striking, but watch her walking and you can see she's got . . . some quality, walks like a dancer, small head erect, walks from the hips, her centre. Where the surgeon will put his knife. Ugh. Hates that women's stuff. Withdraws squeamishly from the window.

He catches Patrick's eye. Must get to that exhibition and

see that portrait. Constance Benson, the lover. Must get to
her. This is it, what he has been waiting for, living this
waiting life for. With the scrap of paper in his hand he
knows, it's like the right key fitting a lock. You have to be
aware, alert. And Tony is. She'll recognise him all right,
recognise that Patrick has guided him to her, that he is the
one she can trust with the elixirs, the one Patrick meant them
for.

And then? But there is no need to think about and then.
Because it will be plain after that. Plain sailing.

FOUR

Evacuation. First it was just a word at breakfast time, a word among many others, scarcely registered. Mother, Father and Alfie all eating their sausages, Alfie talking and talking and being asked please *not* to do so with his mouth full while Connie watched the light dance on the cut-glass sugar bowl. Connie tended to be dozy in the morning, a night owl, Mother said, while Alfie was always up with the lark. White milk in a green tinted glass, a minty colour or pistachio like ice-cream at a party once – *pistachio*, made her think of long curly moustaches though it's a kind of nut which Connie had never seen. But still, the milk tasting thick and cowish so she had to swallow quick without breathing. She hated milk but children must drink it. She was fourteen and hardly a child, yet there was the tall green glass of milk by her plate each morning.

War. That word made her sit up straight, made her skin prickle with fearful pleasure. Alfie was full of it, of course, with his toy soldiers and his drawings of cannons and guns. *We are at war*, Father declared solemnly one morning and Connie flinched, waiting for the sound of a bomb or a gun, but there was nothing, only mother's spoon chinking in her cup and a bicycle-bell pinging on the road outside.

But evacuation was a word that became common and crucial: discussions for and against. Tears came to Mother's eyes at the very idea. Alfie was against. He didn't want to leave his home, his friends, his toys or Matty the Persian cat. But most of all he didn't want to miss the war, he wanted to be in it. 'I will not go,' he proclaimed, his ten-year-old jaw set. But Connie was not so sure. Not that she was afraid of war. She could not believe in it, an abstract thing. War. Thrilling. A fact, yes, but where was it? Autumn turned to winter as usual. The signs of war seemed artificial, black-outs a hysterical reaction yet exciting, too, all that velvety black and the glorious comfort of shut-in light. Christmas came just the same and went again leaving the frosty ash of January. White ferns and feathers on the window for her to copy in her book but no pencil was ever fine enough to catch the detail and breath melted it when you got up close enough really to see.

She wasn't scared of war but evacuation seemed like a door opening into another chance. Chance of what? Connie was ready to step through that door whatever. Home was happy and ordinary, loving and predictable. School had become dull to her. Not that *it* was any duller but her focus had changed. Instead of solids she saw the gaps between them or the light on surfaces, windows, the shiny complex hues of her friends' hair or the apricot fluff of light on their cheeks. She saw how the shadow of her pen fell across the white page and lost her concentration, lost her sentences halfway through. Her marks began to plummet but she hardly noticed or cared. Her body was suddenly aware of itself, aching with the novelty of becoming a woman, the swelling and tingling, the secret wisps of hair and dark of blood – yet she was still a child who had to drink milk and go to bed in summer when the sun was bright against the curtains.

If they were to be evacuated it would be done privately, within the family. Mother would not hear of them going to strangers and Father had a relative. Connie had never heard mention of this relative before. He was a very distant one, second cousin once removed or something. He was a black sheep and he was famous.

'Hardly *famous*,' Mother said. 'He's written a book or two, something *esoteric* . . .'

'Esoteric?'

'Not something most folk would ever bother to read. Some fanciful nonsense about plants. Married to an artist. Sacha-varelle Mount.'

Connie gasped. 'I've heard of *her*. There's a picture in the class-room, it's wonderful, a kind of tunnel through trees. You never told me we were related to her.'

'Well, there you are then.'

Connie felt a breeze blow through the opening door. 'Where?'

'Derbyshire . . . near Bakewell . . . look on the map.'

'Why is the relative . . .'

'Patrick.'

'Patrick, why is *he* not gone to war?'

Mother shrugged. 'Must be some health thing,' she guessed, 'writing, messing about with plants, that's hardly what you'd call a reserved profession, not like your father's.'

In June of 1940 Father procured petrol from some mysterious source and the family drove north to visit. Just to get the feel of the place, Father said. Connie felt her heart lift as the hills lifted around her. The green was so dazzling, so lush and delicious that she had to swallow and swallow against the saliva that flooded her mouth. Driving through the dappled green of a road overhung by a long arch of trees, spots of sunlight floating in her eyes, she wanted to howl and beat her fists on the leather back of Father's seat. 'This is what she was trying to get in her painting!' she cried.

'What?'

'Oh nothing.' It was so fragile and trembling, how could she ever catch it and make it stay? How could she ever catch the green underwater ripple and the swimming spots of gold?

The house was approached up a long bumpy drive. A square grey house, simple like a child's drawing, symmetrical. It was like a town house but planted on a green rise miles from any town. 'Very exposed,' Mother said, frowning. The walls around the fields were made of piled stone. A sheep ran bleating in front of the car for several yards, wiggling its woolly bottom. Alfie laughed. 'It runs like Connie!' he cried and Connie thumped him before she could be stopped.

No one came to the door to greet them though the car's engine and the grate of tyres on the loose gravel of the track must have announced their arrival. Alfie flung himself out of the car first and a collie bounded round to the front of the house its whole body wagging with excitement. Connie unfolded herself from her seat and stepped out. The air was like champagne, like she supposed champagne to taste, clear, precious, heady, and it was *still*, so suddenly still and quiet after the noise of the car that the silence was almost deafening. And then there was the sound of a sheep bleating and the squeal of a swooping bird – swallow?

By the front door was a lilac bush. In London there was blue lilac in the garden, finished by then, but this was white and in its full fragrance. Connie cupped a warm, heavy bloom between her two palms and breathed deeply.

Mother and Father stood by the front door looking ill at ease, the first time Connie had ever seen her father seem uncertain. It made her impatient somehow. 'Why don't we knock?' she asked. The door-knocker was a big fist, fashioned out of black iron. Father grasped it in his own hand which was made to seem small and pale in comparison, and knocked. Flakes of paint fell from the door but that was the only response.

Connie let go of the lilac bloom. The car glinted black in the sun, black with white, blue, grey, green deep in its sheen. In the boot were two suitcases, one for Alfred, one for herself. If they liked it here they could stay, as a sort of trial. 'There is no compulsion,' Father said several times on the journey. Connie felt pity for her parents for the first time in her life. They were scared, more scared than she was. Horror stories of miserable homesick evacuees had scared them. Ill-treatment, exploitation, lack of understanding and then the unspeakable horror of the sinking of the *City of Benares* which had almost decided Mother against letting them go. 'We'll hardly get sunk in Derbyshire,' Connie had snapped. 'But if you don't like it, don't like Patrick or Sacha or anything then you must . . .' 'Let's wait and see,' Connie said, determined she would like it, like them, like everything. And now, just from standing in the champagne sparkle, the lilac-scented stillness, she knew already that she did.

'They should be expecting us.' Mother looked at Father.

'We could just go in,' Alfie said. The dog whined and scratched with one paw at a deeply ridged patch of door.

'We *could* open the door and call.' Mother bent as if to squint through the keyhole. She got hold of the handle, turned and pushed. The door swung open with a long squeak and the dog walked in.

'Spot of oil on that,' Father muttered.

'Hello-o,' Mother called into the dim hall.

'I'm here,' shouted Alfie. They stepped inside. The hall was cool and filled with shoes, boots, coats and a piano piled high with hats. It smelt of dog.

'Look, a note,' Alfred said snatching up a folded sheet of

paper from the piano. Father took it from him and read it. *Do make yourselves at home – or come and find us, we're in the garden behind the house. S and P.*

'Do you think it's meant for us?' Mother said.

'Well, it's not meant for Father Christmas, is it?' said Connie.

Her mother gave her a long look.

'Sorry,' Connie said.

'Well, I think we should make ourselves at home then. Gordon?'

'Suppose so,' Father said.

'I'll go and find them.' Alfie hared off through the hall to the back of the house. Connie pushed open a door that led into a big shabby room where dust-motes twinkled in a shaft of sun between half-drawn velvet curtains. The wallpaper was red, the chairs dumped with clothes, a dog basket with hairy blanket and a bone was positioned in front of the ashy fireplace. On the floor was a pile of papers, the top one a water-colour sketch of trees in their shimmering spring green.

Connie looked up and caught the glances that passed between her parents, the I-don't-think-so pursing of her mother's lips that answered her father's lifted eyebrow.

'Isn't it wonderful!' she said.

'You think so?' Her father regarded her curiously.

Connie hugged him. '*Wonderful.*'

FIVE

A MEMOIR BY PATRICK MOUNT

I consider myself to have been misunderstood in my life's endeavour – the development of a principle and system by which mankind can perfect itself. I have been regarded, I am well aware, as something of a crank. I can only hope that in some more enlightened time my ideas may come to be appreciated. I offer this memoir, not as an apologia to a life, but as an explanation which might be of some interest to the open-minded, perhaps like-minded reader. I will attempt to set down the 'shaping experiences' which led me to develop my principle, philosophy and habit of being.

One morning in my tenth year I awoke to fever. There had been symptoms on the previous day of sore throat, rash, swollen glands and failing appetite but on this morning, in the summer of 1908, it became apparent that this was no trifling childish ailment but a serious illness. I have only to close my eyes to recall the sun shining through the mesh of the muslin curtains and the way the light dazzled even my closed eyelids and beat against my hot temples. Memories are fragmented. There was the sun on the white sheet and sometimes the smell of newly cut grass floating in. There was the sensation of heavy blankets on my hot and aching limbs. My mother would sit beside my bed and wipe my head with a cool cloth. When I raised myself to drink there was always dust floating on the surface of the water even if it was freshly poured. The glass had a design of geometric shapes cut into it just below the rim. The doctor had a red moustache although the hair on his head was dark. I remember the moustache vividly although not the remainder of the man's face. On some occasions the soft drooping red whiskers were stuck together at their ends with moustache wax. One I noticed crumbs of food stuck in the hairs. This doctor had a pleasing smell like cough sweets and liniment. He never failed to address me as 'my little man'. I was confined to bed for a period approximating six months between spring and autumn, missing the splendid summer of 1908.

A crushing disappointment to a small boy was that my father had promised that I might accompany him to one of the Olympic athletics events at the great new stadium at White City. It was to have been an outing to celebrate my tenth birthday. Instead of which my birthday was spent miserably in bed suffering the illness – the diagnosis never quite clear – I had aggravated symptoms of both measles and mumps – which was to leave me with a weakened heart.

I have often pondered that time and the influence it cast over the life that was to follow. If I had spent that summer with my companions in the fresh air, if I had been allowed to go on the annual summer visit to the Isle of Wight, if I had been able to attend the Olympic Games with my father, if my heart had remained sturdy, how differently might my life have progressed?

I would have fought in the Great War, of course, and my life might have ended, like that of so tragically many of my contemporaries, there. Like many a young boy before me, I had a war-like spirit, not averse to battles in the shrubbery,

toy guns and cannons. Perhaps that spirit of war was
sweated out of me that long summer of fever?

One event of that time remains most vividly in my
memory, one that certainly had its effect. The summer of
1908, as I have said, was a remarkable one, weeks of hot
sunshine hardly interrupted by a cloudy day. But the heat
became oppressive towards the end of the summer and one
night there was a storm. I remember my mother opening the
curtains – which were kept closed against the brightness that
might hurt my eyes – to show me the sky that had turned
the colour of clay; I remember the leaves squirming and
darkening on the horse-chestnut tree outside the window,
the leaden sound of distant thunder coming closer and
closer. My mother held my hand as we listened to the
storm's approach and my heart beat with excitement, my
weakened heart. We counted the miles between each crash of
thunder and each flash of lightning. I can still see the way
the flicker of lightning seemed to illuminate the bones
beneath her skin. And then it came and it struck the horse-
chestnut, the crash and the flash occurring simultaneously,
the crack and split of the tree seemed to rip through my
own veins and my mother cried out and held me to her
breast.

The storm that struck and split the tree is the great event
in my memory of that summer and it coincides in my mind
with a newspaper article read to me by my father – as was
his habit each evening while I was confined to bed –
concerning a professor of botany who claimed that plants
have eyes and can see. Forbidden to leave my bed I would
nevertheless creep to the window whenever I was left
unattended to look at the tree. I understood that the eyes
were not like human eyes and naturally no eyes were visible
to me but it occurred to me to wonder if the tree had

25

suffered pain at the strike that had riven it to its waist, twisted it so that the taut yellow of its sinews were twisted against the grain. This I sincerely believe was the germinating moment of the theoretical system I call the Phytosophical Principle and the related practical system Seven Steps to Bliss which I have dedicated my life to developing and refining.

Tony puts down the slim memoir which he has read until he knows it almost off by heart. He stands up, draws the curtains and switches on the light. It's getting dark earlier, he hates that, the shutting down of the year very slow and cruel and leading to what? Leading to Christmas which is fucking shit. Dying trees stuck in pots and covered in tinsel and all that crap. Can't stand tinsel, Tony, puts his teeth on edge.

Time to cook his meal. Feels nearer to Patrick than ever today, feels an odd fizz inside him. What is it? Rinses the white fish fillet under the tap, the water runs cloudy, a fleck of blood escapes from between the dense wet flakes of flesh. It's excitement but not just that. It's . . . vindication. The onion he slices finely, pushing his finger into the slices to make frail rings. It's a mild onion and his eyes don't water. Pours sunflower oil into the pan and tips in the onion, stirs it around as it sweetens and softens. Vindication for this waiting life. Sometimes he has been struck with doubt – cardamom and powdered coriander, a pinch of chilli – waiting for a sign that it is time to move into the new, the Patrick life, sometimes that certainty of vision, whatever, has wobbled and sometimes Tony has wondered what the fuck he's doing here in this Brixton flat, what the fuck he's waiting for. Get a life is something he's heard said, the sort of thing that gets to him if he lets it. Small tin of pineapple in its natural juice, hard lump of creamed coconut which softens as it warms and the white slides under his spoon combining with the fruit juice and the spices. Smells fanfuckingtastic. It will be delicious and anyway, he *has* a life, the sign has come, the waiting is almost over and it's time to put the fish in, set it gently in the fragrant sauce, simmer till it turns opaque.

SIX

Sacha poured the tea. The family sat in splintery wicker chairs in a conservatory that was choked with thick green light filtered through ivy and vine. Dead leaves littered the floor, dead insects, live ones too, spiders with long flimsy legs flowed over the leaves and up the knotty vine stems. Mother made conversation and Sacha responded in kind so it was all artificial though well meant. Father sat with his head back regarding the roof, the fine arched wood and glass-work in sad need of repair. One of the vines twisted with ivy – or maybe it was ivy twisted with a vine – had broken through a pane of glass and climbed outside but there was no air, the broken pane was clogged with dark leaves.

Constance felt Patrick looking at her. She looked boldly back and smiled, a strange twisting in her stomach. This was the black sheep of the family, a famous man and not like anyone she'd ever had to do with before. He looked like someone from the Old Testament or even Russia, Rasputin, someone like that; thin, tall with a black-and-white beard that poured down his chest like foam. His hair was black-and-white too, pushed back from a thin intensely scored forehead. His eyes were large but narrowed as he looked at her, dark but not quite brown. His nose was long and reddish and his lips, hardly visible among all the whiskers, were thin with a little curve at one corner, a gap through which she could see a chink of tooth. This is my relation, she thought, trying to remember what sort, second cousin once removed? She was stirred by the link, however tenuous it might be. He was someone out of the ordinary and he was something to do with her. In the soles of her feet she felt the sort of itch that surely meant that she was about to step into her new life.

Alfie finished his tea and went out with the dog – Harry – to explore. The conversation creaked to a halt and Mother threw Father a pleading look but it was Patrick who spoke.

'Constance, what is it that you do?'

'I do?' She looked at her soft white hands.

'Or wish to do?'

'I wish to be an artist, of course,' she said and felt a sensation like sherbet in her veins.

Father let out a yelp of laughter. 'That's the first we've heard of it.'

'The ideas they get,' Mother said, love on her face. But Patrick didn't laugh or smile. His eyes rested thoughtfully on Connie.

'Yes,' he said, 'good, that's a fine wish.'

Sacha leant forward to offer Constance a pikelet from a plate. She took one, warm between her fingers, wet with melting butter. 'Well, you're in the right place to be an artist, isn't she, Paddy?' she said. 'We'll have to show her the studio.'

Patrick gathered his beard together in his hand and stroked downwards lifting his chin as he did so so that the black and white of it was pulled tight.

'Doesn't that hurt?' Alfie said, suddenly there again, his face dirty, his tie twisted round over his shoulder.

'Alfie!' Mother pulled him to her, straightened his tie.

'A little,' Patrick said, letting go of his beard, 'but a little hurt is sometimes good.'

The air cooled as the sky dimmed to lavender and pale stars gleamed. Mother and Father stood by the front door. Alfie was in bed and Connie stood in the shadow of the lilac listening.

'It's not the mess or the dustiness,' Mother said.

'I know.'

'It's not the dog hairs. It's not Sacha, she seems, I must say, like a sensible type – quite a bit older than Patrick, wouldn't you say? I'd trust the children to *her*, after all she has brought up a son. It's not even Patrick, although . . .'

'Yes, I know.'

'It's well, it's . . . it's the lack of I don't know . . . regulation. You know? You saw how long it took to get that tea together and it was only pikelets for heaven's sake and a pot of tea and it's not even as if we arrived unexpectedly, is it?'

'Not at all.'

'It's not what the children are used to at all – and greeting us with a note! They'd run wild, that's what, if they came here. And I don't want to leave them.' Her mother's voice trembled into tears and Connie stepped forward.

'Oh Mother, it's a wonderful place,' she said, 'I really want to stay. This is where we would be safe.'

'Eavesdropping now!'

'I'm not sure that Alfie wants to stay,' Father said.

'Well, take Alfred home then, we're not Siamese twins.'

'Constance!'

'Sorry, Father, but . . . it's just so glorious and it's well away from the war, isn't it? What war could there be here?'

'We'll talk about it.'

'Please let me.'

'We'll see.' It was no good wheedling. Connie left them

before they could send her to bed and wandered about in the garden breathing in the cooling fragrance of the flowers, watching how the pale roses seeped light, glowing like small planets in the dusk.

And in the morning it was decided that Alfie would return to London and that Connie could stay. 'But think of it as a holiday,' Mother said, 'a trial period, nothing is set in stone and if you're homesick . . .'

'I won't be.'

'We're not talking about for ever,' Father chipped in. 'Understand, Connie, this is a temporary expedient, for the duration only.' Connie smiled past him at the swallows swooping for gnats. They had been left alone to say their goodbyes, Patrick was gardening and Sacha had gone off somewhere to paint.

'If you change your mind . . .' Mother held her at arm's length, looking at her as if she was searching her face for something, or memorising her features.

'Be good,' were her father's last words to her. His kiss was dry on her cheek, her mother's loose and powdery as if she was leaving a trace of herself on Connie's skin. Their embrace, so soft with their breasts squashed between them embarrassed Connie and she pulled away a little too soon.

She stood and waved a white handkerchief, watching the car disappear and appear again growing smaller and smaller on the winding, dipping drive, watching the white flash of Alfred's handkerchief waving back from the window. The air was busy with flying things, the thin squeal of the swallows was like a wet finger on the rim of a glass. She closed her eyes as the car, at last, disappeared. She threw out her arms and twizzled, letting the handkerchief drop, spun round and round and round, her skirt flying out until she was so dizzy she staggered and sank down on the step.

SEVEN

Donna's flat has a sweetish girly smell. In each room there is a bowl of dusty scented petals and dead fragments. The bowl on the coffee table is wooden and the pot-pourri has pine cones in it, twigs, seed-husks. Tony lifts a handful, lets it fall. The sweet dust makes him sneeze. It's good in Donna's flat. It's mostly clean. Donna has this waxy stuff to polish the leaves of the rubber plant with. The plant reaches halfway up the wall. Tony strokes a thick leaf with his finger, cool gloss, no dust here, she must have dusted it before leaving. He can feel the pleasure in the leaf as he moves it gently between his fingers, *caresses* would be the word for the soft stroke he gives it, enjoying the waxy texture on top, the duller veined surface underneath. It's a strong plant, you can feel the force of life in it. Tony has no plants of his own, odd, considering his fascination with Patrick and Patrick's with plants. But when he has settled, when *he* has roots he will root plants to mark the place. And maybe that is not so far away.

Donna has no secrets from Tony. No need to go fumbling through her drawers or her clothes. Did that long ago. There's nothing hidden about Donna. Felt kind of let down to find there was nothing, nothing shameful, not so much as a dirty book or a vibrator in her underwear drawer. She hasn't even had a boyfriend for a year. He likes that she's alone in there, no laughing going on that excludes him, no sex, just her and her telly, music sometimes. They have a chat and lend each other milk, tobacco or a slice of bread. She goes out to work, some local-council kind of thing, comes back, watches all the soaps, goes out mostly on a Saturday night and returns in the early hours alone, sleeps in on a Sunday morning.

Tony stretches full-length on her sofa. Likes to lie like this, feet up on the arm, smoking and watching her big colour TV. A programme about gorillas, such wise sad faces. Gorillas shambling about on their big leather feet, one with a baby on its tit, one stretched out in the sun, feet up on a branch. Tony grins, seeing that he's stretched out just the same. It's good here with the telly and the plants and all, ferns on the windowsill, a spider plant dangling babies, a stubby ginger-whiskered cactus.

It's more friendly somehow than in his own flat. Wouldn't be relaxing like this if Donna was here though, it's just her space he likes. It's female space and female things, accoutrements he gets lonely for. Not another person but another person's things. Sometimes he thinks, when he finds himself feeling lonely – Christ, he even filled in a computer-dating questionnaire once, not that he couldn't get any girl he wanted just with a look – that what he'd like would be a wife who worked. No kids, absolutely no way. A nurse maybe who worked nights, yes, then he could get a job in the day and their paths would hardly cross at all. He'd hardly have to see her. Wouldn't have to eat with her. Can't bear it when people eat in front of him, opening their mouths and stuffing them, the muscular struggle in their cheeks as they chew and then the passage of the messed-up food down their throats. Makes him want to puke. But he does like to cook. Could cook for her, could leave her wonderful things – brioche, pavlova, syllabub – and she could leave him notes saying how delicious, thanking him in a genuine way, he can just imagine it, she'd have that big smart girly writing and she'd sign her name with her initial and a sprawl of a kiss. And he could live with her things, her cosmetics on the dressing-table, her nightie on the chair, the special kind of yoghurt she likes in the fridge, her toothbrush, tampons, bath-oil.

It's ever since he was inside that he appreciates the softness, the sweet smells, the flowery cushion, he hugs it to his chest, the mobile, china birds that chink when you open the door, even the fucking pot-pourri. Inside there was this stink of men, of shit and sweat, farts, testosterone all bottled up and nothing soft; crude jokes and hairiness, bad breath, stiff pricks, almost never a smile or a kind look. He shudders at the memory, buries his nose in the cushion that smells of Donna's cheap scent. Might miss her, the thought jars him, miss someone? He might miss her when he's gone.

No. Getting morbid. He switches off the television which is on about conservation now, and goes into the bedroom. Donna's bed is covered in a pink duvet with rows of white daisies. It's got those matching flounce things to hide the legs of the bed. The pillow-cases match the cover but the curtains don't quite. Beside the bed are two books, romances, both of them have windblown heroines on the front. Donna gets through stacks of this bollocks. Underneath them is her little white Bible with a silver clasp. He's looked in it before to see her childish writing: *Property of* and her name and address. He's opened the Bible to look at the bookmark with a white flower on it and a text: *Consider the lilies of the field, how they grow; they toil not, neither do they spin; and yet I say unto you, that even Solomon in all his glory was not arrayed like one of these.* She says she reads it but the bookmark has been in the same place for months. He lifts up the duvet, the sheet underneath – pink polyester – is fresh. All clean and ready for her return, her convalescence. It's a deep bed, soft, all that pink. Tony strips off his clothes and climbs in.

EIGHT

The road roars. There is no other word for it. It's no wonder people go mad in this constant hostile poisonous din. It's been roaring all night, she'd assumed that late at night it would go quiet but no, there's been no let up at all. Who are these people and where are they all going? It seems to Constance that the world itself has gone mad, mad with movement, everyone exchanging places, restlessly passing each other going north, going south, east, west, roaring away. If someone would just shout *Stop!* then what a hush there would be, what a stillness.

This is a good hotel. Kensington. She asked to be near the park, the idea of the city terrifying after so long. The idea of being near the park was to be near green, trees, above all to have a bit of peace and *quiet* – and Deborah, not the brightest of young women obviously, put her *here* above the roar of Kensington Gore. The bed is king-size, big enough for three. She lies neatly, head centred on one of four gigantic pillows. It's an odd sensation because she doesn't lie down at home. Never uses the bed, not since she slept in it with Patrick. Tends to cat-nap in her arm-chair or sometimes in the kitchen with her head on her little cushion, resting on the table.

These curtains are dark, stiff material, serious curtains not the fluttering kind. You have to draw them with a cord. She tries to pretend the traffic sound is the sound of the sea but it doesn't work. Although the windows are closed and there is air-conditioning she fancies she can taste exhaust fumes in her mouth. Unbelievable that near her home the sea is breathing quietly, lapping on the sand, that her place is empty. That's a comfort, actually. Her place, her things, empty, waiting.

She turns her head and squints at the red figures on the clock-radio by the bed: 2.45. It's no good waiting for sleep because sleep won't come. Stiffly she sits up, hugs her cushion to her, little bit of home that looks so tattered in this setting, stuffing gone all flat, what will the chambermaid think of it? Stiff in her shoulders and neck, not serious, just a reminder, this hot summer has banished her arthritis, please God for ever. She reaches for the light-switch and the lamps on the walls let out a subdued yellow light. She hauls herself off the bed and wanders round the great room with its giant bed, its two sofas at right angles to each other, its television, refrigerator, kettle. The carpet is cold under her feet and catches on the rough skin of her heels. She feels tiny and cold and very alone. On the walls are prints of windmills in flat fields, anodyne water-colours of the pastel variety. Patrick is hanging at the NPG. The lights there will all be off, she doesn't like to think of him hanging in the dark. She rubs her cheek against the cushion and sniffs its familiar smell.

There is a feeling like a stone in her stomach. Is it hunger or is it only her blessed nerves? She perches on the edge of a sofa which seems to snub her, doesn't even deign to dent under her weight. Why two huge sofas? You could seat eight in here. Connie almost laughed when shown the room which could contain the whole of her house easily and still leave room to swing a good-sized cat.

Tomorrow at six-thirty the gallery will fill. People will

mingle and sip wine. Will there be canapés? She adores those fiddly mouthfuls. People who *are* people will be there. Is Connie herself then a *person*? She saw a poster today and it quite took her breath away. Patrick's face, the face that has been hers alone, his eyes met hers through the glass of a taxi-cab window and her heart lurched, like love or fright. Eyes made only of paint, eyes painted with her own brush, yet still her heart can lurch.

He's been dead and gone for thirty years, yet evidently is not dead, not inside her anyway, else how could he have that effect? Just the surprise of it, Connie, nothing more, the surprise of that familiar face in the strangeness that London has become and to top it all her own name CONSTANCE BENSON in red block capitals, oh it's a lark, that's what it is, a nonsense and a lark. So why the stone in the belly? She shivers. Perhaps hunger *is* what is up.

She picks up the menu that is propped like a greeting card. *Room Service 24 hours a day* she reads and a list of what they have to offer: soup and a roll, lasagne, chicken salad, prawn mayonnaise, something called BLT. She is tempted to order it just out of interest, to see what it is and who on earth will deliver it at this ungodly hour – a grumpy woman in a dressing gown and curlers, a boy in a uniform? Yet how can she think of eating at nearly 3 a.m.? She uses the key to her refrigerator instead, what they call a 'minibar'. All sorts in here, much more the ticket, little bottles of whatever you fancy, champagne even, nuts and crisps, a bar of chocolate, even a small fluffy toy duck. She takes it out. Cold primrose fluff, a medallion round its neck: *Buckston Ducks Inc. Don't leave me here to shiver. Take me home and love me. I'm only £3.99. Ask at reception for a gift-box.* She shakes it and its eyes wobble. Whatever is the world coming to? Suddenly she feels quite gay, her suspicions confirmed. Yes, the world gone mad. She certainly won't buy the duck but doesn't replace it in the fridge. She sits it in an ashtray instead.

She takes a couple of miniature whiskies and some salted nuts. It's cold in the room, nothing to switch on or regulate so she gets back into bed, settles herself against the great banks of pillows. She picks up the remote control, flicks through the channels, surprising what there is at this time of night, finds the adult channel, sits with her mouth agape and full of peanuts as a bottom fills the screen, a young bottom pumping and pumping, then a girl's face, eyes closed, mouth wide enough to show the tonsils, head thrashing from side to side. *Yes*, says the mouth, *yes, yes, oh God yes*, which strikes Connie as funny somehow, don't they get theatrical? and she sprays chewed-up peanut on the sheet and switches off. But did she used to thrash about like that? Patrick would have liked it, that's for sure. She gulps some whisky, trying to remember. They certainly did have their moments. One time among the bluebells comes back to her, cool crushed blue and sappy green against their hot skin. Did she cry *Yes, yes*? She watches her reflection in the blank television screen – hair that must be dyed, face that must be painted – and she feels stirred and even less like sleep as she sips and munches, gets up and prowls around again.

Because of the bath and the thick white towels, the ivory cakes of soap in their fluted paper wrappings, Connie decides to have a bath. Sleep is not going to come, not if she waits for it, and who needs sleep? At home she hardly sleeps, she never baths. It is not necessary to bath. You can wash the places that need to be washed with a flannel, a kettle-full of water, splash the face, rub the flannel under the clothes for a freshen up. You can maintain an adequate level of personal hygiene like that, washing the hair monthly or so with Squeezy if it's not too chilly. Not to wash the hair at all, after all, wouldn't harm or kill. But in the hotel bathroom with hours to go before breakfast, Connie decides, just for the novelty of it, she will bathe. She turns on the taps, tips in a bottle of bath-gel so that suds and steam glitter white. While the bath fills she takes off her night-clothes, removes, last, the yellowing vest and pants and with her mind still full of the luxuriant bodies on the adult channel sees in the cruelly lit mirror the thin puckering of her own skin, the sallowness, the low flat pockets of her breasts.

But it is not bad, she thinks, chin set, not *so* bad considering the years. She's trim at least, Paddy always liked to say that she was trim – though there was more of her then. Even *trimmer* then, she tells herself, and though her chin is lifted the mirror weeps and smears her downwards, her nipples looking away from each other as if ashamed. She cups her breasts in her hands, forces them together. *It has been so long since anyone has touched my skin.*

The water is too hot, she gets in and out quickly, turns on the cold tap, her legs stung pink to the knee. The bubbles grow and heap under the taps. She walks about her room naked, cold, the air odd on her skin. It brings to mind some memory, she can't reach it, some sensation like this, air touching her everywhere, no shield or filter, the same air that touches the skin of others, enters others, their noses, mouths, throats, touching, entering her. The unaccustomed feeling of air on naked skin.

When the bath is cool enough she climbs back in, sinks down. The bubbles crackle in the quiet. She lifts her hands to see her fingers webbed with sparkling froth. The smell is something between artificial flowers and sweets, something sherbety, a wet finger stuck in a paper twist of lemonade crystals and sucked.

Air on naked skin. A memory starts to rise. Oh no, not

that now. Enjoy this luxury for now. This warmth, this sweet sweet smell. Keep here for now or else remember something sweet. Patrick and his fingers, the way they conjured joy from her. Sometimes like a magician pulling miles of coloured ribbon from nowhere, the way he pulled sexual ecstasy from inside her even when she didn't think she was in the mood, miles of gaudy silken ribbons and flags and of *course* she would have shouted like the girl on the film. They did it just like that, porno-style all right, yes indeed they did.

She puts her hands on her belly and presses just where she used to feel that first fizz, small throb and ache of desire. Then catches her own eye in the clouded mirror tiles. Why so many bloody mirrors? Who wants to see themselves in the bath? But there she is: old woman floating in a cloud of froth. She struggles up, sobered by the sight. Bath too long for her, she can't relax or she'd sink, has to brace herself against the sides, foam making her itch as it dries on her chest, making her sneeze, feel suddenly chilled. She climbs out, wraps herself in a giant of a towel and with the corner of it wipes her eyes.

NINE

The dream again must be. Tony flounders in deep pink. Knows where he is and that he's dreaming, must be a dream can feel the soft beneath him and the warm and even see pink through his eyelids that try to peel open, but still he can hear the breath in his ear, still feel the flesh and hear the last thread of frightened voice. *Didn't mean didn't mean didn't mean*. Hair against him, sticking, strands of it in spit. Shouting with real voice or only a voice made of dream, throat clogged with horror. Real feeling of soft or is the soft the dream, the dragging and splitting of his mind into horror and comfort and no comfort because it happened. It happened. He did it. A sob close, real, where? Who. No. Donna back. No? You are here in the deep pink bed. Dreaming only dreaming. Cretin.

He pushes himself up out of the deep dream, head up out of the pillows, wet with his drool, with his tears. Reaches for the light. The room falls into order, the walls that surely were crowding in retreat, the ceiling rises high and white and blank.

He gets out of bed which is soiled now with nothing evident, only the scum of his dream brought on by – what? Something soft under his foot, horribly soft, jerks his foot away as if it burns. Reaches to pick it because this is not a dream now, this is only Donna's room, and it's a slipper. A white fur slipper like a bunny with ears and pink glass eyes. Horrid, sweet. Christ al-fucking-mighty.

Brought on by what, Tony?

To be a person who could wear such slippers.

Tension, because it's started. It's happening. The signs are there. Constance Benson in a hotel somewhere in this city. Patrick's portrait hanging where soon he will be able to see and even maybe touch. Signs will follow. Patrick is with and in him, leading, shoving, showing the way. There is no need for nightmares. But Christ they get you when your guard is down, slip like eels into the spaces, the worst things, because only they know the worst things the eels that thread in when you let go and sleep.

When he gets the elixirs there will be no more. Nightmares no more. That's a good thought. Think that one. It is all right and true.

He pulls on his clothes, denim cold and stiff against his skin. Shower later and clean clothes. Mouth tastes foul. In Donna's dressing-table mirror the face is gaunt, new lines running down each side of the mouth to the chin, deep and sharp as if cut into butter with a blade. It's just the electric white that does it, pouring down from a frilly lampshade. All these fucking frills and pink and bunny-rabbit soft. Why does that hurt? Leans close to see the eyes. Maybe Patrick had such lines. Can't think. In all the pictures there is the beard hiding half the face. Why no beard in the new one? Was going to grow a beard to be like Patrick. What now? Why, why the awful dreams?

He notices a vase of artificial flowers on Donna's dressing-table, pinches the stiffened crinkly edge of one. It is all paid for. The dream is not fair. It's a deal. You kill, no, no, not kill but cause to die. Not murder though they tried to make that out, it wasn't murder, it *wasn't meant*. The dreams are not, no way, fair. You've done time. Served time. Time has wiped the slate, should have. Look, you've been through this a hundred times. Get a grip.

But if your conscience thrusts up in your dreams like that – think of it as a shark's fin rising from the water – if your conscience thrusts up a reminder well, that just shows how *good* you are, Tony, deep inside, really deep. You could forget it all, but no, the dream, your conscience will not let you. So you are good. Really, really, good.

Tony makes a smile, watches it stretch his face. A beard would hide his face and his *face* is good. Good angles, jaw-line, cheek-bones. They've all said it, the women he's had. It's that Red-Indian look that turns them on, what with his long black hair.

TEN

In the evening, after her family had gone and Connie had eaten her first meal alone with Sacha and Patrick, Sacha took her up to what she called the studio – even that word thrilled Connie. When the door was opened, the first thing she noticed was a white peaked heap like a miniature mountain range on the floorboards under the window. 'Swallows,' Sacha said, following Connie's eyes. 'It's lucky, you know, *said* to be if swallows choose your eaves.' As she spoke there was a flurry, squeal and swoop and a tiny dark feather spiralled down. 'Paddy likes the window open, likes to hear them, likes them to feel welcome.'

'Welcome!' Connie smothered a laugh. 'Sorry.'

'What?'

'It's just . . . I was just imagining Mother letting there be bird droppings in *our* house.'

Sacha glanced sideways at her, nodded.

Connie looked round the room, a long rectangle with tall sash windows to two sides. There were no curtains or carpets and it seemed a naked room, exciting for being so. The smell was not the smell of swallows at all but of oil paint and linseed oil. But a little connection was made in Connie's brain at that moment and ever after these painting smells would make her think of swallows and of freedom.

It was growing dark and the long room seemed almost

endless, a clutter of stuff on the floor at one end, indistinct. The evening light through the windows was like pink metal.

'I'll put the light on,' Sacha said.

'Wait . . .' Connie held up her hand. 'Sorry . . . it's just that it's such a lovely . . .'

Sacha looked at her approvingly. 'It certainly is,' she said, 'it's very special, the light at this time, the dusk light of summer. It brings out the flush.' She studied Connie's face. 'Not a bloom,' she said, 'not like in daylight, that rose-petal look, deeper than that . . . a glow from within.' Connie felt the glow that came from such approval, her hand went to her cheek. She looked into Sacha's face but could see no glow. The skin was dull and papery, a little crumpled. She was a solid woman, Sacha, solid and unglamorous in her tweed suit, speckled hair cut mannishly short. But there was a shine in her brown eyes, a kind and intelligent shine.

'You and Patrick have a son?'

'Red. Not Patrick's.'

'Oh.' Connie paused, thinking, *Whose then?* but it seemed impertinent to ask. 'Red?'

'Actually it's Martin. Martin Redmartin. So you see . . .'

'Yes. It's nice. Red. Where is he?'

'He's a stonemason, but he's in Africa now.'

'Fighting?' Connie could nave kicked herself. Sacha pressed her lips together until they were white. Frightened, Connie thought, she is frightened. Change the subject, quick. 'Will you tell me about what you do,' she said. 'Your painting and Patrick? Mother says something esoteric.'

A long pause then Sacha shook her head as if snapping out of something, softened her lips, smiled. 'Esoteric, yes. That's a good one.' Connie smiled too, relieved that Sacha was not angry. The light was so pink and the smells so glorious. Everything glorious. She must not spoil it. They must like her, both of them, as she liked them. She was trying hard to feel her feet on the ground, to feel the floorboards through the soles of her shoes because it was so odd, everything, the surroundings, everything, it was so different, almost dream-like – particularly in this strange sheeny light – that she felt she would take off and float if she didn't concentrate. She was longing to be alone. She needed to be alone in order to go over everything in her mind before it faded away. She needed to think it all in order, in images, or else she would forget.

'You know *anything* about Paddy's . . . system of thought?'

Connie shook her head.

'I'll show you something.' Sacha went to the far end of the room where the dusk was thick and velvety and came back with some small canvases. She handed them to Connie who studied them one by one, holding them close to the window.

'They are flowers?'

'What would you say?'

Connie frowned over the strange images. They looked like flowers or something from a medical book, like the book at home in the drawing room that she used to pore over for hours. It had the figures of a naked man and woman, seen from the front in the front of the book, seen from behind in the back. Their skin was made of flaps. If you lifted the flaps you could see the muscles, printed with tiny figures so you could look up the names of the muscles: pronator, supinator, trapezius. If you lifted the muscle flaps you could reveal the ribs, lift the ribs to reveal the organs, pink and red and bluish brown nestled together. With her eyes on the diagrams, Connie would press her hands against herself to try and feel her own liver, spleen, womb, all secret tight and slick. You could lift the skin of the face, too, to show the muscles of the face, the eyeballs and finally the skull. Only that scared her, it seemed such a draughty box.

Patrick's flower paintings were like something from a dream, half flowers half innards. She *thought* them ugly but didn't like to say, wondered if they had a kind of beauty that she couldn't understand.

'I would say they are flowers . . . transformed.'

'You would say right. Patrick has this idea, well, principle, a principle he published in a monograph to, don't repeat this in front of him, universal scorn, I'm afraid, his Phytosophical Principle.'

'What does that mean?'

'Ha . . . well, best you read it. Though doubtless he'll enlighten you himself before long. But broadly it's about the connection between mankind and plants. These paintings came from dreams he had while formulating his ideas. You can see he's no artist!' She laughed and Connie looked at her, wondering is she being nasty or only honest? Certainly the paintings didn't seem much good to her.

'I thought they were like dreams. What connection does he mean?'

'That man could do worse than look to plants for a model of behaviour.'

'What? Oh . . .' Connie could hardly suppress a startled giggle. 'But surely . . .'

'Let's go down now, it really is getting dark.' Sacha held out her hand for the last painting. 'Surely?'

'Surely plants don't do anything, they don't *behave* at all.'

Sacha snorted. 'Come on, let's go and find some supper.'

ELEVEN

The Sunday paper has five main sections. Tony reads the News on Sunday, Travel on Tuesday, Life on Wednesday, and he lasts the Review section for three days. Learns things he really doesn't need to know. The Business section he reads only if desperate. The paper has to last the week. You can't read an evening paper at breakfast time and you can't go out before breakfast, except on Sunday when you have to go out to fetch it. He always reads while he eats his breakfast, Weetabix with milk, a pot of tea, a fag.

Breakfast is one of the reasons he finds it hard to contemplate sharing his life, his space, his peace. If someone spoke to him, say, while he ate his Weetabix which you have to do fast while it's still vaguely crisp or else throw it away and start again, if someone spoke to him then . . . who knows. If someone else crunched or gulped or said a single stupid thing. Because morning is the time when it is hard to hang on, keep on course, and the right bit of the paper, the right consistency in his cereal, these small things . . . well . . .

Wednesday is the day. He showers in Donna's bathroom using her pink grapefruit gel to rinse the dirty dreams away. He smooths and tidies Donna's bed, the sheets all limp and twisted. Should wash them but there isn't the time. She won't mind. Back in his own flat he gazes at his own bed. Good to see it tucked in tight, the cold, starched sheets unspoiled.

The milk is cold from the fridge and he pours it on only after his tea is poured and his fag is rolled. The paper is to the right of his cereal bowl, the lighter to the left. The Review is good to read because it's in the form of a large stapled magazine, not a difficult shape to unfold and keep under control. Tony opens the first page and takes his first bite of cereal. It is right. The biscuits keeping their shape and soft wet bite, the demerara sugar is still crystalline, the milk has not yet made the whole thing to mush. Tea hot, cereal cold. He reads the Contents. Stops. A name jumps out. Constance Benson. He starts, chokes, pauses. It's at the end, the crap chatty bit, At Home With . . . Shakes his head. It's her. It's Constance fucking Benson. It is a sign another sign as if he needs one. He fumbles to the right page, nearly knocks his fag on the floor, picks it up and lights it and looks.

There's a small picture of a tumbledown house under an enormous sky, sand-dunes rolling down towards its gate like waves. There's a red kitchen table with a bunch of wild flowers, there are sea-shells stuck round the frame of a scuzzy window. But the main picture taking up a whole page is golden. The room a dazzle of yellow, chair, floor, light, the old woman isn't much more than a darkness in front of the source of light that is Patrick. Patrick in that portrait, young and beardless with a chin that is so like Tony's you wouldn't believe it. The eyes meet his and his heart tumbles.

He takes a breath of clean hot smoke, a swig of tea and reads:

Portrait artist Constance Benson certainly prefers a life far from the madding crowd.

She lives in a prefab, the only remnant of a settlement built to ease the housing shortage after the war. Long ago the other inhabitants left and there is little sign now of the other houses – temporary dwellings never designed for permanent habitation.

But incredibly the house in which Miss Benson lived with Patrick Mount for several years and has continued to live in for the thirty years since is still standing: a cosy, stylishly dilapidated home.

Mount disappeared in mysterious circumstances over thirty years ago but his memory is still fresh with Benson who has not left her home on the gusty North Norfolk coast since that day.

Although the cosy kitchen with its brightly painted furniture and sea-shell-encrusted walls is the heart of the house, Benson's favourite room is the small loft space which Mount ingeniously converted to a studio for her. It is designed so as to catch all available light and is a triumph of architectural daring. Barely five foot at its tallest point, it has walls that slope down to floor-level on either side.

The studio is kept admirably uncluttered. The only furniture in the room is a miniature armchair, charmingly covered in a faded yellow chintz, which is well suited to Miss Benson's petite frame.

The chair is positioned so that Miss Benson can sit and gaze upon the last portrait she painted – that of her beloved Mount. It is this much discussed portrait which will be the centrepiece of the retrospective of her portraiture which opens at the National Portrait Gallery later this week.

Miss Benson's face clouds when quizzed about the fate of her partner of many years but she says she feels he has never really gone.

This week she will leave her home for the bright lights of London where she will be guest of honour at the Private View of her retrospective show. When asked about her reaction to leaving the solitude of her home after so long Miss Benson laughs. 'It'll do me good to have a bit of a hullabaloo,' she says, 'but I'm looking forward to getting home already.'

It's not surprising. The air is so fresh and the setting so tranquil that London really does seem a world away.

Tony lays the paper down and grinds out his fag. North Norfolk Coast, eh? Thank you – he reads the journalist's name – Lisa Just. Thank you, Lisa. It is happening, it really is. Sign follows sign follows sign. It is going to be a cinch.

Tony takes a mouthful of Weetabix and spits it back in the bowl. Bloody mush. Bad omen. If breakfast goes wrong it always is. Have to start again now, the whole thing, fresh tea, fresh Weetabix, fresh fag. The brown mush slops heavily into the bin. Tony rinses the bowl, dries it on a white tea-towel, arranges two more Weetabix one on top of the other, fills and switches on the kettle, rolls another cigarette.

TWELVE

The air roars and the plate glass trembles its reflections of umbrellas and traffic. Through the reflection is the bright peace of the window displays, the perfect people in their perfect clothes. They all look so stern, the plastic? plaster? people, stern and attenuated. September and already they are got up for winter. Connie stares at a model in a long grey coat, black fur collar and trim, pale face, smooth as an eggshell, serious, the lips unpainted, the head smooth and bald but each eye trimmed with a stiff birdwing of lashes.

Connie pulls herself away from the window and in the slipstream of a crowd, enters the store. The air is utterly fake, such a perfumed assault of clashing scents it makes her teeth ring. She goes forward between the bottles and the brightness holding her breath, goes between hosiery and handbags to find the escalator which sweeps her upwards towards Ladies' Fashions.

She has not bought a new item of clothing for thirty years but today she will. Like it or not she will be noticed at the private view, noticed in the right way. She's not having them sniggering at her in her old stuff, daft old bat up from the sticks, not having them humouring her. She'll knock their eyes out, for Patrick's sake. It's just a matter of getting into the spirit of the thing, shopping, dressing up. She's still a woman after all under all the shabby layers, with a woman's taste for luxury still there, still stirrable.

Rising up the escalator she breathes in fabric, electricity, wealth. Purple she is hit by first, silver, royal blue, the colours hum in the brilliant light, mirrors glint back the dazzle of party frocks. Then there are darkness, deep greens and browns and behind everything, more than anything, black: velvet, satin, silk and wool, matt and shiny, pure black and black with a sheen of blue or brown or deep red. She takes a breath. How does a person choose? In a long mirror she catches herself amongst the racks of clothes and turns her head away before the reflection can belt her one. Scruffy old woman. No, only on the outside, no, no. But still she can feel the eyes of an assistant boring into her from behind, critical, accusing, *What are you doing here?* She fingers some jumpers, aware of the eyes, unable to concentrate, to think. The jumpers are appliquéd with penguins and flowers, scraps of wit and silk. She turns eventually to confront the eyes of the figure behind her and finds it's only another dummy done up in purple that is looking nowhere, that has, in fact, no eyes.

Connie smiles at her own foolishness. She relaxes, puts a Fisherman's Friend in her mouth, tries to think properly. The skirts and the dresses seem enormous, even the smallest sizes are long enough to trail behind her on the floor. People seem to have got so *big* these days, so unnecessarily, so *vulgarly* big. The fabrics are luscious, such a long time since she's felt or smelled new velvet, slithery satin. She finds a rack of silk blouses, muted mauves and pinks with a white bloom on them like a peach – or the tenderest private human skin. She picks up a sleeve and rubs it against her cheek. She gets herself into a dreamy state, a kind of trance, hardly looking or trying to think but rubbing the fabrics between her fingers, smelling the newness of them, getting bolder and

burying her face in a velvet dress, nuzzling, finding herself
wanting to suck the velvet wet like, as a child, she used to
suck the corners of sheets.

And then there *is* an assistant, real and breathing, a
towering girl all legs and lashes, small sharp head perched
up there somewhere near the ceiling. 'Need any help,
madam?' she says polite enough but with an eloquent flick
of her eyes over Connie's shabby coat.

'Purple, do you think?' Connie says. 'I want a whole new
get-up. Would this suit me?' Indicating the dummy. 'Dress,
coat, hat, the lot.'

The eyes travel down to the splitting shoes. Connie looks
down, too, her best shoes but obviously they'll have to go.
She'll have the works: shoes, stockings, underwear.

'I'll leave you to browse, shall I?' the girl says, and bolts.
Connie grins. This could be quite a lark. But even underwear
is not as simple as it sounds: racks, shelves and stands of
difficult straps and scraps of lace, shine and sheen and peep-
show stuff, Wonderbras, strapless, nude-look, uplift, balcon-
ette – the thought of her old vest makes Connie come over
queer. She needs a rest before she can think straight. She goes
to the coffee shop for tea and a bun. The nearest thing an
extortionate *pain au chocolat*, all greasy flakes and bitter
sludge, not ideal, but fortifying, at least.

As she munches she reads a leaflet advertising beauty
products. *Twenty per cent off our Exclusive Range for Store
Card Holders. Open a Customer Account today.* Ho hum.
Gel de Bain Moussant, Gel Exfoliant Moussant, Gel Min-
ceur, Galbe de Buste. Breast cream? She could do with some
of that, frowns at the memory of her breasts in the hotel
bathroom mirror looking so . . . forlorn.

And then the memory hits her, the deep memory brought
back by the sensation in the hotel room, the sensation of air

on naked skin. Her nails cut into her palms as it comes back. The studio. October, the sky a blaze of blue, the fire lit, flames pale in the sun. Sacha wanted to paint her nude, standing and looking out of the window, paint her from behind but slightly turned, head almost in profile, hand on the window frame. She had never been naked except for the quick shivery duck between bath and bed, between clothes for night and clothes for day. Strange to let her dressing gown fall and for her limbs, her buttocks, her belly, her breasts – which nobody had ever seen since they had grown – her neck and most of all somehow the vulnerable place between her shoulder blades to be naked, to be seen. She was aware that the air Sacha breathed was able to travel freely and to touch her skin. But Sacha was so businesslike, almost brisk, that she was hardly embarrassed. Actually after a little while of the interesting warmth of the fire on one side of her, the slight chill through the glass on the other, she began to enjoy the bareness, looking down at her pretty body, its creaminess, thinking, *This is mine, this is me.*

A happy moment before.

And now the other memory, the bad one, the one that will always be attached.

Patrick coming up the drive, head down, approaching the house. She watched his long-legged scissoring stride, thought, *Something is wrong.* He stopped and looked up, quickly before she had time to withdraw, looked straight at her nakedness through the glass and though it was too far for their eyes to meet, Connie felt a flinch as their gazes intersected, a sudden hotness on her front, almost a flushing that Sacha might have caught with her paints, a fleeting rosiness.

Patrick on the stairs, then Sacha saying, 'Have a break, I'll make tea.' Connie pulling on the gown and settling on a low stool by the fire. Patrick in the room, the fresh raw-air smell of him as he approached. A feeling of shyness, pride, what would you call it . . . coquettishness? so, so foolish, before he opened his mouth and told her the worst. Words that are not in her memory, that her mind rejected. The heat of the fire against her left shin the last sensation, the last coherent memory before a period of confusion in which there were things, of course – an egg in a yellow egg-cup for some reason, Sacha's tweedy arms, stars needling frostily through the curtain gap . . . oh this and that . . . but most of all there was loss.

Mother and Father and Alfred gone, the house gone. Just gone. A direct hit and why were they not in the shelter what oh what oh why . . . Gone. Her mind stopped still at that.

'Finished, madam?'

What? Connie trawls her mind back to here and now, to the leaflet advertising Galbe de Buste, to the empty teacup. 'No,' she says as a girl with a tray stops at her table. She grabs her cup and holds it against her chest. 'No. I haven't finished.'

The girl squelches a mouthful of chewing gum at her and shrugs. 'If you say so.' She goes off with her loaded tray. Connie watches her little bottom under the green nylon overall. That girl must be about the age she was then. She sighs and lets go of the empty cup.

THIRTEEN

Tony wanders between his own flat and Donna's, trying to pace away a morning that drags on and on. He turns on Donna's TV, just gibberish for kids, tries music but he can't stand Donna's taste in music. Can't stand music anyway the way it goes on and on wordless, on and on and tries to mess up your brain with all its tricksy rhythms. Quiet is best, or the sound of traffic. Traffic is OK.

It's gone cold. Rain lashes the window. A yellow leaf splayed like a hand sticks and slides down the glass. Tony piles Donna's post neatly on the table. All junk. Tragic. He touches the compost in the plant pots, moist still. You don't want to over-water, that's worse than letting them dry out, she says. No need to be here then. Funny how he prefers being here than in his own place. Means to keep out, but can't. Women's things. Should he go and visit her in hospital? Should, because once he's gone that might be it. Might not see her again and she is, he supposes, a friend. The nearest thing he's got. Never been good at friendship, Tony. Doesn't need people, that's the thing. But Donna likes him. And he can like her ... can he? Because there's no ... doesn't fancy her at all. No danger there.

Getting sorted in his head. Not in actuality sorted but he has a strategy. First off, see Benson, go to the Private View. If he can't get in he'll hang about outside and get a glimpse of her at least, introduce himself, at least, begin the process of knowing her. She won't trust him till she knows him, she won't give him a thing till she trusts him. They must not be strangers, not when they've so much in common. Patrick in common. Then go to the exhibition, have a look at the new portrait of Patrick, find out what there is to know. There will be a sign. Find out exactly where she lives. There is sure to be a sign and then he can go there. And it will all fall into place, he can practically feel it inside him, starting to fall.

He cooks his meal in Donna's kitchen with Donna's pans. His own food though, he wouldn't stoop to nicking food. A simple lunch, pasta with anchovy sauce, delicate, salty, a ten-minute meal and stunning. Does Benson like pasta, like anchovies? Soufflé, that's the sort of thing, for an old person, old but sophisticated he guesses, cheese or mushroom per-haps? In one of Donna's cookbooks he finds a recipe for a prawn and asparagus soufflé. Ah, comforting and posh, that's it. What could be more right than that?

Picture me as a boy of thirteen, pale, puny, interned. I had been all but forgotten by my friends. My only companions were my parents, my tutor and the gardener with whom I spent much time. Except for interminable Sundays, my days had a similar pattern. Each morning my tutor came and we trawled wearily through Latin verbs, algebra, capital cities. After luncheon I had to rest. My free time I spent in the garden or in the greenhouse.

'Do you think it natural,' I overheard my mother say to my father, 'a boy of his age so transfixed by plants? What does he think he's going to grow up to be – a gardener?'

'Oh leave him to it,' my father replied, 'he does no harm. And the fresh air will do him good.'

I had an image of my weak heart like a mouldy plum,

with a soft brownish place into which one could push one's finger with no resistance. The rest of it beat in a weak fluttering way, not the regular strong boom-boom, boom-boom I had heard when, as a smaller child, I had pressed my head against my mother's chest.

During my convalescence I had overheard the doctor say, 'If he catches a chill or strains himself . . . well . . .' An unspoken warning that had left me acutely aware of the softening of my heart.

The garden was long. There were stone steps that led down to a lawn edged by herbaceous borders, a shrubbery, the greenhouse and behind the shrubbery where the garden narrowed there was a triangle of scrubby soil and weeds, a compost heap, a gloomy laurel bush with leaves that looked spattered with whitewash, a privet hedge, a stench of cats. This became my private place.

Here out of sight of the house, I used to do a most curious thing. With the doctor's warning about the danger of strain ringing in my ears, I tested my weakened heart. I ran on the spot and skipped with a length of old washing line. I have often wondered whether I was trying to die, but perhaps there was no such morbid intention, perhaps it was only an innate wisdom telling me to exercise in order to strengthen the muscles of my heart. After these first tests of endurance my heart would beat fearfully, a stuttering rush of beats that caused me to sink to the ground trembling and exhausted, but the more often I repeated the test, the stronger it seemed to grow. It was secret, this strengthening of my self, my system. I did not speak of it, or speak of how much better I felt because I had grown to appreciate the status and privileges of the semi-invalid. I told the doctor that I still felt faint often, that I suffered palpitations in the night that woke and scared me, because I had no wish to return to school where I would have fallen far behind my fellows. I liked my afternoon rests, my solitude, my tutor who in an occasional fit of frivolity would sometimes agree to lay aside the books and play cat's-cradle with a length of green string or recite long passages from Edward Lear's *The Book of Nonsense*. I was relieved, furthermore, that my father no longer expected heroic feats from me in the realms of sport or commerce and that thus I would not disappoint his expectations. And best of all I liked to have time to spend amongst the plants.

The more time and attention I paid the plants the more my attention was repaid. I became increasingly aware that they, no less than animals or humans, were sentient beings. I vividly recall my first inkling of this and the experiment that followed.

First I must introduce the gardener who came to us on Tuesday and Friday. His name was Percy Greengrass – I am not sure to this day whether that was his christened name or whether he adopted it himself. I do suspect the former since he never exhibited a single other sign of whimsy. He was old, near-sighted and bad-tempered. His eyes were small and further hidden between whiskery folds of skin and craggy eyebrows so that I never felt myself to have been seen by him, a feeling that gave me a curious sense of invisibility and freedom. He rarely spoke to me, or even seemed to notice me but did tolerate the dogged way I followed him about without complaint.

Greengrass had no special feeling for plants, or rather no consistent attitude. Although he rarely addressed a remark directly to me he muttered and mumbled to the plants, mostly a litany of complaint about work, his wife, food, life and the 'blinding' world in general. But there was one plant that he seemed to hate, a big scarlet pelargonium that stood on the corner of the bench by the greenhouse door. My mother was particularly fond of this flower and Greengrass was required to make cuttings for plants for the borders and for the house. I fancied that whenever he directed his curses at the plant – he called it a tart, and a stinking whore, expressions which I didn't understand – it would shudder, fanciful notion you might think and perhaps you would be right. The plant was by the door, perhaps it was the vibration of the doorframe or the breeze that made the plant seem to shiver, but when I entered, speaking softly and affectionately to the plant, there was no such motion. However, explanations could be found for this anomaly, perhaps Greengrass's greater weight caused more disturbance, perhaps he jolted the doorframe more when he opened it.

However, the notion that attitude might affect a plant interested me and I begged from Greengrass two cuttings. I took two of equal size, both small sturdy plants with between four and six leaves apiece. I kept one on the windowsill of my bedroom and one similarly placed in the spare upstairs room used as a study by my tutor and me. I chose these two positions because the windows were on the same side of the house, with similar levels of light and temperature.

I watered the plants exactly the same amount and gave them equal amounts of attention – with one difference. I spent ten minutes each morning and evening praising one with great affection, admiring its leaves and stalk, talking encouragingly of the soft roots pressing down through the soil, giving it love. The other I criticised and shouted at, branding it a puny, ugly plant, using the words tart and whore, threatening to kill it one day, saying that I hated it. At first there was no difference, both seemed to grow apace

and both attempted to produce a flower-head. One I
pinched out gently, explaining to the plant that this was for
its own good, that it needed to be bigger and stronger before
it flowered, apologising for the discomfort I caused it, the
disappointment, saying that one day it would produce the
most beautiful flowers ever seen. The other bud I ripped off
saying, 'We don't want to see your ugly stinking whorish
flowers,' saying I'd never let it flower, sneering at its
impertinence in trying.

After a period of several weeks, to my excited amazement,
the experiment began to show results. The loved plant
flourished, soon grew too big for its pot, great soft leaves
stretched towards the light and it tried again and again to
flower, showing great vigour, I would almost say enthusiasm
for life. The pace of growth of the hated plant slowed. It
didn't die, it just grew more slowly, the leaves smaller and
meaner, a paler green, even a little sickly and yellow round the
edges, and the frequency with which it attempted to flower
was far less than that of the first until in the end it stopped
trying. It hurt my heart to see the sadness of the hated plant
but I forced myself to keep up the hatred, let no pity soften
my scorn. After about three months I brought the plants
together on my own windowsill and saw how astonishing the
difference. The loved plant at least twice the size of the hated.

I swapped them over, and reversed the treatment and
with a few weeks the difference was less. I tried the
experiment again, this time with broad bean seeds grown in
water – exactly the same result, though even more dramatic,
since the very speed of sprouting seemed affected by my
attitude to the seed. When I became sure of the plants'
sentience, of their response to feelings both positive and
negative, I could no longer bring myself to hate the plants,
it hurt my own heart to see how they suffered.

These particular experiments came to an end but my view of life, of the world, of the possibilities therein had been irrevocably altered and I was a step nearer to the development of my principle.

Tony wipes a slice of bread round his plate to mop up the gritty anchovy sauce. Puts down the book which he hardly needs to read, knows it off by heart. Looks at Donna's plants, all of them glossy, green, happy. She must be good to them. Once he'd explained to her about Patrick, about his theories, and she had listened and nodded in that way of hers, arms crossed, wry expression on her face. Even told her about the Seven Steps to Bliss, and how a few drops of one of Patrick's elixirs could transform a person – not told her, though, that it was his intention to get the elixirs because she would have asked questions. Why do you want to be transformed? she might have asked and what could he have said to that? No, she never would have understood. *Some people*, is all she'd said, pulling a face.

The leaves are cool between his fingers, he praises the plant like Patrick would have done. 'Good plant, lovely, beautiful leaf, mate.' Feels a right prat, would if anyone could see or hear. He loves the story of the first experiment, though, feels satisfied whenever he reads it. People in general are so stupid, so narrow-minded, not to recognise the genius of Patrick. Still, that's good for Tony, good, shows how special he must be, to know, to *know* that Patrick was absolutely right, to sense that what Patrick invented is the thing that could save him from himself. Can't touch a woman ever again because if he does, well . . . don't think about that . . . but there is this other way of being happy, more than happy, of achieving bliss.

Tony actually loves Patrick whose childhood is so vivid to

him he can smell it sometimes, if he closes his eyes: the hot stink of tomato plants behind glass, the cat-piss under the privet, the sourness of the white-splashed laurel leaves.

Patrick's childhood is more vivid to him than his own, his own he doesn't want vivid. No way. It wasn't a proper childhood at all only a kind of waiting, he can't count it as *childhood* not in the sense that there was any fun or play, or anything *to* remember, nothing he wants to remember at all.

FOURTEEN

Grief is like another country. Connie travelled there for months. Her heart, not just her heart, her womb, stomach, liver and spleen all contracted and blackened; her eyes were dazzled by strange brightness. The sun never stopped shinning that autumn and winter. She'd squint at it, puzzled. One day it shone on a light frosted crust of snow and Sacha forced her out to walk in it. She walked as if hypnotised by the breaking of the crystals underfoot, the softness beneath. It was so white, like careful celebratory icing on the smooth branches and twigs of the beech trees. She thought how Alfie would have delighted in scuffing up the snow with his heels. She remembered the earth- and grass-stained boulder they used to roll up on the lawn at home, the belly of the snowman, how heavy it grew, how it creaked as they pushed it picking up squashed berries and bird-droppings, how hot inside their coats they got, their woollen gloves huge and clogged, wet fingers numb. How in the thaw the snowman would be the last thing to go, how it would sit on the lawn for weeks, a grubby nub, gradually shrinking until it was gone. And remembering that, she started to cry.

This was a new place again and it was as if before – that numb dazedness – had been easy, had been nothing. Now the tears came in waves that engulfed her, that she gave herself up to until she thought she would go under and drown. The ugliness of grief dismayed her, no romance in the chapped skin, blocked nose, eyes rimmed with red.

Sacha, sitting by her bed, didn't try and stop her crying like Mother would have done. Connie wanted her mother to soothe her but then it was her mother for whom she grieved: she ground round and round in that terrible cycle of realisation and pain. And Alfie, dear little war-loving Alfie . . . and Father. It was too much and she felt her heart break in her chest, thought that was just an expression before, never knew that a heart could really break. Sacha there saying, 'That's good, good, Con, you cry. Cry.' Sacha's hand bigger and rougher than her mother's would have been. Connie stared and stared at it, the thick thumb, the dry texture of the deeply fretted palm, the minute brown hairs on the backs of the fingers, the paint or ink stains beside the nails. Not the soft white scented hand for which she longed – but when she looked up there was such tenderness in the brown eyes, lucky Sacha's eyes were brown not blue like Mother's or Alfie's, not grey like Father's. Sacha solid enough to hold on to, a still thing in the sweeping grief, a big, dry hand.

Sometimes in the midst of her grief Connie would have an awareness, just for a moment, like a swimmer coming up for air, of something else that Sacha was feeling. And that was fear. Although she never said so, Connie knew that Sacha was thinking about Red in Africa and sometimes she would find a thread of strength to hope, for Sacha's sake, that he might return home safe.

But mostly Connie couldn't get past her own pain to wish or hope for anything. Patrick was kind too. He didn't know what to say to her but he would bring her things: a fat white hyacinth in a pot, a branch of fir cones, brown acorns, scarlet butcher's-broom. He wanted her to take some mixture he'd made from plant essences but Sacha absolutely forbade it.

When he came to her room he'd stand awkwardly wringing his hands, his beard wild, his eyes bright with sorrow till she wanted to tell him it was all right. But it was not all right. It never would be right again.

And then one day the windows were opened and there were daffodils, daffodils everywhere. Such *yellow* and a soft greenness in the air. Walking then on legs that had grown weak, sometimes with Sacha, sometimes with Patrick, spotting the way the bracken grew curled up in tight foetal buds; leaf spears everywhere; green sparks igniting on twigs; birdsong, she felt the spring in herself.

One day feeling the hot roll of a tear down her cheek – why? Oh something Alfie would have liked, a grass-snake perhaps or a bird's nest, she felt bored. Bored with tears, impatient.

New again, a new feeling like one of the bracken fronds beginning, just beginning, to unfurl and then the tickle of a smile that started in her diaphragm, a tickle stretched by her lips curving up, the tilting of her eyes, a rush of pleasure. The first moment she forgot and smiled, chuckled, laughed: she was walking with Patrick that day, they paused by a pond in the wood and were confronted by the shocking, hilarious, preposterous sight of frogs, dozens of them, hundreds, clinging and clambering and croaking. 'Mating,' Patrick said and to her horror and delight scooped up a ball of frog, a female sandwiched between two males. 'See how they grab on,' he said, trying to disengage one but it was impossible. 'Only the first one gets it, but still this other fellow won't give up. Sometimes they're so desperate for it, the males, that they drown the female, drag her under in their struggle to mate.' He crouched and replaced the frogs at the edge of the pond. He lifted and held out to her a clotted mass of jellied spawn that made her shudder, then smile. 'Touch,' he said, and her smile turned to a chuckle and then a laugh that almost hurt it had become so strange to her. Not funny, nothing funny really, but it was the breeding frogs that first made her laugh.

The day of the frogs, the day she laughed again and her heart started to mend – not mend entirely because a heart will always bear scars – was the day Connie began to experience a new guilt. Her grief had been threaded through with guilt that she had lived while they had all died. She should have gone back to London with them and died too. Or at the very least she should have persuaded Alfie to stay with her, when really she'd been *glad* that he had gone back, glad to be left to start her new life alone. She remembered the white hand-kerchief fluttering from the car, Alfie's farewell. That guilt was such a staggering weight to bear. And guilt that she was rich too, not rich but comfortable, had *benefited*, all Father's investments and what have you, hers.

But with the spring and the gradual lifting of her spirits a new guilt grew. Not something she could ever voice to a soul, not a worthy or explicable guilt like those she'd gulped out one dark night to Sacha. This was a sneaky feeling of exhilaration that caught her now and again, caught her unawares: that she was *free*. Free to be who she wanted. Young and free and happy, alive in her lovely body. This feeling she weighed down as if she was piling stones on a light puff of silk that wants to rise in the breeze, weighing it down with deliberate sadness, focusing on all that she had lost until she caused the breeze to drop, the silk, her spirits, to drop.

FIFTEEN

You could get used to hotels. You collect your key from some smart piece at reception, you press the button and you step into the lift which is carpeted and mirrored so you can stare into your own eyes as you rise. You only have to remember your floor, master your key-card – what is wrong with a proper key for goodness sake? – then you shut the door behind you and it is all yours, the great bed made up for you in your absence, all tidied, the bathroom stuff replenished, thick dry towels. It is private and thrilling.

Connie flings her bags on the bed and lies down. She has spent £500 on clothes, lipstick, shoes. It makes her dizzy to think it. *Five hundred pounds*. A sin. Thirty years ago she could have lived for a year on that, royally. Her last coat cost £3.12/6d, that sum sticking in her head for some reason. Patrick was there when she chose that coat, fidgeting because he hated shops, but she made him help her choose and the pinkish tweed was a good choice only now it's finished with. She runs her finger down the chipped buttons. She may never wear it again, not now she has her new and snazzy London look. The assistant at the PAY HERE desk hardly blinked as she wrote her cheque, as if people spend like that every day – well, most likely they do.

She lies on the huge bed feeling tiny, her ankles together, her hands folded on her stomach, but it's no good. She's too tremulous to rest. When she shifts the bags crackle. She gets up and takes off her old coat, her dreadful shoes. Fingers trembling, she opens the first bag, almost afraid to look at what's inside – things that are like scraps of dream carried back into daylight. She bought everything in a rush in the end, getting impatient, not wanting to be in that hot shop for ever.

From the bag she takes out a silver-striped box, under the lid folded in black tissue paper is the first item: a glossy green brassière trimmed with lace. She tried it on in the changing room, amazing item, amazing feel, she's never worn such a thing before. Strange what it does to the whole body, that feeling of grasping, two silky palms cupping her breasts upwards and together, giving her a shape, an attitude, that makes her want to jut her hip and toss her head. She takes out a pair of matching pants, not very warm pants by the look of them, a scrap of silk, a scrap of lace held together by shoelaces, and the cost! She holds them up to the light, almost nothing there. Complete extortion, that's what it is. Still, it's a shame to be a woman and never know what it's like to wear such a pair of pants, to wear a silky uplift brassière, anyway, that's what she told herself in the lingerie department and it may be true.

She arranges the underwear on the bed – how Patrick would have liked that, or would he? You never could tell with Patrick – and takes out the other things, a green dress with a hundred buttons, knee-length, quite demure, a purple velvet coat and hat, black tights, lipstick and shoes . . .

She saves the shoes till last, hardly breathing as she removes box from bag, lid from box and lifts them out one by one. Shoes she's never seen the like of before, dream shoes. The feeling when she saw them on display was like . . . like love . . . the nearest she's felt since . . . goodness knows.

The shoes are green suede, soft and bright as velvet grass with small heels and buttoned straps and each one is sprinkled with diamonds. Not diamonds, you fool, she smiles running her fingers over them, only paste or what have you but still, they glitter like diamonds, like ice-crystals on grass. Something her father used to say . . . oh! Twinkle Toes when she danced by the fire, or on the lawn, now she'll be Twinkle Toes all right in her new get-up. Tonight she'll show them, no fuddy duddy old recluse, Constance Benson, nothing to smirk behind her back at. She'll show them and she'll show Patrick, too. How proud he'd be, proud of her all done up in her new togs with her glittering shoes.

SIXTEEN

He washes up the pan, the plate, the wooden spoon, the fork. Dries them with Donna's 'Desiderata' tea-towel and replaces everything in its exact position. The kitchen clean and shiny. Next time he cooks it might be at Constance Benson's house. Feels a whizz of adrenalin in his veins. Time to get ready, shower again and shave and dress. Because then it will be time to go.

He sees her, midget in a purple hat with a tall blonde bitch. He's been hanging about outside the NPG in the pissing rain since they chucked him out, watching the taxis spewing out the chosen few. He recognises Benson immediately, a silvery shock up his spine. *This is it, this is real.* The face is old, of course, but still there are the same deep eye-sockets, slightly beaky nose, curve of high brow. Constance Benson in the flesh, Patrick's lover. Hard to see it, she's so teeny and gaudy, like something carved on the side of a fairground organ. Still, this is it, it is happening. He steps forward.

'Excuse me.'

Benson would have stopped. Her eyes flick to his face but the younger one, who is sheltering her for the two-metre dash with a white umbrella, urges her on and Tony has to back away. What do they think he is, some beggar? Some nutter? That he is dressed so smartly seems not to have registered. His shirt, even wet with London rain, is the cleanest most gleaming thing in the entire vicinity.

'You don't understand,' he says, 'if I could just have a word with Miss Benson . . .' But what word? What word could there be? He hasn't rehearsed this, hasn't got a frigging script. He waits for Patrick to help, *trusts* that Patrick will help but Patrick lets him down. He should have filled Tony's mouth with the right words, the words that would have stopped her in her tracks, made her look, made her *see*. But no, there is nothing there. The tall bitch gives him a look like a chip of cut glass in his eye and hustles Benson away up the steps and through the doors.

He nearly loses it then. Walks in the rain with the light splashing up round his ankles, feeling sick. Gets on the Victoria Line at Oxford Circus, numb, wet, warm, almost steaming in the crush. Arm above his head he hangs in the crush aware of the smell from his armpit, anxious reek, odd, a vegetable smell, like sap from hogweed or something, tough and sour, something vaguely remembered, a river bank, hedgerow trampling and crushing. Forget that childhood shit. He stares at an advert for contact lenses, thinks about that bitch's eyes and Benson's, which did look at him. Must get her alone, be alone with her, must find her.

Just wait. Just have faith. All things come to he who waits. There will be a sign, a further sign and then it will be all right. She will give him what he needs. Then his life will start. All right?

But . . . if it never comes . . . if there is nothing . . .

The train, almost empty now, stops in the tunnel just short of Brixton and Tony catches the blank eyes of a youth, looks away quickly, notices the sheen of nylon over a pair of fat knees further down the carriage, sees the flat meaningless glossiness of both, gets a pain in his gut that almost doubles him. Not pain, not in the usual sense, but a sensation of nothing . . . an ache . . . an awful glimpse. Like a voice saying *You are a fool, this is all nothing, this is nothing.* What? Like a knee in the heart.

He groans aloud, curious eyes swivel and he turns it into a yawn, feeling like the fucking dick-head that he is. There was no voice, not really, and with a jolt that shakes him out of it the train starts and the knees cross showing a paler glimmer of thigh and the eyes of the youth opposite narrow and spark. The train stops, doors open to spill him out. And there on the platform before this . . . this *fear* can really get a hold, there in front of him is Patrick – on a poster. And those eyes anything but empty meeting his. And what is that but a sign? Get a grip, Tony, don't lose it now. The fear lets go, sighs off down the hot tunnel. Stupid. But human. After all he is only human. Tony pauses by the poster. Smiles at Patrick, 'Thanks, mate,' he says.

SEVENTEEN

Everyone is so tall and the noise goes on over her head. Connie has drunk several glasses of red wine and cannot prevent herself smiling whenever she looks down at her twinkling shoes – though her plastic teeth must be black by now. Not that the shoes are comfortable, they squeeze her big toe joints and tilt her forward so she has to lean back and that gives her a nag in the lower part of her back. High heels are hell.

'Do you paint at all, Miss Benson?' a young man asks, the umpteenth time she's been asked that tonight. He smiles down at her, head tilted in anticipation. His teeth too are wine-stained, she frowns and runs her tongue around her own.

'It's a lovely party,' she says.

'I very much admire your work.'

'Such a long time ago, dear.' Someone fills her glass, offers her something from a tray – asparagus on little bits of biscuit. She puts it in her mouth, it's her least favourite of the circulating tit-bits, can't understand all the song and dance about asparagus – soggy, wee-wee smelling stuff. Wine good though, tough, puts a fur on the tongue. The young man has three studs in one ear and many rings in the other, otherwise he's smartly dressed with a thin tie that looks like leather. Wonderful. Patrick would surely have had rings in his ears, piercings. She saw in a magazine in Deborah's office that some of them have all sorts pierced, nipples, eyebrows, navels, even their what-nots. She likes it, sort of tribal, though she'd draw the line at the foreskin if she was a man. One woman here has at least thirty studs and rings in her ears and nose and a Celtic design tattooed on her neck. Makes you wonder about the rest of her. She, like most of them, is dressed from head to toe in black. Connie stands out all right in her green.

'And do you still paint?' The man persists.

'You've asked me that,' Connie says. 'I do like your ear-rings, do you call them ear-rings or is that sissy?'

He shrugs, sulky and theatrical. 'Call them what you like.'

He reminds her of whatsisname, the photographer chap. 'Are you a homo, dear?' she says and the poor man chokes on his wine. Oh it's lovely to be old, you can be quite outrageous.

Photographs are taken and she's glad she's made the effort with her dress. True she *is* the only woman not decked out in black, a sore thumb at a funeral springs to mind, but then it distinguishes her, too, the rest of them like a foil. She smiles brazenly at the camera, sod the teeth, and raises her glass, poses beside Patrick, feeling his eyes warm on the green of her dress, the purple of her hat which she kept on in the end because she never did get round to getting her hair dyed.

'You've been offered a huge sum for the rights on a new edition of Mount's Memoir,' a voice says and Connie squints to connect it to an aubergine mouth.

'Is that so?'

'I wonder, Miss Benson, how does such a renewal of interest in Mount affect your personal memories?'

'Not a blinking jot.'

'And I believe negotiations are underway for the film rights?'

'I never could allow it.'

'Not in favour?'

'It would be pure porno, you see.' Connie pauses. 'I could do with the spondulicks . . . been shopping today . . . the cost of things! Like my shoes?' She kicks up a foot and catches the owner of the aubergine mouth smartly on the shin. 'I do beg your pardon,' she says, but the mouth and the shin have gone.

The voices are like a cloud above her head. She wanders below it breathing in perfume, alcohol, breath. She is on a level with bosoms and armpits, sees the red mottled top of an arm squeezed into a too-tight sleeve, sees a man with a smear of something white – horse-radish? – on his lapel. Once, shortly after Patrick's going, she tried to drown but she couldn't stay under. Her head *would* come to the surface, her mouth would not open to the sea and as she gave up, came up, gasped the air into her burning lungs, a seagull swooping down close to her head gave a derisive laugh. Why does that come to her now, submerged by voices, fogged by drink? Deborah comes across to her, long flat body explicit in her tight little dress. How does her lipstick stay so exact? 'How are you doing?'

'Very well.'

'Good.'

'Except for my feet, killing me.'

'Mine, too . . . just say when you're through. Shall I introduce you to . . .' and more questions, more photographs and something much more agreeable to eat, little toasts that taste of prawn with seeds all over that get stuck under her denture. Connie forces her tongue up underneath and champs it back in place.

'After the death of Mount you never painted again . . .' a voice breathless with romance and yet borne on breath that

78

reeks of garlic. Someone almost as short as Connie though three times the breadth at least with most improbably coloured hair.

'Did I not?' Connie tilts her head playfully to one side and her hat slides. She clamps it back.

'Your inspiration died with him.'

The face is innocent and sincere, the eyes soft. This is a person who has yet to be hurt. The last mouthful of wine tastes sour, her mouth sore. Only choice now to flee or to carry on drinking. A bottle floats past and she holds out her glass. 'Sorry, dear?'

The voice more hesitant, curling up at the end. 'Your inspiration? Died with him?'

'If indeed he died.' This wine white and acidic. She swills it round her mouth. At least it might bleach her teeth.

'You think he might still be . . .'

'He would be ninety-nine, but then I'd put nothing past Patrick.' Connie laughs, looking at the credulous face. 'No, dear. I'm certain that he's dead. I didn't feel like painting for a long time, I wouldn't put it no grander than that. More grandly, rather. Would you . . . if your what have you . . . boyfriend or so on snuffed it? Would you feel like painting?'

'Well, no, I suppose not.'

'Do you paint?'

'Well, no . . .'

'Well, then.'

People are thinning out and Deborah finds her. 'Had enough?' she says. 'A great success, I think. Let's get a cab.' They make their way out between hands and smiles and continental-style kisses from people she's scarcely met for God's sake! Gusts of alcoholic breath, promises of all sorts, articles, dinners, even a TV documentary. And someone wanting to write her biography. Now, there's a thought.

'I'm pooped,' Connie says. 'I want my bed.'

'Nothing to eat then, not a quiet little supper? I know the sweetest Italian . . .'

Connie can barely shake her head. Quite suddenly she has had it. She longs to ease off the pinching twinkling shoes and the hot velvet hat, to unfasten her bra and remove the irritating lace knickers that have crawled up between her buttocks, to find an interesting little bottle in the refrigerator, to fill her pipe and climb into bed. Maybe a few peanuts. Maybe room-service, try one of those BLTs. Maybe even the adult channel again, a few minutes of young pounding flesh might be just the job to send her off to sleep. Maybe, maybe not. But what is utterly crucial is to be alone. In the rainy flash and roar of the London streets, Connie has a clear sharp stab of longing for the sea and for the peace of her own place beside it.

EIGHTEEN

Patrick is everywhere. People are stopping in front of him, leaning forward to read the titles, dates and notes mounted beside each portrait. Patrick like a prophet, bearded and wise; Patrick close-up and in the distance; Patrick in profile and Patrick head-on. Here he leans over a spade in a green, green garden. Here in similar pose he seems the dark centre of a brilliant flower. Here he bends over his desk, reading glasses slipping down his nose. Here he holds a purple orchid in his hand. And here is the new portrait in which, suddenly, strangely, he is young.

Tony stares at the face, the look in the eyes that is . . . a *blaze* almost of outrageous, knowing, bliss. Tony grins, understands. That is the bliss that will be his. Feels proud and jealous at once. Jealous that other people are staring at his Patrick. Liked it best when nobody knew, when Patrick was obscure, was his alone. But there has to be a price for this, *this*, what is meant to be, what he has been waiting for.

Patrick. The Seven Steps to Bliss. *Only stay open*, says Patrick from somewhere in his gut and Tony is, *is* open, more than he has ever been before, open to what comes next. A woman moves in front of him, gets in his way. She's looking at the portrait of Patrick in the garden with the hills behind, in the foreground are huge leaves – rhubarb? Patrick dwarfed and yet magnificent. It's a clumsy painting, early, he sees from the dates, yet it has caught Patrick's movement, his foot on a spade, hands brown on the handle, a moment of concentration. The woman is wearing black, a thin black dress, short sleeves. Her arms are very white. He stands close behind her, very white, and there are tiny moles above the elbow. Below the elbow the arms are downy, long light-brown hairs. Maybe she feels his scrutiny. She turns and frowns at him but he smiles.

'Like it?' he says.

She looks back at the painting. 'Yes . . . it's charming . . . kind of naive . . . but really it's the later stuff I love . . . more substantial, I guess.' She moves away. The scent she leaves behind her is like almonds, very faint. Tony feels the leak of saliva inside his cheeks. Follows her to a portrait of a woman.

'Sachavarelle Mount RA,' he reads. 'Substantial enough for you?' She laughs but looks at him oddly. She can't weigh him up and that's how he likes it. Keep 'em guessing, Tony. Leans forward as if to look more closely at the picture and breathes in the almond smell that seems to be coming from her hair, fair, flyaway hair. The material of the dress clings and he can see the shape of her shoulder blades, a ridge that must be the back fastening of her bra. Her back must be so very white. With little moles like on her arms? Would the bra be black like the dress, or white like the skin, or . . .

Sachavarelle Mount RA sits on a wicker chair, in a conservatory perhaps. Plants everywhere, a cup and saucer balanced on her knees. Her face is solid and pink, many pinks, when you look close you can see how many shades of pink and grey and even blue go to make up that colour, clever stuff. She's big, hair heavy grey, eyes warm and wet looking like a kind dog's eyes and there is a dog, a black-and-white one sleeping by her feet.

'Now this is what I call great,' the woman says.

'His first wife.'

'*Only* wife – he never married Constance Benson. And not just a *wife* either. Brilliant in her own right. Seen her stuff in the Tate? Landscapes, still lifes? And some great pictures of her son.'

Tony shakes his head. He knows the paintings exist, of course, but they haven't seemed important, oblique to his purpose. Now he feels irritated that he has to say no. 'And *her* portrait of Benson, here in the twentieth-century room. That famous nude by a window . . .'

Tony shakes his head again.

'You *must* know it, it's on a book cover, a book about women's art that went with a Channel 4 series . . .'

He likes her dress, the smell of her hair, the sprinkle of pin-point moles on the white of her arms. There's a mole beside her mouth that disappears into a fold of dimple when she smiles. He forces his eyes away from her and meets Patrick's. Patrick was a goat all right, but Tony must concentrate, stay open, must not fall into this trap of attraction which in any case he could never follow through, must never. That is where the danger lies. He cannot have happiness in that way. That is why the elixirs are vital – another route to bliss. All the same something inside him stirs at the scent of her. If he could only touch her skin, smooth down that flyaway hair, that would be enough. As his gaze lingers on the skin of her upper arm, the texture changes. Goose-pimples?

'What do you think of this?' She stops by a portrait of a bloke with blue eyes, very rough hair.

'OK.'

'*This* is Red, you know, Sachavarelle's son. I read somewhere that she had some sort of affair with him.'

'What, Benson?' He snorts. Load of bollocks.

She shrugs. 'I was going to have a quick coffee,' she says. 'Fancy one? Then I could show you the Mount.'

He pauses.

'Only if you've time . . .' She looks down, folds her arms across her chest, her cheeks gone very red.

'OK. A quick coffee.' Approval on Patrick's face? 'Just quick, I'm . . .'

'I haven't long either,' she says.

Somewhere, Tony read Patrick described as a sexual adventurer. Odd way to put it, makes Tony think of jungles, mountains, torrential rivers. Sex is far more dangerous than that. Awful memories, the shocking looseness of a big breast, reek of fingers more clinging than onions that you have to scrub and scrub. No. No more. And the way a head will loll suddenly even when you didn't mean –

No, oh Christ no, not here in the bright and pictures. Look at the tiles on the floor and how square they are and what colours. And look at her neat legs in thick tights, the short dress and Doc Martens. She is the sort of woman he would like, if. Nothing wrong in thinking that. Nothing wrong in a cup of coffee. Slim and trim, small breasts, smell of almonds almost a baby smell. Intelligent, too. She walks ahead of him bulging bag over one shoulder. Feels good to be walking with a pretty woman in a public place. In her smile a promise? You don't want the promises but you like the promise anyway.

She pours three little tubs of milk into her coffee and tells him about her job. She's a journalist, well, *reporter*, she wrinkles up her nose, tells him about the shit jobs she usually gets.

'How old are you?' he asks.

'Blunt, aren't you?' He waits. 'Twenty-five.' There's a long pause, her cheeks are very red now, from the coffee, or from his eyes on her so close.

'You?'

'Thirty.'

'No!'

Where is this leading?

She giggles. 'Well, I'm glad we've got that straight.'

He drinks his coffee black. When she picked up three milks he assumed they were to share, now he doesn't want to show his error by getting up to fetch some more. It's bitter coffee.

'And you do?' she says.

'Write,' he says.

'Oh?' She looks pleased. 'Write what? I mean would I have heard of you?'

He shrugs, swallows coffee, looks off into the distance.

She laughs and the tip of her tongue touches her teeth which are a little crooked in the front, one crossed slightly over the other. His finger itches to touch the mole on her cheek, to feel her flesh dimple round it when she smiles.

'Books,' he says. What does it matter? Won't be seeing her again. He could say any old bullshit, anything at all.

'Fiction or . . . ?' She is ready to be impressed. But he can't decide what it is he writes. 'Gawd, it's like pulling teeth!' She is a giggler. Tony hasn't giggled for a long time but he remembers the feel of it, lifting up the lid of his desk to hide himself from the teacher, the rubbery pencil-shaving smell as the giggles burst in him and out of him like bubbles.

'I'm doing a thing about Mount,' he says.

'Really?' She waits for more, a strand of hair stuck to the corner of her mouth.

'Actually, I don't talk about a piece while it's in here.' He taps the side of his head.

'Oh I understand.' She is suddenly serious. She brushes the hair away from her lips. Christ, she is adorable. He looks away.

'I did a piece on Benson,' she says.

Everything seems to go very still. 'What?'

'At Home With . . . it was sheer luck, the woman who was assigned went into early labour – little boy, really *sweet*, called him Mercurio though poor thing – so it was luck but I jumped at it, of course.'

Tony forces his mouth to move. 'You.'

'I interviewed her, yes. God it was a scream! What she gave us for lunch!' Tony watches her speak. This is different. Of course it is different. *This is it.* This girl is the sign and signal, the focus, the point at which meaning starts. 'I've always loved her work,' she is saying, 'so the chance to go to her home . . .'

'You've been to her house?' The rest of the cafeteria is a blur and this woman shines, pale hair, scarlet cheeks, the mole coming and going as she smiles and speaks. He wants to grab her and squeeze out what he needs to know, but cannot do that. She has been sent and he must honour her. Feels something in his gut like Patrick rubbing his hands randily together. Of course it would be here that the sign would come to him. And of course, Patrick *would* make the sign in the shape of a shaggable woman. Not that he will.

'Yes and it's like in the middle of *nowhere*, you know? And really . . . *ramshackle*. All the same . . .' She sips her coffee. 'All the same it was very nice, sort of quaint. She's got sea-shells stuck all over the walls. It's romantic, isn't it? All that stuff about how they loved each other so much . . .'

Tony makes his face smile and relaxes. She isn't going to disappear.

'Have you read Mount's Memoir?'

'Got it here.' Tony pulls his battered copy from his jacket pocket.

She gasps. 'This is *so* weird,' she says. She opens her bag and rifles through, pulling out the same book. 'Coincidence or *what*? I've never even seen another copy.'

'I don't believe in coincidence,' Tony says. Her eyes are small but they are the lightest blue.

'It's funny though, isn't it?'

Tony looks at his watch. 'Gotta go.'

'Just come and see the painting of Constance Benson first.'

'OK.' Can't hurt, can it? Can't run, anyway, not without more . . . more to go on.

The painting is hung on a perspex wall. It is sky through glass. *Sky Before the Fall*, it's called for some reason. In front of the window a nude girl stands, slim and shimmery pale. Her long brown hair hangs down her back in a plait, the tapered end just touching the cleft between her buttocks. She is turned so that the small point of a jutting white breast is visible, and the cheek and the edge of her slightly smiling mouth. It takes his breath away.

'This is the only portrait of Benson by Mount . . . not really a portrait painter. Well, it's hardly a portrait, is it, not in the usual sense. I wonder . . .' She pauses. 'I wonder how Sachavarelle felt when Patrick and Constance got it together. I wonder if she minded, I mean. They all lived together for quite a while before Sachavarelle died.'

Tony shakes his head. 'It's Afuckingmazing,' he says when he can speak, and the woman giggles.

'Lisa,' he says, tearing his eyes away from the painted flesh.

She turns and stares at him. 'How do you know?'

'Ah,' he says.

She blinks, then laughs. 'You saw the article!'

He nods. 'Lisa Just.'

'Well . . . I'm . . . flattered.' She looks down at her toes, twists her hair round her finger. 'So, what's yours?'

'My what?'

'Your name! Gawd!'

'Tony.' His eyes go back to the painting. Something about the juxtaposition of flesh that is almost ethereal in its paleness, like something temporary, a trick of the light and the sky that seems solid. Christ, he *could* write something about this, something quite poncey if he set his mind to it.

'Well, Tony, nice to meet you.'

'You're going . . .'

'Yes.' Opens his mouth to ask, what? Where she lives? What? Can't let her go, needs her to tell him what next. But before he can speak she reaches into her bag. Her face has gone very red, it's amazing the way she goes from white to pink to red and back again. 'Here's my card,' she says. 'If you feel like a drink sometime . . .' Her eyes meet his for a moment, terrifyingly genuine, and his heart lurches.

'See you,' he says, as she walks away. Watches the sway of her hips until she has gone and then, with his heart beating hard, he slips her card into his wallet and turns back to *Sky Before the Fall*.

NINETEEN

'I can't move,' Connie said, licking a trace of gravy off her index finger.

'She's a wonder,' Sacha agreed.

Betty, Sacha's friend, grinned. 'Only a pie,' she said. They were sitting on the lawn, beside them empty plates bearing remnants of a rabbit pie and glasses with the last few sips of pea-pod wine, both of which Betty had brought for Sacha's birthday lunch. Patrick had gone off to his beehives and the three women lounged on the lawn. Betty stretched out her long legs, Connie looked at the straight brown hairs on her shins. A tall woman, nearly as tall as Patrick, with a big humorous face, lots of teeth.

'But *such* a pie as never was,' Sacha said.

Betty threw back her head and laughed, then yawned. 'I wish my boys were half as appreciative,' she said. 'Speaking of which, I have to be going, my sweethearts.'

'Not yet,' Sacha's voice was persuasive.

'Yup. Must get back.' She stood up, gathered her fuzz of grizzled hair into a bun and tied a red scarf over it. A bead of sweat trickled down the inside of her knee.

'Bye,' Connie said and took the last swallow of the warm thin wine. Sacha went to see Betty off then sat down on the lawn again sighing.

'She's nice,' Connie said, but Sacha said nothing, just

gazed at the gate through which Betty had gone. They sat in silence for a long drowsy time then Sacha said, out of nowhere, 'It takes a year, you know. The first cycle of mourning.'

Connie started. Harry loped out and lay down with his nose by a gravied plate, flipping the tip of his tail up and down hopefully. It was such a lovely June day, the weather so perfect you'd have liked to bottle it. A day just like the day a year ago when Connie arrived with Alfie and her parents. A year that felt like twenty. Looking back to that day was like looking back on herself as a child, another kind of creature altogether. So innocent. There are those who have suffered and those who haven't and that is the biggest difference between people. Connie thought, looking at Sacha's face, that is a greater difference than between men and women, or adults and children.

The smell of lilac and the dazed murmur of the bees brought the memory of her arrival back to her, stealthily, overwhelmingly, pushing her back till she lay flat on the grass, the sky pressing down as if it had fallen. She no longer grieved all the time. She had hours some days when she forgot her grief but it was as if she couldn't get away with it, a few hours off were paid for by more acute grief later.

'A year,' she whispered.

'After a year you can no longer think *this time last year we* . . .' Sacha said. Connie turned her head and blinked up at Sacha, rainbowed through the prisms of wet on her lashes. Sacha did understand. Sacha had suffered. She had loved someone before she loved Patrick, a man called Miles who had been thrown and trampled to death by a horse just days before their wedding. Sacha had told it to Connie one day, her voice flat, her eyes on the window down which rain was streaming. 'We were riding on the South Downs, a windy, sunny day. He had hair the colour of conkers in the sun. I thought, *I am so happy, I am happier than it is possible to be.*' She had given a humourless laugh. 'That taught me. Never, Connie, *never* take anything for granted. I was ill after, sick as a dog on what should have been my wedding day – with what turned out to be Red.' Her hand had gone to her belly and a shadow had flitted over her face. Red still out in Africa, the news sporadic. Sacha *so stoical*, never speaking aloud the fear that she lived with every day.

Connie lifted her heavy hand from the grass and touched Sacha's knee. Without her, Connie did not know how she could have lived through the first winter and spring. Sacha was so solid and kind but not intrusive. She never said, 'Everything is all right.' She never said, 'Don't cry.' 'This is terrible,' she said instead, 'this might be the worst thing you ever know. You must cry, you must grieve. And it will change you for ever. But you will live.'

They remained on the grass for a long time, quiet. Connie closed her eyes. She breathed in Harry's doggy smell and the smell of Sacha, paint and sweat; the scent of lilacs and wallflowers. She could hear birds, bees, breathings and rustlings, a little yelp from the dreaming dog. The sun was hot on her eyelids. She lay on the ground until the sky began to lift. An ant tickled her leg and she sat up to brush it off. She hugged her knees to her chin. She was wearing a summer dress that Sacha had made for her out of an old one of her own, faded blue and flowery, loose and cool, but still, sticking to her skin in the heat.

Sacha's forehead was deeply creased and her mouth pursed in a way that made her look fierce and old. 'Thinking about Red?' Connie asked.

Sacha shook her head impatiently. 'You know what I think?' she said. 'I think it's time you began.'

'Began what?'

'To paint, of course.'

'No.' Connie frowned at her knees under the stretched material. The idea of doing something, something new, was too much to contemplate. It was all she could do to hold herself together. Patrick came round the side of the house, his bee helmet under his arm.

'A charming vision,' he said. 'Two females in repose. And dog,' he added, crouching down to rub Harry's head. He put his helmet on the grass. A bee crawled lazily across the visor. He unbuttoned his thick canvas shirt and took it off. He sat down between Connie and Sacha. The smell of him was strong, the hairs around his nipples shocking black against his whiteness. Connie looked harder at her knees.

'I was just suggesting to Con that maybe it's time she took up the brush,' Sacha said.

'Got stung,' Patrick said, showing them a swollen redness on his wrist. 'And what does Connie say to that?'

Connie shook her head and looked towards the house. The sky reflected blue in the windows. A tortoiseshell butterfly landed on Patrick's arm.

'Look, Con,' he said and extended his arm towards her. The butterfly rested on his skin, opening and closing its wings. 'What do you see?'

'I see a butterfly on your arm.'

'Try again.'

It was a game he liked to play. Sometimes Connie liked it though it was hard. And she was too hot. It annoyed her, *he* annoyed her the way he'd never let her slide away, always made her engage with him in a way that was demanding, but . . . she looked at his intense face . . . but made her feel approved of, too. Made her feel important. As no one else had ever done. So she played along. 'I see peachy brown, speckled, pink swell, small black fuzz of lines and green beneath, a moving thing now doubled, trembling. Gold, orange, brown, the lightest shadow . . .'

'No!'

'Wisp of grey, no deeper flesh . . .'

'And that doesn't make you want to paint?' said Sacha.

'I wouldn't be any good.'

'Good is subjective,' Patrick said. 'You're right. Undoubtedly some people won't think you're any good. But it scarcely matters. To be doing, absorbing yourself . . . forgetting . . . colour . . . light . . . space.'

Both of them looked at her, expectantly, hopefully even. This pressure was new and unlike them. They must have planned this, decided behind her back that it was time to chivvy her. She jumped up. 'If I try to paint, it will be when I'm good and ready,' she said, smoothing down her skirt, flicking another ant to the ground. '*And* if and when I'm ready it won't be butterflies I paint.' She stalked off into the house where it was cool and dim and dusty. What would it be then? she asked herself, but glancing back out of the window at Sacha and Patrick together on the lawn she knew it could only be them. The grey and the black, the dark cushions on the grass, the million greens of grass, leaf, shadow, hill, the white feather of dog-tail, the yellowish pale of skin and the speckled sparkle of blue air, pollen- and sunshine-filled. She could see it in paint when she closed her eyes, in patches, *freckles*, of light and shade, graduations of colour so fine you wouldn't believe it. For some reason she held her breath and tiptoed as she climbed the stairs into the swallow- and linseed-smelling studio.

TWENTY

Tony loves hospitals. Loves the bare shiny floors, the clink of metal on metal, the high white beds with their boiled clean sheets. Loves the nurses in their uniforms, though he's disappointed that they're wearing blue polyester-looking things, like housecoats. If it was up to him there would be more starch and whiteness. Yes, the wife he will never have could have been a nurse, a night nurse, and they would rarely meet – and when they did she might look like Lisa. Those small blue eyes, the fair hair piled on her head with a starchy cap. And as he lay alone at night between hospital-tight sheets he would be proud to think of her at work.

Maybe it's because he loves hospitals that he's visiting Donna. Maybe it's because he likes her, yes, something is stirring in him that feels like *like*. Lisa set him off, that frightening open glimpse into her, into her eyes. And Donna . . . well, he may never see Donna again. Donna has only been a part of his waiting life. When he sees Lisa later that will be the end of it and he may never return to the flat. So maybe he is here to say goodbye.

Visitors swarm through the entrance and they all have something with them, flowers or carrier bags full of fruit and chocolate. Of course, that's what you do on a hospital visit, you take a present. Goes into the hospital shop, looks at the chocolates but she might not like chocolate, did she say, he can't remember, that she was allergic to chocolate? She's one of these people allergic to everything, allergic to life practically. Best off with a book or magazine but most of them are crap in here and he doesn't know what she's got. Chooses a box of tissues, different colour ones in a flowery box. Tissues are always useful and you can't go wrong with something useful. Goes up in the lift in search of Donna's ward.

He sees her before she sees him. She's reading, not looking around, obviously not expecting a visitor. Her bed is opposite the door with its panel of criss-cross patterned glass. There are curtains drawn either side between her and her neighbours. Her hair is tied back from her colourless face, her eyebrows are fine raised lines. Is she really reading? She looks kind of defiant. He feels shy of her in the high neat bed and almost loses his nerve, but she looks up before he can turn.

'Tony!' It's like a fucking lightbulb's switched on inside her face, makes him feel bad.

'Hi.' Hands her the bag. She puts her hand in, eyes huge with surprise, and brings out the box of tissues.

'Oh . . . ta.'

'Didn't know what else.'

Light's off again. Looks as if she might cry. Christ, he's done his best. But then she shrugs and smiles. 'Very useful,' she says.

'That's what I thought.'

'Sit down.' She gestures to a chair which makes him way below her. He can't think of anything to say. Shifts around. Her book slides off the bed, he picks it up, another crap romance. Tragic.

'Well,' she says, 'didn't see you as the type . . . to visit, you know.'

'Said I might.'

'Still.' She smiles at him, the smile that makes crinkles at the corners of her eyes. Her eyes are not blue, but muddy green.

'So . . .' Shifts his eyes down to the green honeycomb blanket with the shape of body underneath. 'How was it?'

'I was asleep.' She laughs at the expression on his face. 'All according to plan . . . two more days I'm out of here. How's things?'

Tony nods. 'Fine, great actually. Donna, reason I've come, I'm moving on.' Her eyebrows meet. 'Something's come up, work and that.'

'Oh.' She smooths the folded edge of the sheet over the blanket. Her nails are bitten right down to their soft pink beds. 'Can't offer you anything . . . except water . . . water?'

'No ta.' A long silence. He wishes he hadn't come.

'I fucking hate cauliflower cheese.' The voice of a visitor behind the curtain is raised.

'What can I bleeding do about it stuck in here.'

Donna lifts her eyebrows and grins. 'They're always at it, hammer and tongs,' she whispers. 'So . . . what sort of work?'

'Not a job exactly, more an occupation you might say.'

'Girl?' Something funny in her voice, a little twist. New. The woman behind the curtain is crying now.

'Christ, I'm sorry,' the man says, 'I'll eat the fucking cauliflower cheese, only stop crying, baby, stop fucking crying.'

'Shall I lend her a tissue?' Donna says.

'Actually I did meet a girl, at an exhibition.'

'*Exhibition?*'

'Art. Lisa, gave me her number.'

'Going to ring?'

He shrugs.

'What's she like?'

'Blonde, blue eyes, kind of pretty.'

'Sounds nice.' Her hand goes to her own hair, stringy with grease, fiddles with the ratty rubber band. 'What were you doing at an exhibition?'

'Looking.'

'You don't say.'

'Patrick Mount's portrait and that . . .'

'Course. Well, ring her then. What you got to lose?'

'And where's my bleeding Lucozade you promised?' The woman, recovered now, demands.

'I'll miss you when you've gone.' Donna puts the raw end of her thumb into her mouth.

'I watered your plants.'

'Ta.'

'How old are you?'

'Why?' She starts to laugh and grabs her belly. 'Ouch! Twenty-two, why?'

'Just wondered.' Wants to go now, been and done it and now he wants to go, can't think of another thing to say, hates goodbyes. There's something he ought to say, something kind or comforting, but he can't think.

'Funny sort of present,' she says. She presses down until the perforations give and tears out the oval cardboard shape from the top. She plucks out a yellow tissue and wipes her nose. 'Very nice, very good tissue that,' she says stuffing it up her pyjama sleeve. Is she taking the piss? 'If you'd brought grapes you could have eaten them all like they do on the telly.'

'Didn't have grapes in the shop.'

'Doesn't matter I'm . . .'

'Allergic to grapes?'

'No, joking.' Their eyes meet for a second and he looks away.

'Best be off.' He stands up. What he should do, he realises, is kiss her. Kiss her on the cheek because it's goodbye and she is a friend. She likes him and he . . . he does like her. Is she expecting a kiss? Her eyes are dry and bright as she looks into his face. He leans towards her. Her skin is sallow and sheeny with grease, he can see the open pores beside her nose. Can't. Can't put his lips against her skin. Actually can't do it.

'See you Donna, take care.'

'Yes.' Her voice is very small. He leaves fast, whack through the swing doors along the corridor where a woman in a dressing gown totters along, a drip on wheels attached to her arm. Makes him go weird. Stops by the lift, finger hovering by the buttons. Can't do it. Something makes him go back. Stops by the doors of Donna's ward and looks through the chequered glass. She is clutching the box of tissues to her chest but he doesn't think she's crying. Thank Christ for that. Turns away and this time makes it down in the lift and out.

Goes in the first café he sees and pulls out his book. The same book she, Lisa, had in her bag. Nice name that, Lisa. Coincidence, she said. But it is a further sign. Watches his tea get cold. The tannin forms a patchy ginger skin on top. When he stirs it the skin breaks into geometrical fragments, clings to the spoon and the sides of the cup. Won't see Donna again. Raises the cup to his lips but puts it down. Wasn't tea he wanted in any case, just a fag and a place to sit out of the wind while he makes up his mind whether to ring Lisa or not. Whether to ring her today. The woman who served him is Australian, pretty, dark hair cropped very short, a straight look, sensible, long-fingered. 'Coming up,' she said when he asked for tea. 'Can I git you anything to eat?' as if she cared almost, took a personal interest. He felt sorry to say no and sat with his back to her to stop himself staring. What is it with him? Women everywhere all of a sudden and he can't have them, that decision is made. Laughs at a sudden realisation. Patrick! Of course, it's Patrick guiding him, noticing, steering him. Rolls a fag and opens the book at random. This page! Yes, Patrick is behind this all right, randy bastard. Grins as he reads:

As the attentive reader will be aware, it is one of the highest tenets of my system that one should take pleasure, where it does not give pain, wherever one can in order to increase the amount of pleasure and therefore joy and therefore good in this world. It is enjoyment that lends strength to the plants which nourish the air we breathe and return it, purified, a thousandfold to mankind.

Human and animal sexual activity, when it is of an enjoyable nature, gives pleasure to plants in the vicinity – and even to plants at great distances if they are personally attached to the participants. (See appendix for precise data.) Suffice it to say for the purposes of this memoir that the galvometer shows highly increased vibration in plants exposed to human orgasm.

For a male, and in some rare cases, for a female, novelty is one of the greatest aspects of sexual enjoyment and therefore I have made it my life's work, and occasional sacrifice, to seek sexual novelty (enjoying, I would estimate, upwards of five hundred women). However, when Constance Benson came into my life I discovered how a rather different sexual pleasure can occur in the context of a deepening love. Constance Benson has been and remains the love of my life. My wife I loved, too, but the love between us was always tempered by the love she had first given to another man – the fiancé who died in a riding accident – and our marriage from the first was based on understanding rather than passion. After the first year of our marriage we turned aside from each other in the physical respect alone. We both had lovers and sometimes early on, we had conjoined experiences – what have been commonly and crudely described as *orgies*, by my critics.

Sacha, Constance and I lived harmoniously together for eight years until the sad occasion of Sacha's death, after which my heart was given solely to Constance with whom it remains. Sexually I have never understood the reasoning behind fidelity but emotionally there has been only one woman for me since she entered my life.

Tony pulls out a Rizla and smooths it on the table in front of him. To ring Lisa now or not ring her now, ring her tomorrow? He needs another sign. Pinches out tobacco and rolls the paper into a tight cone, slicks his tongue along the shiny edge. Listens to the Australian woman behind him, 'Can I git you anything to eat?' asking someone else, with just the same pretence, as if she cared. But maybe that's just because she's Australian. Are they really friendlier? Thinks of Donna and her pinched little face, reluctant smile and her pile of crap romances. If this one speaks to him again, then he'll go straight out and ring Lisa. That's it. Signs will come via fanciable women, of course they will, he's getting the hang of this now. If not, then what . . . ? Flicks his lighter and breathes in smoke.

'Nobody iver tell you those things kill?'

Tony looks up at her face. She's standing behind him, a tray of crockery in her hands. He likes the way she wears a white apron over her jeans, and the shape of the muscles in her thin arms straining with the weight of the tray. 'Thanks, doll,' he says, gathering together his book and fag stuff.

'Doll! I like that!'

'See you,' and he's out of there heading for the nearest phone.

'Fucking pom,' she calls after him, but when he turns round she's grinning.

He has no phone card and there's a queue for the coin box. Almost gives up. But no, Patrick won't let him, he won't let himself. A windy corner – the wind sprung up from nowhere. Sky suddenly dark. A whirlpool of rubbish blows round in the gutter, crisp bag, cellophane, even some yellow leaves – though there are no trees in sight. Suddenly it's autumn, just like that. Pulls up the collar of his jacket, hunches into it, hands in pockets. Finally gets into the old-fashioned pissy-smelling box. Gets the card from his wallet, money from his pocket, only 20p, Christ. Lifts the receiver, puts in his coin, breathes in as he presses the numbers. What will he say? Probably isn't there. Should have rung the work number, dick-head, why would she be there at this time? Just about to put the receiver down when there's her voice, breathless.

'Sorry, just got in. Machine on the blink.'

'Lisa?'

'Speaking.'

'It's Tony?'

'–'

'From the Benson . . .'

'Oh! *That* Tony.'

'So . . . how are you?'

'All right . . . good.'

'–'

'So?'

'Look, I'm in a box, money going, fancy a drink or . . .'

'Er, yes . . .'

'Meet me at Leicester Square Tube at eight . . . we're going to be cut off . . .'

101

'OK.'

'OK? Which ent . . .'

But the line has gone dead. Tony listens for a moment to the quiet of it. Steps out of the box and into the wind. *Here we go*. Feels kind of loose and light all round his heart. This is it, the process starting. Three hours and he'll be with her and he won't get too close. Only needs directions. Won't hurt her and he won't get too close. And once he's got to Benson and got whatever he needs, the recipe or the elixir itself, then it will all be different. His proper life will start. The wind hooes round the corner and he clatters an empty Coke can along with his feet.

TWENTY-ONE

They let her have the studio. For those hot summer months Patrick worked in the garden tending his beehives and growing the victory vegetables as Sacha mockingly called them and they *were* splendid vegetables, creamy earth-tasting potatoes, the sweetest peas, lettuces big enough to fill your arms. He spent the rest of his time in his shed, doing some kind of experiments with the essences of plants, something that was secret and so absorbing they sometimes did not see him for days until he emerged with an odd dazed smirk on his face.

Sacha cycled off and set up her easel outside whenever the weather was clement. Sometimes she went to Bakewell to shop and visit Betty or Betty visited her. But usually Sacha painted, she took to painting in the kitchen so that the oily linseed smell infused the entire house, crept even into the taste of the food. The pastry she made to surround the fruits and vegetables of the garden was leathery with a linseed tang and sometimes even a streak of colour so that Connie, in her first giant burst of creativity, really felt that she ate, slept and breathed painting. Her dreams came in images and when words entered them it was often the names of pigments – burnt umber, raw umber, raw sienna, cinnabar green.

Three months, sometimes sun, sometimes rain sluicing and gurgling in the gutters, but three months spent in another existence where form was broken into planes, where edges became apparent where there were no edges before, edges between light and dark, soft and hard, real and reflection or shadow. And edges dissolved, too, into the subtlety of graduation. And the edge between grief and joy became subsumed in the fierce concentration to capture the form and nature of a moment.

And then October. A day, the day, the anniversary of the day. She did not paint on that day. It was not blue and blazing like last year, but a day of dull low cloud, the brown leaves a squelching porridge as she tramped through the beech wood with Patrick. It was her first day away from the studio. She had taken lately to sleeping in the studio on a folded pad of blankets so that she could lie in the first light and gaze at her work of the day before until she saw what was needed and hauled herself straight up to her easel. Patrick and Sacha had not seen what she had painted. After the first day they had submitted to being kept away.

'For a while only,' Sacha had said.

'I don't want you to look or I won't be able to work properly,' Connie had tried to explain. 'I'll always be worrying what you'll think. I don't want your . . . your . . . judgement.'

Sacha had nodded sagely. 'All right, until the first burst wears off.'

Connie had frowned, thinking what nonsense, this will *never* wear off, this fever for colour, this sudden urgent reason for being that was stronger than the need to eat or sleep or see another person: the need to paint.

But now, listening to the wet sucking underfoot, the scattering of rain on leaves, watching the dark stains spreading on the beech trunks, Connie knew that it had come. The end of the first burst. Today she did not need or want to paint. Today she was tired. It was because of the date, of course. This is the last day I will be able to think *this time last year*, she told herself, remembering Sacha's words on a hot day that itself seemed years ago. Alfie would never be eleven, would never be a man. Mother and Father would never see her grown. She thought this deliberately harshly as if poking at an exposed nerve but though the pain was there it didn't overwhelm her. There was even relief. That year over, that year done.

'Jay,' Patrick said from behind her, making her jump. She stopped to look up at the pinkish dun of the bird, a leaf fell as she looked, twirling slightly on its fall, and then another. Patrick stood close behind her like a pillar. She leant back against him to feel his warmth. She could feel or sense the soft of his beard against her head and smell something greenish. His arms came round her from behind and held her tight. It was the first time they had touched, Connie and Patrick, although she and Sacha were always hugging and touching each other's hands and hair. The rain pattered high up in the branches and some bird sang.

She rested her head back against him. 'I don't think I'll paint any more.'

'Ah, so it has come. Sacha said it would. You will paint, my love.' She could hear the smile in his voice. 'And when are we to be allowed to see the fruits of your endeavours?'

Connie pulled away and began walking. They had come to a place where the wood changed quite abruptly, the beech trees giving way to pine. A flat wooden bridge spanned the stony river that gurgled beer brown, already swelling with the autumn rain. She crossed the bridge, slippy underfoot, without looking back though she knew he was behind her. Between the sudden lofty pines the air was charcoal grey and chilly. It was quieter, no bird-song and the ground almost dry. It was a shivery place, less friendly than the beech wood where there was lightness between the spreading branches and colour in the undergrowth, where Patrick had pointed out a ring of fly agaric, vermilion spotted with white, nibbled at the edges. 'Some mice having a good time of it,' he had laughed, stooping to break off a small piece of toadstool and put it in his mouth. Connie had not been surprised – Patrick tasted everything, leaf, bark, petal, twig – but had shaken her head when he offered her a morsel.

Little rain penetrated to the ground between the pines and the ground was soft, earth and dried needles, their footsteps were silent. Connie pulled her coat more tightly around her and thought about her painting. Twenty old canvases and boards Sacha had given her to paint over and she had made twenty puzzling paintings. Each one was a craze of colour. Each one had made utter sense as she worked on it but that morning in the watery gloom of the studio she had not known what they were, or what they were for, whether she could even *call* them paintings in any sense other than that they were arrangements of paint on canvas. That was why she had come downstairs and announced her intention of going for a long walk and only then, when she noticed the look that had passed between Sacha and Patrick, had she remembered the significance of this day. She had been deliberately avoiding knowing the date, hoping it would pass her by unnoticed. But the calendar on the wall would catch her eye.

Seeing Patrick receive Sacha's look and knowing what it meant seemed to wake her from a dream. She had felt she was an artist, that she had found her calling, found a new kind of sense in life, the smell, colour, texture of paint, a new way of seeing. But now it all seemed an illusion, a kind of spell she'd been under. *Why?* She thought of the squares and oblongs of colour. *Why and what for?*

'You can see them,' she said over her shoulder. The dark wood made her uneasy. The towering trees had a definite and different presence from the beeches with their generous rounded limbs. The pines grew straight up, making dark in their competition for light and the carpet of pine needles was almost sterile apart from the occasional yellowish nub of a toadstool head pushing up. Patrick caught her up and put his arm round her. She let him, appreciating the warmth. She liked the way he listened to her, took her as seriously as any other adult. Treated her like a woman and a friend. She smiled up at him, lovely funny man with his spindly limbs and cascading beard.

'What do you smell of?' she asked wrinkling her nose. It was something like leaf-sap, something like incense, sweet but a bit sickly, too.

He drew his arm tighter round her and stooped to sniff his fingers. 'I will tell you all,' he said, 'when the system is further developed. Indeed I may ask your assistance.'

'How?'

'Some experiments on the effects of my elixirs.'

'What are they for, your elixirs?'

'That's a trade secret,' he said, tapping the side of his nose. They walked along in step and left the darkness of the pine wood, walking through a plantation of young firs barely six feet tall, intensely green, spangled with raindrops constantly shaken and shot to rainbows by the hopping of birds. Sunshine had escaped from a slit in the clouds and Connie squinted in the dazzle of it.

'There was a most . . . desolate atmosphere among those pines,' she said.

'Naturally. Trees have their own cultures, atmospheres, moods.'

'What?'

107

'Beeches are congenial, most deciduous birches are particularly playful and the rowan, well!' he chuckled. 'And these
young firs, like children. Do you feel it?'

'Mmmm.' Connie removed herself from under his arm and
walked ahead a bit so that she could grin. She could never tell
whether he was having her on.

'Mature Scots pines are possibly the most antithetical to
repose or pleasure. Though yews give them a run for their
money.'

'Oh look!' In the wet grass was the sudden mauve of a
cluster of autumn crocus. Connie crouched over them noticing the glitter of wet on mauve and green, tender petal
against coarse blade.

Patrick trampled along ahead of her and she followed,
watching the water brushed from grass and bracken splash
about his legs, the brown corduroy of his trousers growing
dark with the wet. He stopped suddenly and turned, held her
in his arms against his chest.

'I'm all right.' Her voice was muffled against his coat, her
nose full of the funny smell. His lips brushed the top of her
head.

'Are you sure, love?'

'Yes, just that I keep thinking of what it is I am.'

'And what are you?'

'An orphan,' she said. 'Isn't that a horrid word? Sounds
like awful.'

'Orphan,' he said slowly. 'Sounds like fantastic, too. And
you're not just an orphan, you're also an artist. Should I kiss
you?'

'You haven't seen yet. Compared to Sacha's . . . No!'
Connie pulled away from him and shivered. Her hair was
wet and her shoes soaked. She walked fast back the way
they'd come, her face burning. What did he mean *kiss*, a

fatherly kiss, or a friendly kiss. Or did he mean . . . she could scarcely believe that he meant . . . She could not look back at him. She hurried until she was almost running. He could not have meant a lover-like kiss, could he? Could he? She looked behind her but he was not following. She sat down on a fallen branch to get her breath back and waited for the shock to come. But it did not come. So he really saw her as a woman, did he? She realised that she had a great big grin on her face – and it was that that shocked her.

TWENTY-TWO

'The focus of your sensational retrospective has undoubtedly been the last portrait of Patrick Mount.'

'Undoubtedly.'

'Are you happy with this emphasis?'

'Which is that?'

'That Patrick's portrait . . .'

'Well, I rather think that was the point of it, dear.' She sees Deborah – who has seated herself discreetly a couple of tables away – twitch her lips. Why they had to come to this chilly café where even a cup of tea cost upwards of a pound, she doesn't know. She reaches in her bag and pulls out her sorry scrap of cushion, lifts her bottom and sits on it. 'Terrible chairs,' she says. Whoever heard of metal chairs? This man has the most enormous stomach, she can see the texture of the hairy skin pressing against the thin lemonish cotton of his shirt. He's not a fat man otherwise. She can't take her eyes from this curious rotundity. He's sipping black coffee from an absurdly small cup. He has great thick fingers, she wonders if he has a wife who enjoys them.

The table is too small. It has spindly legs and wobbles which is a most irritating thing in a table. Connie clucks her tongue and sighs. She's fed up with all this palaver, had enough. This is the third interview today, the first one was over the telephone, a disconcerting experience, her mind wandering, bound to have made some *faux pas*, and live radio, too. But who cares? Just get this over and she can go home. She aches for home. On the floor beside her feet is a brown-paper parcel. Paints. She could not resist them. The names of the colours, the pristine tubes, packed fat with all that gorgeous pigment. Not that she has any intention of painting. All inspiration gone. She realises he's said something and is waiting for her answer.

'Sorry?'

'Been remarked upon the . . . strangeness.'

'What strangeness?'

'That this last portrait of Mount when he was . . . what . . . late sixties looks more youthful than any single other . . .'

'Well, none of them are useful.'

'Youthful.'

'Yes.'

'Yes?'

'Yes, it is odd, isn't it?'

'Any explanation?'

The back wall of the café is one huge mirror. Connie is in there, tiny, face brown, hair black with its bone-white stripe. *Is that me? Am I really so small?* Despite her purple coat she shivers. The man waits. His face is a study of perplexity. A finger of mischief wags inside her. Might as well enjoy herself.

'Explanation of what?'

He sips his coffee. 'With this retrospective and a general upsurge of interest in alternative culture, interest in the . . . the *fate* of Patrick has been rekindled. What's your attitude to that?'

Connie shrugs her shoulders. 'Do you think I could have a spot more tea?' The man inhales patiently and catches a waiter's eye.

'Anything to go with it?'

'Do you know what I could fancy? It's something I haven't had since I was a girl. Brown-sugar sandwiches. Could you ask him for a brown-sugar sandwich. No crusts.'

He gives the order and the waiter gives her a soppy look. 'That's a new one in here.'

'Maybe you'll start a trend.' The man winks across at Deborah. 'Now,' he taps the end of his pen on the table, 'where were we?'

'Search me, dear.'

He frowns over his squiggly page.

'Is that shorthand?'

'My own version . . . ah, your attitude to the renewal of interest in the final *whereabouts* of Patrick.'

'Well, he'll have passed on by now.'

'But on that day in 1960 what? Five? Can you cast your mind back . . .'

'Of course I could if I so wished.'

'But you don't wish?'

'I do not.'

The waiter is back with a tray of tea and coffee but no sandwiches. 'Excuse me, madam,' he says, 'would that be demerara or muscovado?'

'Oh . . . muscovado I should think. As far as I'm concerned Patrick disappeared from my life on that day. He may have absconded to Patagonia or joined the Foreign Legion or been spirited away by fairies for all the difference it makes.'

'Has murder crossed your mind?'

It's as if the breath has all been knocked out of her. She opens her mouth but nothing comes to her to say. Deborah half rises from her seat but he waves his hand.

'I'm sorry, Miss Benson, perhaps that was crass.'

She forces a breath in, a voice out. 'It most certainly was.'
There is a pause. 'I did love him, you know, despite his . . .'

'Of course you did. I'm sorry.' The sugar sandwiches
arrive garnished with a sliced-up strawberry and a sprig
of mint. The waiter puts the plate down with a flourish,
almost a little bow. What does he want? Applause? 'Despite
his . . . ?' the man prods. Connie nods at the waiter. She
swallows her indignation and an odd feeling of panic and
eats the strawberry before she replies.

'His . . . well, you will know about him, you will have read
his book . . . his eccentricity you might say which was, in the
end, trying.'

'Trying?'

'Yes, trying.'

'Right.' He taps his pen in a staccato rhythm while she
nibbles the corner of her sandwich.

'Takes me back,' she says. 'You're wobbling the table,
dear, do you mind?'

'Sorry.'

The waiter is there. 'How is it?'

'It's splendid, thank you.'

'I understand you want nothing to do with any film
version of the story . . . you and Patrick Mount, your life
together, his . . .'

'You understand right,' Connie says through a mouthful
of bread and sugar. 'If they want to make a film, well . . . I
might go and see it but otherwise . . .'

'It would be odd to see yourself portrayed on the screen
. . . ?'

'Mmmm.'

'All right, let's change track.'

'Tack?'

'I have been reading Mount's Memoir and the Seven Steps

113

to Bliss. I understand you were involved in the development of his principle.'

'Phytosophical. No, he'd sorted all that out before he met me.'

'His process then.'

'Yes, dear.' The table wobbles again. 'Could you lean your weight on it or something? He leans forward and presses his elbow down. The table edge digs into his belly. 'I wonder who they'd choose?'

'?'

'Which film stars.'

'Were you involved in the experimentation?'

'The other thing, of course, was cinnamon toast.'

'He developed seven elixirs.'

Connie feels sorry for the man all of a sudden with his dented paunch and his fruitless squiggles. 'He never perfected the seven. Let me think, there was Pleasure, Harmony, something, something, Euphoria, Bliss. Is that seven?'

'An extraordinary idea, an extraordinary thinker.'

'An extraordinary man,' Connie agrees, finishing her sandwich and wiping a gritty trail of sugar off her chin. 'But do you know, living with someone extraordinary can be very . . . Sometimes I wonder if I had chosen an ordinary man life might have been . . .'

'Easier?'

'Oh I don't know, dear. One life or another life, what's the difference?'

'Quite a bit, I'd have said.'

'Did you want to talk about my painting?' Connie has a sudden memory of Patrick's skin, the amazing tenderness of it as she pulled the razor over his cheeks and chin. Her heart lurches inside her, the sandwich a mistake, sugar too sweet, she doesn't like sweet. The shock of that accusation, not accusation, suggestion, just a word. *Murder*. The very word in connection with Paddy sickens her. She sips her tea to try and take away the sweetness. He is going on and on, questions, questions, but she can't listen any more, can't think. Patrick, Paddy . . . she looks over at Deborah who catches her eye and comes across.

'Sorry,' Connie says. 'Sorry,' to the man. Tears rise in her eyes which have been dry for years.

'OK. OK.' He puts his pad and pen away.

'I'll get a cab,' Deborah says and Connie, looking up, catches the look that passes between them – a look of exasperation, amusement and pity. And it's that look that tells her that she can bear no more of this, not another single thing. She must go straight home.

TWENTY-THREE

The sun came out again, weak and nebulous. The paintings were propped up all round the walls. Not twenty, nineteen. Connie sat on her pad of blankets, knees drawn up to her chest, heart bumping against her thighs. She watched the backs of Sacha and Patrick, watched their shadows falling across her work that seemed so facile, pointless now. Neither of them spoke. Harry, who had followed them up, walked round sniffing at the paintings, his claws clicking on the bare floor.

Connie's palms were wet, her cheeks burned. In a moment she knew they would turn and speak to her. They would say something kind. Neither of them were cruel people. What a waste of canvas, she thought, what a waste of beautiful paint. Sacha would find her something else to do: sew or garden, or learn to play the piano. And that would be that.

Sacha moved aside and a ray of watery light quivered on Patrick in the vegetable garden, a small bent shape, foot on spade, the vegetables and flowers exploding round him, scarlet runner-bean blossoms stretching forward as if out of the painting, drawing the eye in to Patrick. A cheap trick, maybe. How would she know? The greens – yellow-green and blue-green and everything in between and cobalt and chrome – scarlet, Patrick's brown corduroys, the dark intense shape of him in the heart of the brightness. It was what she meant, her heart began to lift, but then she blinked and saw it again as they might be seeing it, childish, an exaggeration. You might even call it ugly, all that clashing of vegetation and the gardener practically lost within it, almost laughable maybe. And laughable certainly, the first one. Patrick and Sacha on the lawn, Patrick's naked back a luminous patch, almost a vacancy beside the sturdy blob that is Sacha, the dog's tail like a snake, the grass a vulgar, unmodulated green. Compared to Sacha's work . . . oh she cringed at her own cheek.

The room darkened and rain lashed the window. Connie felt cold. It was cold. Autumn suddenly come, after an Indian summer, swallows gone, time to close windows and light the fire. With a weary sigh, Harry settled himself beside her, nudging her leg with his damp nose. She stroked his silky head. She couldn't bear this silence. Why didn't they speak? Why didn't they at least look at each other so that she could intercept their look and know for sure how disappointed they were? Appalled. Poor them. How could they tell her kindly that her three months' toil, urgency, her three months of *purpose*, were a waste of time? All for nothing. Still, she thought, letting go her legs, flopping back on to the blankets and staring up at the stained ceiling, at least the time had passed, that was something. That year was gone.

The door banged. They had left the room, gone downstairs without a word. How *could* they? Harry hauled himself up and followed them. Connie stayed where she was, staring at a thread of cobweb hanging from the ceiling. She scanned the plaster for a spider but couldn't see one. She remained motionless listening to their footsteps on the stairs until she could hear them speaking downstairs, their voices low. A tear rolled sideways into her hair and she scrubbed it away. The dreary sound of rain again, the sunshine gone.

She hauled herself up and went to the window, pressed her

face against the glass. All grey out there, even the green grey, everything grey, the sunlight of a few moments ago impossible to believe in. She looked back at the terrible mortifying canvases with their dolly bright colours. Funny that she had painted so gaudily while she was mourning. What would she do now? She hated Sacha and Patrick for their silence. They should know, Sacha especially should know how much that hurt. That they had said *nothing*. She could leave. But where could she go? The sickening punch of grief again. Nowhere to go. It was war and she was alone, an orphan. Awful. With a shiver she remembered Patrick's arms around her, *Fantastic. Should I kiss you?* How could she stay? The wind got up and leaves whirled about like dark snow.

'Con.' It was Sacha calling. 'Con, coming down?'

She hesitated. Felt almost a revulsion thinking of them down there, talking about her, judging her. What did it matter what they thought anyway? The first tendrils of a headache crept round her forehead. It was so gloomy in the room, gloomy and cold. The wind moaned.

'I've made tea,' Sacha called.

The big brown teapot and half a fruit cake waited on the kitchen table. The range warmed the room and the lamp was lit which made it seem darker and bleaker than ever outside. The windows were steamy. The curtains should be drawn if the lights were on, even though it was only afternoon, what if a stray German bomber . . . ? But Sacha and Patrick were careless about the blackout, almost contemptuous, and at that moment Connie hardly cared.

'Gone quite wintery,' Sacha said. She smiled at Connie as if nothing was wrong. 'You all right?'

'Headache.' Connie sat down and received a cup of tea.

'Difficult day,' Patrick said. 'Headache, heartache, no doubt.'

How *could* they say nothing? They should understand. But she could not bring herself to ask what they thought. She didn't care what they thought. But it was cruel of them not to say.

Sacha cut the cake into three huge slices. 'Might as well finish it off,' she said. 'I'm baking later. Want to help, Con?'

So this was it. She was to learn to cook. That was her sentence, something useful and wholesome. Nothing wrong with cooking. She would like to cook. But it felt all over now. The summer a dream. Flour and sugar were to be her canvas; carrots, spinach, blackberries her palette. That would be it. They would garden and paint. Patrick conduct his lunatic experiments and she would feed them. She would be the cook. She swallowed against a lump in her throat. She would not submit to that. She would not stay.

'Not hungry,' she said as Sacha pushed the plate towards her.

'It's good,' Sacha said. 'It's got carrots and honey for sweet – no butter. I enjoy this rationing. Stretches one's ingenuity. Try it.' Sacha took a bite, made happy chewing noises. 'We must get you some more canvases, paints – oh it's a trial, this war, a bloody nuisance. What we need is to get you to some galleries – Paddy, we must invite Waverley, see what he advises.'

Patrick nodded, his beard sprinkling crumbs. 'Yes, yes.' He met Connie's eyes and gave her such an admiring, approving smile that her blood seemed turned to honey in her veins. She sat absolutely still, scared to breathe too hard or move too suddenly. They looked at her, both of them, waiting.

'So you . . . you don't hate them?' she whispered.

'Hate!' Sacha laughed.

Connie raised her two thumbs to her mouth and nipped the ends with her teeth.

'You must know that they are . . . well, we are stunned . . . Paddy?'

Patrick nodded, beaming. 'Oh yes yes, so fresh.'

'Fresh, yes, fresh, unselfconscious, they come from the heart – the use of colour is . . . stunning . . . oh yes, you need focus, direction blablabla, training. They will say naive charm . . . training? Yes or we can ignore all that if you like . . . whatever you like . . . what you must remember, Connie, what you must *know*, is that you have real ability. Do you know that? Real talent.'

Time stuttered and slowed. A whole beat lost. Connie pulled a sliver of carrot from her cake and chewed, trying to stop a stupid grin. What to say? She could not think. There is nothing that could make me happier than this, is what she thought at last. This moment would remain for ever in her memory: warm kitchen, rain lashing the steamy windows, brown teapot, cake – and most of all the excitement on Sacha's face, the way Patrick's eyes bathed her in warmth. 'Thank you,' she said at last.

Sacha smiled. 'So we'll bake this afternoon? It's Christmas pudding time. Now that *will* take some ingenuity. What we'd do without Paddy's bees . . .'

Patrick got up from the table and rubbed his hands together. He put one arm round Sacha's shoulders, one round Connie's and gave them a squeeze. 'Call me when you get to the stirring bit. I want to make a wish,' he said. He picked up the big black umbrella from beside the back door, winked at Connie and went off out to his shed.

Connie watched Sacha bend down to take the big brown mixing bowl from a low cupboard. She noticed how broad Sacha's hips were, how her own hands were soft and trembling and most of all how a smile was spreading gradually through her, tugging upwards from her footsoles to the roots of her teeth.

'How's your headache?' Sacha straightened up and rubbed her hip.

Connie put her fingers to her forehead. 'Completely gone,' she said.

TWENTY-FOUR

Patrick is definitely with him pushing his eyes towards the woman, strap-hanging, gum-chewing in a short tight orange skirt. Imagine the warmth of the back of her leg, smooth in its black nylon, how it would feel to slide a hand right up from her ankle to her thigh inside that tight skirt. No harm imagining that, is there?

The train slows, Leicester Square. Tony stands, the train lurches and he is thrown against the wearer of the orange skirt. She grins round at him, bold grin, squelch of fruity gum between her teeth. He squeezes past and off. A shudder. Christ, it could be so easy. A cold wind blows down the stairs as he mounts on to the wet street. Seven-fifty-five and they didn't agree which exit. Have to wander about like some prat. Looks good though, clean hair tied back, best faded Levi's, black leather open to show white shirt. Yes indeed.

Stops at a flower stall. Should he buy flowers? Say it with flowers – say what though? Seems appropriate somehow, a tribute to Patrick. His gut is tight. Can't remember what she looks like. This is stupid. Shouldn't be here, should be anywhere but here. Burrowed under Donna's pink duvet? No. Because he has received the sign. Patrick has pointed him in the right direction, provided the clue he needs to continue and now it is up to him. She isn't there. What if she stands him up? No. Buys a bunch of tall blue flowers, the man says they're called irises. Their stalks bleed wetly through the wrapping paper. Now he feels a complete prat, hanging about in the pissing rain with a bunch of flowers. Crosses the road, nearly hit by a taxi, gives it the finger. Not at this entrance either. A drop of water trickles down the side of his face. A woman gives him the eye, black hair, short black shiny coat. Christ, they do ask for it, the bitches. Not bitches, *people*, not to think like that, Tony. Could give *her* the fucking flowers and leg it. Forget it, go home, give up. Then what? Life, what's the fucking point?

Another circuit of the entrances. Eight-ten now. About to bin the flowers when she arrives. Fair hair, pale fake-fur jacket and that face. *Her*, yes. She scans the pavement before she sees him, smiles, pretends not to notice the flowers. 'Here.' He shoves them at her. Her smile is better than he remembers, soft lips, pale and sort of padded. No lipstick, good, he doesn't like lipstick, but a bit of stuff round the eyes. Nice. Classy. They stand for a moment, smiling, what to say?

'Sorry I'm late,' she says eventually. 'Took the bus, stupid, forgot about the traffic.'

'OK. Walk?' Tony suggests. She looks up at the sky from which street-lit rain is falling steadily.

'Just for a bit,' she says, 'should have brought my brolly.' They walk down St Martin's Court pausing for a moment to look at some second-hand books.

'Always keep an eye open for Patrick's stuff.'

'Patrick?' She looks blank, then registers. 'Oh, Mount.' Pleased she remembers, of *course* she remembers. They should probably eat, he realises, but he doesn't want to eat, or watch her eat. Doesn't even want to touch. Would be happy just to walk with her all night, drifting around the noisy lit-up streets with her beside him, close but not touching. But that is not the way these things are done. Shop windows, theatre fronts, umbrellas, the perfume of women, the bulk of men, a bleat of music, a warm blast of beery air from a pub.

'Drink?' she says. They walk past the pub. What to answer? They'll have to do something. She's getting wet, her hair, her furry jacket clotting and glittering with wet light. The question hangs in the air like a little wire poking. This is ridiculous. He stops. She waits, he looks at her, flowers cradled in her arms like a baby. He thinks of Donna with the box of tissues in her arms. How these women hold things close to their breasts, to their hearts. Men don't hold things like that. He feels like a man in a boat drifting further and further from the shore. From sure. *Help me*, he thinks. *Patrick*. It was Patrick who nudged him to notice Lisa in the gallery, the thin material of her dress and how it suggested what was underneath, how her pale hair smelled of almonds.

'Or film?' he suggests, 'or dinner?'

'Oh, do you mind much if we don't eat?' she says. 'Sorry, but I had a huge lunch . . . or you could eat and I'll just have a drink.'

'Fine.' Something gives in his stomach. Another sign that this is right. This is *all right*.

'But we must get out of this rain,' she says, 'and I could use a drink. Here?' She stops at the entrance to a basement wine bar.

'Sure.' He follows her down. The cellar is bright and busy but they find a table, order a bottle of Chardonnay and some olives. A jazz band in the corner begins to play as soon as they settle, the double-bass plunking away like a fuzzy heartbeat. A tide of voices rises all around them to compete. Lisa runs her fingers through her wet hair. 'God, I must look a sight.'

Tony smiles. 'I'm not complaining.' The red is back in her cheeks. She could never lie, this one, that colour would always find her out. She takes off her coat, stretching her arms back so that he can see the shape of her breasts, small, good, the faint outline of a white bra under a thin white sweater. Sexy/clean. Finds he is not scared.

'Nice sweater,' he says.

'It's my best one.' She grins. 'Cashmere, got it for Christmas last year. Feel.' She holds out her arm and he touches the soft sleeve.

'Mmmm.' They are both in white. He sees them for a moment as a stranger might, fair and dark, an attractive couple. 'Trouble is it's white and because it's cashmere I'm afraid to wash it.' She giggles. 'Look, it's a bit grubby here . . .' She draws attention to the wrist and he wishes she hadn't, it doesn't look grubby, he doesn't need to know it's grubby. Picks up his wine and takes a swallow, at least that tastes clean.

'So, tell me about yourself.' Lisa smiles at him over the rim of her glass. She picks up a fat green olive and bites into it. Her teeth are very white and small, almost like milk teeth. Finds he's not revolted by the sight of her nibbling the olive. But what to tell? No way is he dredging up all that psycho-babble stuff, childhood trauma, all that. And Christ knows he'll not mention the worst. Four years inside. Oh yes, just the sort of thing to make a good impression on a girl.

'Nothing much to tell.' He should have concocted something, what has he said already? That's he's a writer.

'Go on.'

'You first. Tell me about you.' Clever Tony to slide out of it like that. And she does, she tells him.

'I'm second. My big sister Judy, she's the clever one really. Cambridge – English and Philosophy. Works for the Open

University, got two kids, she loves kids, two girls, she's going to keep on till she's got a boy. Me, I don't know, don't know about kids yet . . .' She talks on, parents, brother-in-law, university, work and while she talks he watches her mouth and does half listen, rolls a fag, eats an olive or two, good olives marinaded in garlic and lemon. Have to try that, wonders if Constance Benson likes olives, little twang of excitement knowing soon he'll be there. Lisa will give him directions and then he'll be away. Tomorrow. Why not? But first there is tonight. Lisa's tale is ordinary and pleasant, peppered with anecdotes in which she says or does something daft, is the butt of some joke. Self-effacing. She can certainly talk. How it must be to have a past that is such an open book.

A tall woman comes down the stairs, hair falling like a blackbird's wings beside her face. Red mouth. Not his mother, of course it's fucking not, her hair will be white now if she's even still alive . . . funny to think he doesn't know if she's alive or dead, having severed contact will never know. And anyway what would she be doing in a trendy West End wine bar on a wet Thursday night?

Lisa giggles at something she's just said. Pulls himself back, nods, tops up her glass. The band starts an arrangement of 'Ain't Misbehaving'. '*Love* this.' She leans forward, elbows on the table, chin cupped between her palms, rapt, like a child listening to a story, except that the way she is sitting, her elbows push her breasts together. His cock twitches and he feels the flush of guilt that he still feels, that is ingrained in him deep as his response to his own name. *She* made him fear sex and she is a bitch for that. Can't stand to hear piano, all right this jazz piano, though it makes him uneasy. It's classical piano, the endless Chopin, Debussy, Tchaikovsky, played always a bit too fast, a bit too hard, played furiously at night when he was in his bed trying to sleep or read a book. Anger returns to him if he lets himself remember that, shouldn't let himself remember that, *won't*. But rage almost, even here in the safe bright cellar with this safe bright open book for company. She meets his eye. 'Aren't they great?' One by one he straightens out his clenched fingers. 'Great,' he agrees.

Rolls another cigarette, his hands are trembling. The deep . . . what is it? . . . *hypocrisy* of the fucking woman. Yes, he's talked it through with a shrink, yes, all very interesting, very illuminating, any idiot could see what was the matter with him, it's how to put it right that is the problem. That's why he needs Patrick. Patrick. Even the name calms him a bit. Like, almost like, love.

Concentrate on this sign who is smiling and saying something else. *Concentrate*, Tony. You couldn't call her beautiful. Pretty, sweet, attractive, touching, sexy in a kitten way not a cat way not like . . . better if she'd had him aborted. Better if she'd had him adopted. Better anything than to give up a career as a concert pianist and stay at home, bitterly bringing up baby, watching the glitter and glamour roll further away, further and further out of reach, while the little brat grows fatter and messier, staggering, dribbling, crapping. Repulsive.

'Yes?' Lisa tilts the bottle towards him. He nods. Her fingernails are short and natural. Good. Fingers on him. No. Feels sick when an erection starts. Not right. She made him like that. She took the piss whenever he got stiff, far back as he remembers, she slapped him, called him dirty, filthy, looked hate at him if ever his hand strayed anywhere near. She hated that part of him and she made him ashamed, more than ashamed, made him frightened, made him hate it, too. Could have killed her. Should have, maybe, and the fury of it is still there, a deep scorch mark inside.

What if he said to Lisa with her blue eyes and her baby teeth: 'Hey, I'll tell you about my childhood. One time, I was only a little kid, maybe five, already afraid of touch, afraid especially of the feelings in my little prick, the way it sometimes got stiff. Scared, really scared of that feeling, not understanding what it meant only knowing it was something awful, something good people didn't have. The night I woke up feeling sick. I never went to my mother's room at night – not allowed. You weren't allowed to sit on the bed, the cover was slippy blue like ice. I was sick on the landing and couldn't clean it up myself. Tried to clean it with toilet paper but it got worse and worse, bits everywhere. Terrible stink and warm slime on my fingers that made me sick again. Must have gone to her room and knocked. No answer. Thought I heard her voice. Thought I heard her say, "Come in." Opened the door and stood there . . . I did not know what . . . wet myself. Hot, heavy wet dragging my pyjamas down. Ran. Ran to the telephone to call the police. I knew all about 999 for the police. Because a man was killing her. He was on top of her squashing and squashing. His arse is what I saw, big hairy arse with a deep black crack and her face all twisted, eyes shut, mouth open, voice coming out all wrong. The lady on the phone asked what service I required and I said police that someone was killing Mummy but then suddenly she was there beside me, snatched the phone and laughing in her pretend way, not even smiling, said *sorry*, hair everywhere, face when she looked at me . . . repulsed. That's what it was. She was repulsed by me. Wet and stinking. It was the man who cleaned me up, washed me, found clean pyjamas. That man had a nice face and I wondered if he was my father. Never saw him again. Could have killed her then if I'd been bigger. After that I would lie awake at night wishing to kill her, to get on top of her and squash her dead like I thought the man was killing her. And then I'd have nightmares that she'd died. And who could I call for? Not that I ever could have called for her.'

What would you think if I told you that, Lisa? Would you giggle, wrinkle up your pretty nose and think it kind of cute? Would you feel sorry for me and say you understood? But it would be a lie. *You* could not understand, with your nice little life, with your trustfulness. Christ, don't look into my eyes like that, blue eyes. You don't know me. Nobody does. I could wring that white white neck.

Tony gets up, jolts the table, knocks over the wine bottle, pushes his way through the crammed tables to the Gents'. Shuts himself in a cubicle just to be alone. To let his face slip, jaws open in a silent scream. Presses the heels of his hands into his temples and the sound he makes is a small boy's moan of terror. Stands for a moment, touching nothing, fastidious even in his terror, waiting for it to pass. He's damp still from the rain, with sweat, the clammy, smoky air of the cellar slick on his skin. Unbolts the door and washes his hands with cold water and slimy liquid soap that makes him shudder, dries them in the screaming hot air of a machine.

Wants home. Could leg it, just go, leave Lisa to the jazz. Need never see her again. She'd get over it, narrow escape though she'd never know it. Always wonder what happened. Keep 'em guessing, Tone, oh no no no it's sick that's what it is, makes him feel sick . . . *Dirty boy, you dirty repellent boy.* Rush of applause, a guy pushes in through the door. Tony leaves. This is a test. You must be strong. If you run now you will forfeit the information you need. It's like one of those fucking fairy stories or something. Except it's not the princess he wants to win, it's freedom from the princess. There she is, sitting in the smoke, fair hair just drying all fluffy, looking about her, a bit anxious now. But she is not the prize, she is the test he has to pass. All he has to do is charm her and get her to give him the key. Not try to screw her, not hurt her. That would be his downfall. Just ask her the way then he'll be off. That's it. OK? Pushes back between the tables and sits down.

'You all right?'

'Fine.' He forces a smile.

'Do we need another bottle?' She's shared the last of the wine between their glasses. Doesn't know. Yes. No. But what else? It's all right for a bit longer. Because what when they're out of here? It's warm here, quite safe. The band having a break. Might as well be here as elsewhere. Reaches for his wallet.

'My shout,' she says. She gets up and he watches her go to the bar. Tight black jeans. Hips slim as a boy's – but more curved than a boy's. Other men watch her, too. Not that he's any right to be proud. Rolls another fag.

'You're very mysterious,' she says as she sits down again. She pours the wine. He smiles a mysterious smile.

'Go on,' she urges, 'tell me something about you. Star sign or something. No, let me guess.' She regards him thoughtfully, the tip of her pink tongue nipped between her lips. 'Gemini? Libra?'

He shakes his head.

'Aquarius?'

He sips his wine.

She laughs. 'I give up. What?'

'Don't believe in that crap.'

'Something else then. What kind of music do you like?'

'You've got lovely eyes,' he says. Just the perfect thing to say.

She shakes her head. 'I can see you're going to drive me mad,' she says.

*　　*　　*

130

Quarter to midnight on the shivery street. The rain has stopped but everything is wet and water gurgles in the gutters. His ears are full of a rushing sound – from the loud music maybe, from having to concentrate on Lisa's soft voice through it. Hasn't been in the West End this time of night for . . . Christ knows. Somehow couldn't bring the subject round to Benson in the wine bar, too much noise and she got on to the subject of writing, how she wants to write a book, and it took all his wits to appear in the know. Write a book? Aren't there enough of the fuckers already? Beggars in doorways. Keeps his eyes averted, been there, done that. Lisa slips her arm through his. Doesn't mind, a friendly arm only, firm inside the furry coat. 'It's been a really nice evening,' she says.

'Yes.'

'Think I'm a bit pissed.' She looks up at him, a teasing sideways look, 'only a *bit*.'

So now, if he wasn't Tony, what would happen? They would make another date. Presumably this counts as a date. They would both go off home, looking forward to next time. Or would she want it now, tonight, might she invite him back for coffee and kiss him while the kettle boils, take him to her bed, let him see and feel her naked skin? Would she do that? Stupid stupid girl when there are such monsters about. Tony is beyond it now but knows the danger. Sex. That is what it is about, sex or a promise, or sex and a promise or sex as a promise.

They have reached the tube station. They stop. 'Well . . .' she says. 'I'd better find a cab.' He doesn't look down but he can feel her eyes on his face. The top of her head comes only just above his shoulder, she's smaller than he thought and slight in that big coat. The thing that tightens his chest is almost tenderness, but tenderness shrivelled immediately by a blast of anger. Because he can't.

'I'm . . . going away for a bit,' he blurts, 'if not I'd . . .'
What, *what* would he do?

'Where?' Her voice is small, a sinking in it as if she's
disappointed.

'Norfolk,' he says.

'Well, that's not the end of the world!'

Somehow she is in front of him now, somehow she has got
his arms to go round her back. Her hair still smells – through
the cling of smoke – faintly of almonds. It's like hugging a
toy, the thick fake fur quite safe. Her arms tighten round his
back. He has an idea.

'I'm going to see Constance Benson . . . in connection
with, you know . . .'

'Your book? Lucky you. She's wonderful.'

He nods his face against her hair.

'Trouble is, I'm not sure where I put the address, the
directions . . .'

'Driving?'

'Train.'

'But it's *miles* from any station – the back of beyond. Can't
think what the nearest station . . . King's Lynn?'

'Did you say you'd been there?'

'Give us a minute,' she says. She lets him go and fishes in
her bag for a notebook and pen. 'Turn round.' She leans the
notebook against his back and scribbles something. 'There.
Directions from the village anyway.' She comes round in
front of him again, tears the page from her notebook and
gives it to him. He puts it in his inside pocket. She waits for
his arms again and he does it, grateful, relieved he's got what
he wants, he gives her a hug.

'Ring me when you get back?' she asks. And then, 'Oh
no!'

'What?'

'I've left my flowers . . . I put them down by the table . . . oh *no* . . .'

'I'll get you some more,' he says into her hair, 'next time.'

She's quiet for a minute. Can he feel her heart or is it his? 'So there is going to be a next time?' she mumbles against his shoulder. 'I thought . . .'

'Next time,' he repeats, a sinking in his heart. A promise made and he hates to break promises, that's why he hardly makes them. Before he knows what's happened she's reached up and kissed him lightly on the lips. Soft brush of dry lips, barely warm, a pause when he could have kissed back, kissed properly, but didn't. She must have been on tiptoes, sinks down again. An empty cab comes round the bend. She leaps out, hand up, and it stops. Likes the way she did that, assertive, confident. As the taxi carries her away her fingers might have gone to her lips, she might have blown a kiss.

On the tube he takes out the scrap of paper. There's an address and instructions, go through Wisborough, past shop and straight down unmade-up road by sea, about one and a half miles. PS I fancy you! the exclamation mark fat as a balloon with a flower for the dot. So girly. So much the sort of thing his wife the nurse would do. Folds the note carefully and puts it in the breast pocket of his shirt. So. That is done, the test is passed and he is on his way. Need never see her again. Shuts his eyes. *Thanks, mate*, he mouths.

TWENTY-FIVE

On the 1st of May Connie rose with the sun. It was her sixteenth birthday. She pulled a sweater over her nightdress and tiptoed down the stairs of the still slumbering house. The clock in the hall tick-tutted, not five o'clock yet. She crept past the sleeping dog and slid her feet into Sacha's Wellingtons, cool and gritty inside to her bare feet. She opened the door and stepped outside. It had rained overnight and the world was clean rinsed for her, the bird-song in the shadowy trees rose to a crescendo as she stepped on to the soaking lawn and her heart lifted as if it too would sing.

She liked her birthday being on the 1st of May, a special day. Her mother used to tell her the story of how she had woken with labour pains at dawn on that day, how she had crept up and out and walked in the garden while father was still asleep, holding her hands around her big hard belly and talking to the baby that moved in there, the soon-to-be-born stranger. And when her mother had told her that Connie had felt that she almost remembered it, absurd of course, how could she? But it would have been just such a morning.

Connie pressed a hand on to the flat space where her womb was. Unbelievable that a child could ever grow in there. *We nearly called you May*, Mother used to tell her every year, but Father thought it too indefinite. May? Like a question. So they christened her Constance May. *Constance is definite, don't you think? And it suits you.* Constance would nod but privately wished she had been May, a taller girl, fairer, less serious, less constant. Only now, now that everything had changed, she wondered if she was different. She wondered if she knew herself at all.

She walked through the garden to the trees which were alive with the rustle and song of birds. She stopped and looked back at the house. The windows flashed in the rising sun. From the open door a trail of her own green boot marks was printed on the silvered lawn. This is my home, she thought. And I am Constance but not constant. I am more *May?* Patrick and Sacha are – not quite my family but my *people* now. What was the feeling that flooded her at that thought? Not sadness or loss or joy. Not even regret or gratitude. It was more a sort of hunger, but not a hunger for food or anything she could imagine.

She walked on between the beech trees. Up through the wood, spellbound by the stillness of it. Filaments of spider's web spun between the trees broke across her face. She stopped in a clearing beneath a great beech, her favourite tree. She looked up at its smooth grey trunk. There was a hole for an owl and dark tracings, too, that looked, if you wanted them to, like eyes. She put her face against the bark, not as smooth to touch as you'd think, pleasingly rough and cool. The sensation of the tree-trunk against her forehead and the flat of her palms filled her with calm. She stood for several moments like that pressing against the tree, in a daze or reverie, no particular thought in her head. And then she heard Patrick's voice: 'Conn-ie, Co-on . . .'

Her first reaction was to hide. Why hide? Oh just that she was relishing her solitude. She turned her back to the tree and there he was, striding towards her up the path, pyjama trousers tucked into boots, shirt open, beard halfway down his chest.

'Happy birthday,' he said. There was a dewdrop on the end of his nose.

'How did you know where I was?'

'Got up early. Glorious . . .' He gestured around him. 'Door open . . . looked out . . . what do I see but a trail of little footprints? What could I do but follow?' She felt uneasy at the brightness of his eyes. 'Follow a maiden into a wood at dawn on her sixteenth birthday and who knows what might happen. The 1st of May at that!'

'Nothing will *happen*,' she said.

'Sit down a minute.' He hunkered down beside her, his back against the tree. She looked down at the top of his head where the hair was thinning a bit, then lowered herself down beside him. 'Don't worry,' he said.

'I'm not.' They sat for a while, listening to the sounds of the woods, watching the sun strengthen enough to begin to penetrate between the leaves. Patrick moved himself far enough away from the tree to sprawl full-length. Connie drew her knees up to her chest, her nightdress pulled tightly over her knees. If she looked at his chest she could see the throb of his heart in the tender place below his breast-bone where the ribs splayed apart. Milk-pale skin, a scatter of freckles, the copper edge of a nipple fringed with black hairs. She wished she had not come out alone, wished she was in the kitchen with Sacha getting breakfast ready.

His eyes were closed. She was beginning to think he had fallen asleep but then he said, 'When I was a child, I had a revelation.'

'Oh?'

'A chestnut tree struck by lightning, split . . . outside my bedroom window.' Connie waited for more, used by now to

136

Patrick's ponderous way with a story. A breeze stirred the leaves above them. *I am sixteen*, she thought, lifting her chin. *I am a woman*. If anything the skin of Patrick's chest was blue and the leaf shadows rippled so lightly he could be underwater. Imagine that in paint. 'I felt its distress,' he said, 'as plainly, as obviously, as if it spoke to me in words. As if it cried.'

'How did you?' Connie asked. Thinking, If I am a woman why do I feel just like a little girl?

'Just felt it,' Patrick continued, 'and knew that plants are sentient beings. Sentient beings. I have become convinced, of a higher order than the animal kingdom – in which I include *Homo sapiens*.'

'Oh?'

'Yes, Con, do I hear disbelief in your voice?'

'*No*.' Connie was glad his eyes were closed, she could let herself grin up at the dancing leaves. 'Go on then.'

'Our senses, for instance, take our five senses . . . discounting the others for now . . .' Connie settled herself more comfortably and stifled a yawn.

'Sight, sound, taste, touch, smell . . . crude, *crude* mechanisms, Con.'

'But,' she could not help herself, 'they are the only way we . . . we know the world. *Know* it. How else can we know? And plants . . . Patrick! Plants don't have eyes, ears . . . they can't feel.' She saw that he was smiling, his eyes still closed, a small spider struggling in his beard.

'I would submit,' he said, 'that the five senses by which we . . . how did you put it? *Know* the world are precisely what stop us knowing it.'

Connie sighed and recognised in her own sigh the long-suffering note her mother had sometimes . . . when? . . . oh it is so sad the way the memory slips. Maybe when she was getting Alfie to explain how he had ripped the knees out of yet another pair of trousers. Her heart contracted and she lay down, let gravity draw her close to the earth.

'These senses are but crude interpretations,' Patrick said. 'They catch the most obvious blunt manifestations of existence, light . . . within a certain spectrum: colour . . . within a certain spectrum: sound . . . again within a certain spectrum. So we exist only within a certain spectrum. Doesn't mean that's all there is.' He waited but Connie said nothing, felt the hardness of the forest floor against her back, a twig digging into her hip. 'Our senses are a primary method of perception only and limiting because most human beings are content with that much, that small amount of what there is. Most feel no need to search deeper for the whole *being* on a cellular level.'

'I don't understand what that's got to do with plants,' Connie murmured, 'but don't say more.'

'The human brain is pathetically primitive in comparison with even the simplest of single-celled plants,' Patrick continued. 'How much can your brain know at once? How much can it see, think, experience at once? Two things, three, fifteen? No matter. A single plant cell can know far more in one instant than you can ever hope to know in your entire life. That is why I am endeavouring to utilise the wisdom of plants in my elixirs . . . what I am doing, Connie, will revolutionise the way mankind experiences its world.'

'Oh Patrick, how can you know what a plant knows?' Connie jumped up, impatient, brushed bits of leaf and twig off her sweater. 'I'm going back for my breakfast. Coming?' She looked down at Patrick. He was wonderful, of course, in his original way – but he did go on a bit.

He opened his eyes. 'I've bored you,' he said, getting up. 'Bored you before breakfast and on your birthday, too! How can I repair the damage?' He put his hands together as if in prayer.

Connie laughed. 'Not bored *exactly*.'

'You little witch.'

'I'm starving. Let's go.'

Patrick held her arm. '*Hush, wait*,' and as he spoke, the air rushed with silent wings, and there like a ghost looming through the trees towards them was a huge white bird. 'Owl,' Patrick whispered, 'snowy owl.' Connie waited with her mouth open as it flew, almost floated, by. They stood in silence for a moment, looking at the place where it had disappeared. 'There's a birthday present for you,' Patrick said, his voice soft with awe. 'I've heard that fellow many times but never seen him.'

'Beautiful,' Connie said.

'Yes.' Patrick turned and put a finger under her chin. 'Sixteen,' he said. 'How does it feel?' He had sleep in the corners of his eyes. She wondered if she did too, blinked. How oddly fascinating to be so close to another person, close enough to smell him, to see every pore in his skin, every separate hair in his long soft beard, the hairs all black or white, none of them grey. And suddenly she felt very naked underneath her nightdress.

'Don't know yet. No different.'

He let her go. Her gaze fell to his belly, the soft hairs that grew there and a stiff slant under the striped material of his pyjama trousers. She could not pull her eyes away.

'Yes?' The thing twitched. Her face flooded with dark blood. 'Don't worry,' he said. 'I wouldn't touch you for the world, not without your say so. But you can see what it thinks of you.'

The blood was throbbing in her face, her ears. She should turn away, she should walk quickly to the house. Nothing wrong had happened and nothing wrong would happen. She should turn and walk away.

'You know our – Sacha's as well – views on physical love. We each have other lovers.' Connie wondered about this. Patrick disappeared for a few days now and then but Sacha? Where were her other lovers?

Connie half laughed, her voice coming out strangely.

'And we must find you a lover, eh? Now that you're sixteen.'

'But . . . I don't know.' How shocked, how mortified her parents would have been. But her parents are no more. And that is why she is here, why this is happening to her. This is it, this is her life. Here, this Patrick standing before her looking so funny and lovable, the baggy flop of pyjama material at the top of each boot. If only he hadn't followed her. Why did she leave the door open, leave her footprints clear as arrows pointing her direction? She lifted her face and their eyes met. A kind of fizz in the air like sherbet or electricity. She looked down at his trousers again.

'Patrick, can I . . . ?' She could hardly bear to make the words.

'Can you . . . ?' His interest was entirely caught.

'Can I touch?' How could she be saying this? Asking this? Even *thinking* it? Curiosity maybe, and some sort of madness just because it was her birthday and it was dawn, past dawn now. Because fingers of light were opening the spaces between the leaves. And she felt safe with him. He would never harm her. He loved her and she, she realised, she did love him. What kind of love? Who knows? He would like it that she asked to touch, he would approve of her daring. Stupid how she had flown from his kiss last year – he had never tried it again. She just wanted to know . . . needed to know . . . she just could not imagine what it must feel like . . . his . . . penis . . . the strange thing that grows and moves and twitches. She saw Alfred's when he was a baby but this . . .

'Yes!' He sounded delighted. 'How sweet you are! And I understand. When we find you a lover you don't want to be too surprised.'

Connie nodded, true or not she didn't know. But her fingers itched to touch the thing that was pushing up now, almost straight. She took it in her hand under the cotton. It felt hot and solid. A little patch of dark wet blossomed through the cotton at its tip.

'Take it out and look,' Patrick said.

It seemed almost to leap out of the opening of his pyjamas by itself, purple and swollen like something bruised, something that must surely hurt. It was too big and raw. She snatched her hand away.

'I'd better go.' She walked fast, wiping her hand on her nightdress, not liking the hot smooth sensation the thing had left on her palm, wanting to get away from it, from him, to be with Sacha. Poor Sacha, whatever she thought about sex, whatever she did, surely she would not want Patrick to be showing his thing to Connie. Although *I* asked, she reminded herself, it was *me*.

The thought of the owl came back to her, the great soft whiteness of it, suddenly there and suddenly gone. Like a ghost, yes, and her knees weakened for a moment: the ghost of whom? As if maybe it was her father, warning her, warning her, *no*? No, no, no, of course not. She ran as fast as she could, as if she was being chased, pelted between the trees and across the lawn and into the house where Sacha, like a barrel in her old brown dressing gown, was just putting the kettle on.

PART 2

NORFOLK

ONE

The sound of an engine, the scrunch of wheels on shingle. Tony's belly lurches. This is it then, this is Benson back. Not ready, no meal cooked, this is not how he meant it to be. He doesn't know what to do. Hide? He drops to the floor on his knees, ridiculously behind the table, as if she won't be able to see him there. Get yourself together, man. Footsteps. He waits for the door's opening, hands flat on the floor, filthy with sand and hairs and God knows what, heart crawling along his throat. But then a hammering on the door. Who the . . . what the . . . ? What to do? Hammering again, a voice, 'Miss Benson, yoo-hoo . . . Anyone there?' Tony stands, heart sliding back into place. Goes to the door and opens it.

'I'm looking for a Miss Benson.' There's a delivery van parked outside and the bloke's got a big flat brown-paper package, waist-high leaning against him, and he's holding a receipt book.

'She's not here, right now. Can I help?' Tony's voice comes out smooth as butter. 'I'm a friend . . . well, relation.'

The man hesitates. 'Well, I ought rightly to deliver this to her,' he says.

'I'm expecting her any time,' Tony says. 'Just about to get the dinner on.'

'I ought rightly to come back.'

'Up to you, mate.' Tony holds his breath.

The bloke pulls on the lobe of one ear, then removes a pen from behind it. 'You'll sign for it?'

'Sure. Unless you'd rather wait for her. As I say . . .'

'No.' He hands the pen, which is warm, to Tony. 'Reckon that'll be OK. You'll make sure she gets it, like?'

'Sure.'

He looks around. 'Live here, do you?'

'Just visiting.'

'Bit isolated for my taste.'

'Yes, well. Horses for courses.' Tony signs his name and gets his hands on the package. Knows already what it is. Here is Patrick delivered unto him. It's all coming together, it's magic, that's what it is, sheer fucking magic.

Shuts the door and waits until the van has gone, the sound of the engine died completely away before he takes a bread knife and saws through the string. It's well packed, as it should be, layers of brown paper, taped together, a wooden frame, sheets of bubble wrap – and, at last, Patrick.

'Hello, mate,' Tony says. His voice comes out tender, like it's never come out before, he's embarrassed by the sound of it. Runs a finger over Patrick's face, familiar but strange, old and young at once. Close to you can see the brush strokes, how the colours blend to create the moulding of the flesh, strong face, long nose a bit reddened at the tip, the peaceful set of the mouth, the flecked eyes, kind of greenish, that look out at him so . . . so blissful, so almost, *loving*. Nobody has ever looked at him like that. Not his mum. Not girls. Even Donna, even Lisa, it's not love he sees in their eyes – not that he wants to – it's *want*, they all *want* something, that's all that kind of love is, want and then disappointment. But not this. This is pure platonic love. Nothing physical in it even, it's above all that, it's one mind loving another mind, even after death. *I love you*, Tony whispers, then flushes, looks around, not that there's anyone to hear. But he laughs as if there is, fuck *off*, he mutters, and looking into those eyes again knows Patrick understands. This is *Patrick's* face, the last portrait. And here is Tony in the place where Patrick lived. It's all coming together now, Christ, he's getting warm.

TWO

It has been a delight and it has all been far too much. London is left far behind where it belongs. The countryside has changed its colours even in the short time she's been away. Another palette – greens and greys, slashes of bright berry red, flaming bracken blur together, a wet sparkle. Not that she's crying, it's just one tear. Her heart lifts with the excitement of it and relaxes in her all at once. She strains her eyes for the first sight of the sea. Remembers Alfie, how fiercely they'd compete, she and he, on summer holidays, to be the first one to see the sea.

Connie slides along the seat as the taxi turns off the main road. A small road now, low between hedges, towards the scattered village – church, shop, houses, not even a pub – then they will be off the road proper and there will be the first glimpse of the sea, *her* sea, and then she'll be at home where she so badly, badly needs to be.

Church against sky, a wavering spire. 'You'll have to tell me when,' the driver says.

'Past the shop,' Connie says. 'Actually, dear, if you don't mind stopping a mo I could pop in there.'

He pulls up outside the Spa shop and gets out to open the door for Connie. 'Take your time, I'll have a fag,' he says.

In her new hat and coat she can see she is, momentarily, a stranger to Barry who is serving, his mum on her weekly trip to Cash and Carry. Connie is comforted realising it's Thursday and that is so. Nothing changes here except the weather.

Barry looks up. 'Miss Benson!'

'Like it?' Connie does a little twirl.

'Shit hot,' he says. Poor lad, Connie thinks, looking at his blubbery lips, the lick of greasy fringe, the speckle of blackheads beside his nose, he's probably never had it off, probably never will. He'll help his mother in the shop till she drops. Then what? She doubts if he's got the nous to manage it himself.

'There were a man looking for you, Miss Benson.' Connie picks up a bag of nuts, a pint of milk.

'What sort of a man?' Getting properly run-down in here, she notices, just the contrast with all those bright and shiny London shops. But still it doesn't do to let things slip too far. There are filaments of spider's web in the corner of a shelf, the lino floor-tiles have broken corners, there are grubby thumbprints on cereal boxes. If they don't keep it up to scratch they might get closed down – then where would she be?

Since she's in a car she might as well load up. She looks out between the notices stuck on the window at the driver, having his fag. Something flirtatious about the way he leans back in his bonnet, a flourish in the way he exhales the smoke. Yes! Connie chuckles as a girl comes in view, a girl in jeans and one of those draughty tops that show the midriff.

'He were a nice man,' Barry says, 'long hair. I told him where you live. Mum says I shouldn't of told him. She give me a row, she did.' His bottom lips turns down as if he's going to cry.

'It's all right, Barry,' Connie says. 'You did well.' Apples, a box of russet apples, she runs her tongue regretfully round her teeth. She turns to the shelf full of tins, picks out soup, corned beef, spaghetti and a tin of chicken ravioli which is a new line in the Spa shop.

'And you'll want your baccy.' Barry reaches it down for her.

'And what else?' Connie smiles. She's got a soft spot for poor Barry.

'Whisky,' he says. He fetches her her customary half-bottle of Famous Grouse.

'No, I'll take a whole one,' she says.

'Feeling flush, Miss Benson?' He giggles wetly, excited. This is a high point for him, a few words exchanged with an old woman. But then, Connie reflects, what is a high point for me? Shutting the door on myself on my own? What else? Biscuits, peanuts, cheese, tea-bags, pork scratchings, Bombay Mix. 'Big box of matches,' she says.

'So I'll tell Mum you're not cross about the man?'

'It'll only be some journalist. No, tell her I said you did well.'

'You've been up London?'

'Yes.'

'What's it like?'

Connie paused. 'It's not as good as here,' she says, 'you're far better off here.' Barry grins and Connie remembers him sitting up in his pram outside the shop, the very same grin on his wide red face. How time has catapulted forward.

'When did the man come?' she asks.

'Yesterday, I think.' With the tip of his tongue pinched between his teeth, Barry rings the purchases into the cash register and packs them into bags. The door jangles as the driver comes in to buy more cigarettes and help Connie carry her shopping out to the car. As they jolt along the unmade road and the sea blinks at her in the mild sunshine, Connie's spirits rise. Soon she will see the roof of her house. And that is a high point for her. Coming home.

THREE

At last I come to the heart of my achievement – I allow myself to make this claim despite the fact that ultimate perfection still eludes me. The progress of this memoir has overtaken the progress of my researches and the development of my system. I will however attempt to explain – in terms suitable for the layman – how my Phytosophical Principle can be put to practical use in order to enhance the life of mankind.

Before I do so I must interrupt myself to say that one of the sadnesses of my life is the lack of recognition I have received for my work. I can only conclude that such a system as mine – derived from the higher consciousnesses of our fellow green beings – is too sophisticated for the common human mind to grasp. I have not only received no recognition during my lifetime, but my ideas have very often been greeted with contempt and derision. It is commonly the fate of the pioneer into human consciousness to be ridiculed and the mark of the higher mind to take this ridicule in its stride, to refuse to be deflected from its greater purpose by the stupidity of those that surround it.

My last humiliation I regret deeply because by implication it directed scorn on others engaged in similarly directed research. My public demonstration of plant psychic life was ill-conceived, I fully admit, due to a factor I had neglected to take into consideration. The audience contained an element whose hostile and negative emanations upset and confused the philodendron which was thus unwilling or unable to co-operate in its normal manner and sat dumbly in its pot making me the butt of much ridicule.

I repeat that I deeply regret the backward step this represents in the progress of understanding, especially where it also reflects on the work of other vegetal scientists and psychologists. For this I apologise unreservedly. I believe the philodendron itself was also contrite: in subsequent private experiments it never regained its former vigorous level of response and soon perished.

Here, finally I offer to my reader:

THE SEVEN STEPS TO BLISS:
A LIFE-TIME'S SYSTEM
Being for the gradual achievement of perfection,
peace and enlightenment.

(Note: Plants hold the key within them to the perfection of human experience on earth. In my earlier teachings I preached that mankind might look to plant life as a model of behaviour. I am not too proud to retract, in part, that advice which isn't in all cases practical and applicable. I suffer, like many thinkers, from being taken too literally. However, I do still assert that plants are of a higher consciousness than man. Within each single plant cell there exists a sensitivity and awareness of the cosmos far in advance of the purely subjective and limiting partial experience given to man with his five crude senses.)

By extraction, by a method secret, a spiritual essence from a variety of plants, the species of which must likewise remain a secret, plants which have been nurtured in an atmosphere by turns meditative and sexually charged, I have been able to manufacture a series of seven potions. I over-reach myself, I have manufactured six of the series and it is my life's ambition to complete the system which is as follows:

THE SEVEN STEPS TO BLISS:

Being SEVEN ELIXIRS with effects on a continuum. ONE to SEVEN drops to be taken. WARNING: promiscuous and unsequential use of these potions may result in DERANGEMENT or DEATH.

The system:

POTION 1: PLEASURE: will ease physical and mental pain and induce a feeling of contentment.

POTION 2: HARMONY: will remove physical pain, ease mental suffering, induce harmonious and pleasurable feelings.

POTION 3: HAPPINESS: will induce a feeling of mental sharpness, physical well-being, strength and intense happiness.

POTION 4: JOY: problems that seem insuperable will dissolve like Scotch mist, the body, intellect and mind will be bathed with light-heartedness, laughter, joy.

POTION 5: ECSTASY: will induce feelings of utter physical balance and strength, mental agility, spiritual well-being. The physical world will appear suffused in a golden light.

153

POTION 6: EUPHORIA: will induce feelings of physical and mental perfection, spiritual enlightenment, possible spontaneous orgasm.

POTION 7: BLISS: feelings of extreme physical, mental and spiritual bliss, spontaneous and prolonged orgasm.

(WARNING: When the seven-drop stage of the seventh stage of the system is reached the orgasm may be intense and so prolonged that the individual experiences temporary freedom from the mortal restraints of his physique which may be distressing if witnessed by the uninitiated.)

Tony closes the book and puts it down. His hand has crept to his crotch and he snatches it away. All this talk of spontaneous orgasm. Gets up. 'I'm here,' he says to Patrick, 'look at me, *here*.' And soon Benson will be here, too, and she will show him the way, give him the stuff. Course she will, why not? And then the quest will be complete. He punches the air. Yes! But cool it. Take a deep breath. Cool, now, cool.

He stands back to admire the table. Sun slants through the window, smeary and speckled with salty sand, but he'll get that sorted later. The table is set for one. Not just set, arranged for one, *arranged*. Tony has scrubbed the table, scoured it, bringing up a greasy froth of grey, and now the surface is golden, light seems to shine up from the grain of the wood. The plate is blue. In a yellow jug he has arranged some wild flowers – yellow spiky things. He has washed a glass, found a blue-and-white-checked napkin and folded it beside the plate. It looks like a painting, or an advert for something. And the room is warm with the smell of cassoulet. Cassoulet, beans and herbs, sausage and strips of belly pork, bought in Brixton and carried down in his rucksack, recipe copied from a book. Decided against soufflé in the end, it needed to be something that could cook a long time and wouldn't spoil. Soufflé needs an audience for the moment of its entrance. Ta-dah! He's opened a bottle of Cabernet Sauvignon from the village shop, fortunately they do have booze – dicey moment when he realised he'd forgotten it – a dusty bottle, the label wrinkled as if it had long ago got wet. But still, it's decanted into a jug so it can breathe and be ready for the welcome. He sloshed some of the wine into the pot and drank a small glass, just a taste.

Christ, how he enjoyed the cooking. Hasn't enjoyed anything so much since . . . can't think. Maybe never. Cooking is always good but cooking for someone else, someone you want to nourish and impress . . . that is total. He was absorbed, that's it, his mind on nothing else but the slicing of the mild white onions; the crushing of the garlic with salt; the colours of the carrots, white beans, green; purple sausage, pale damp fatty pork. Just as well he thought to shop before he left London seeing what's in that village shop – and that poor tosser behind the counter. Christ!

His stomach growls. Pours another mouthful of wine. Wishes he knew when she'd be getting here. What if it's not today but tomorrow? or the next day, or what if it's not for weeks? But no, she'll want to be home, she'll be here and the food will keep, its flavour will improve.

What is it he feels as he surveys the warmth and colour in the room – crazy place, sea-shells stuck all round the doors and the window like a sort of frame – as he inhales the smell of his own cooking? Can't quite place it, not a customary feeling – it's benevolence or something like – beneficence, that's it. Not a common word but then he's not common, Tony. He appreciated Patrick right from the beginning, not like the ignorant, common people who couldn't understand, who only mocked. What common guy would have had the initiative not only to get here, not only to dare to seek his fortune but have the imagination to prepare this feast purely as an act of . . . homage – there he goes again – for a woman he had never met? Homage on Patrick's behalf. She'll get a bit of a shock when she gets here, he's prepared for that, prepared for a hiccup while she takes in the news that he's here, as a sort of disciple of Patrick's, guided here by Patrick himself, and she is not alone any more.

He's searched everywhere for the elixirs, little dark bottles they'll be, or phials, each one numbered. But there's no trace. No panic, no need to turn everything over. She'll tell him where they are, or hand them over. It's a dump, this place, nothing but a glorified shack. And Patrick lived here? Dark old bedroom, mushroom-smelling, a lurch to the floor if you step too hard. Toilet out the back, no bathroom let alone a shower and he takes that hard. A cake of Imperial Leather on the draining board studded with crumbs and hairs, a stiff and tatty flannel hanging on a pipe by the sink shows *she* washes there. Disgusting to wash your body where you wash your plates.

But this room, lived-in kitchen, is OK and upstairs, well up that ladder, is *the* room, the room in Lisa's article. You'd never believe it, dwarf-sized – the ceiling maybe five foot at most, sloping away to the floor. Patrick must have had to crawl. But it's full of brightness. There's something right about it, about the room, about his being here, a feeling that after all he's been through at last he is home. Like that game, cold, warm, warmer, hot! Very very warm now, almost scorching himself on what he's after. Almost there.

There's a faint whiff of old pipe smoke and a little clay pipe like something from an archaeological dig. And dead insects on the floor, wasps mainly, flies, moths. Why so many bugs? And boxes of photographs. Treasure. Patrick inside and outside. Patrick with his flowing beard looking like a fucking prophet. Patrick naked in one, dripping, like Neptune just emerged from the sea. Hung like a frigging horse, well, he would be. Patrick and Sachavarelle, Patrick and other people, Patrick with a girl, slim, dark with a straight look. Benson! She's hardly changed, except for the change from girl to old woman – that look is just the same as the one she gave him in the street, chin lifted, sort of brave. Prickly, alert, sharp. She couldn't be other than clever with a look like that. And thinking of looks, eyes . . . holding the picture of Benson, Tony sits down, wedges his hips into the tiny armchair. Those other eyes suddenly assault him with their openness, their lack of guile. Lisa. It strikes him suddenly like an insight – though really it's obvious – that Lisa is lovely. That if he wanted a woman, was capable, Lisa would be the one. But he is not capable or safe and when that comes back to him, it comes with such anger that he screws up the photograph in his fist.

Gets up and goes down the ladder. Sees the table – set by some fucking fag by the look of it. Takes the flowers from the vase and crumples them, wrings them between his hands. Swigs from the jug of wine, spills a long red splash down his white shirt. Shit. Kicks the leg of the table and a glass topples to the floor but it doesn't smash. Wants a smash. Presses his foot down on the glass. Hard. Leans his weight on it, why won't it fucking smash? and then it does, feels through his trainer the crack and give and scrunch of broken glass.

Then he's out of it, legging it down the path, running awkwardly through the shifting sand of the dunes to the flat wetness where there is no one now and where he tries to scream but a scream won't come, only a kind of sob.

FOUR

Here is the house, settled and complete. Her own place. At long last. Oh it is grand to be home. No place like it, cliché or not. The tyres of the taxi grate on the gravel. The driver carries her luggage and shopping to the door. She tries to unlock it. The key turns but the door won't open. She struggles the key in the lock, turns it again and it opens. Funny. Surely it hasn't been unlocked all that time? It's warm and welcoming inside. She's proud to have the driver see it, bright in all its colours. He puts the bags on the table, her suitcase by the door.

'Good to be back?' he says and she looks up at him, has a shocking thought. He's got a ring in one ear, she does like that in a man, and stubble on his chin, a sort of jaunty set to his shoulders, long legs. Good gracious, it's been an age and she feels odd, experiencing a surge of something, something almost forgotten, something very like lust. Yes, it is lust. She bites her lip. What would he think if he knew? It's been years since she's felt that, surely, *years*. All that jolting about in a taxi must have brought it on.

He hangs around a bit and she realises that it's a tip he's after – the journey itself was paid for in advance. She takes a fiver out of her purse, *feeling flush, Miss Benson*, hands it over. He stuffs it in the pocket of his jeans, tight jeans that cling to his narrow hips. 'Ta,' he says. 'Well, I'll best be off-ski.' She watches him walk to his car, get in and drive off, too fast down the rutted track.

Something is strange in her. Yes, that old strange achy heat. But no, that's not all, something else is strange. The place has been empty and yet – it is not cold but warm, it's too welcoming – and too clean. The table clean. And something else . . . no . . . a smell of food. She goes to the cooker and puts her hand on the white enamel. Warm. She steps back, her heart doing a funny flip in her chest. And white. Cleaning the cooker is not something she does, but it is white. She comes over queer. Goes back to the door, shoves it open for the fresh air.

Someone has been in her house. She looks back at the room, takes in the changes. Nothing bad. Come on, Con, be rational. Someone has been here, that's all, someone has been here and cleaned the table and the cooker and . . . she goes back to the cooker and stoops to open the door . . . and cooked her a meal. The heat hits her, the thick meaty smell. The old casserole dish is in there, she can hear whatever's inside it bubbling. She closes the oven door quietly so as not to disturb it and sits down on a chair beside the scrubbed table. She takes off her hat.

So, someone has been in. But not to be alarmed. Not a burglar or an ill-wisher, or a breaker and enterer, because nothing is broken. She has only been entered. Nothing, as far as she can see, has been taken. What is there to take? The only valuable thing she possesses is Patrick's portrait, which she sees with a start is back, is propped up against the wall. Someone must have brought him back and unpacked him. He looks all wrong there, shadowed and low down – but still he's home, undamaged.

Nothing to be afraid of. Some kind person has been here and cooked and cleaned. A well-wisher, not an ill-wisher.

She digests this. Who on God's earth could it be? There are no neighbours and she doesn't know people in the village, not properly, only to nod, smile, exchange a word, a Christmas card to Barry and his mum. Barry's mum? No. Someone from a distance then. The man Barry directed here? But who? Nobody knew when she was due back. It should have been tomorrow, she could have stayed another day, planned to do the Tate for old time's sake, but couldn't bear another single question, another single night suspended above the roaring streets. Not that she didn't enjoy the luxury . . .

Who then? Who has been in the house? There's some squashed ragwort on the draining board. Most peculiar. If it's meant to be some sort of message she doesn't get it.

She goes outside and lifts the flowerpot by the door. The key has gone, of course. Too obvious, she's been told, that's the first place a burglar would look. But her answer: I'd rather they opened the door with a key than smashed the windows or the door down, makes sense, doesn't it? She prowls round touching and checking. Her feet crunch on broken glass and she stops. Some breaking then. But only an old glass. Probably an accident. The sink has been cleaned, the enamel which has been dark brown for as long as she can remember is cream swirled with scratches. Even the tap has been polished, she sees a distortion of herself as she peers at it. There's something different about everything. She exchanges a shadowed glance with Patrick. It's as if everything has been moved and put back in not quite the right place.

She climbs the ladder, stopping halfway up, suddenly afraid that someone might be up there, waiting. She pauses a moment, listening, her head just below the level of the trapdoor, then dares to rise, her voice stuck in her throat ready to call out to . . . to greet or . . . she doesn't know. She turns her head to survey the room, relief slowly settling in her because no one is there. No one is waiting for her to emerge. Not even Patrick, who she will bring up here later, return to his rightful place. She climbs up and in. Turns once in the golden light, her arms outstretched, it *is* good to be home – then freezes when she sees her photographs strewn on the floor, carelessly fanned out, face-up, face-down, the black-and-white, the sepia, the coloured.

She sits down on her little chair, which surely has moved. On the floor is a screwed-up photograph. Oh dear. She picks it up and smooths it on her knee and meets her own eyes. Has a sudden start, remembering the moment, Patrick's voice: *I'll steal your soul*, and how it had made her shudder. Only a girl, then, where? After Sacha?

Yes, it was after Sacha's long illness, after the funeral. They'd gone to Cornwall for a few days and taken lots of pictures as if to confirm that *they* were there, *they* were still alive. Connie had felt awful to be enjoying herself, swimming, dancing, making love, had felt awful about the unworthy thought. *He's all mine now*, because Sacha had never been an obstacle between them. And she had loved Sacha like a kind of sister/mother/teacher.

Patrick had asked her if she wanted to get married and she'd said no. Not because she didn't love him, but they had been together so long by then, what was the point? *All right then, you little witch*, Patrick had said, snatching up the camera, *then I'll steal your soul*. She remembers the start his words gave her, remembers raising her chin to the camera feeling a small tug at something in her chest. What they used to call heart-strings. Thinking, How I love him but he cannot steal my soul.

Why this photograph? This one screwed up? A horrible stupid thought, feeling. That Patrick is here. Patrick has cleaned the cooker and made a stew, just what he would do.

Patrick screwed up the photograph in which he tried to steal her soul. Connie's lips are dry. She licks them. She looks at her own clever face in the photograph, scored now with crumples and cracks. *Don't go gaga now*. Someone has been in the house – why probably a journalist – someone like that – someone looking for secrets, that woman who wants to do her biography? Yes that, of course, that. Not the other thing, stupid. But why screw up a photograph, any photograph, why this – the soul one? No. It is not Patrick returned. Think like that, you daft bat, and you've had it.

He did cook. He liked things cooked in a pot for a long slow time. Rabbit, chicken, a swede, carrots, a handful of herbs. The pot would last for days, topped up with more vegetables, until a rim of scum would form around the top and the cooker would be splattered with brown crusts, dried filaments of spinach or what have you. Then Connie, in a fit of energy, would throw it out and scour the pan, boiling kettles of water and making her hands pink and wrinkled, scraping scabs of food from the enamel. Did she *really* ever have the energy for that? And Patrick would grumble and she would cook for a few days, omelettes usually with mushrooms or chervil, boiled potatoes, separate things, pretty on the plates. And then she'd get tired of it, having to think about food, and Patrick would take it up again, humming as he chopped onions, and the smell of a new stew would rise to the studio where she'd be, mixing with the smell of paint, and she would smile. Feeling love for him, hearing love from him even in the sounds of his chopping and stirring and humming. And after all, it was a healthy way to eat. Approved of these days, no doubt, all those vegetables.

Oh the smell does bring it all back . . . that smell now . . . complex, sweet stew smell. But not paint, the smell of paint has long ago faded. She did so love the smell of paint and food together. This nourishing smell . . . oh but why and from whom?

The presence of Patrick is very strong. The widow of Patrick Mount, someone called her in one of those articles, but she is not a widow because she was never a wife. He did try to persuade her but she couldn't do it, couldn't take Sacha's place like that. Sacha was his only wife. And Connie found to her own surprise that she had no desire to be a wife.

When Red proposed to her she did consider it. Being a wife. Being Constance Redmartin. How would that have been? In her nostrils is the memory of woodsmoke, oil paint, the scent of a young man's skin. That salty taste, the crisp of hairs on her tongue. *Marry me*, Red had whispered, his weight on her, *have my babies*. Oh the gift of a young man's lust. No clever tricks, like Patrick, no memory in Red's fingers of the hundred other women's bodies that she sensed in Patrick's. Just the pure hot charge of love and lust.

But that was *ordinary love*, Patrick said when she told him. *What we have is extraordinary. You*, he said, running his long index finger down in a steady line from between her eyes, over her nose, lips, chin, neck, between her breasts and resting it just below her navel, *are made for more than that. This love, our love, is extraordinary*.

He didn't want her to have other lovers. *Believe me, it would never be better than this*, he said. Rich coming from Patrick who had so many women. Almost a joke that *he* should preach monogamy to her. He would promise not to but then he would. He could not resist a willing woman. It means *nothing*, he'd say, as if that made it all right. But he still wanted her to be faithful to him. She wasn't having that, of course, and early on she dabbled. She took quite a few to bed but Patrick was right. It was never as good. And she wanted her energy for painting. Painting and Patrick, that's where her energies went, creative and romantic. And anyway Patrick was so grumpy about it whenever she slept with anyone else that it was hardly worth the bother.

Extraordinary love. It is hard to remember. So hard. You can remember having feelings, but the feelings themselves are impossible to recall. Her head knows she loved him but her heart feels nothing now. Her heart is asleep. If she listens with her whole body she can just hear its sluggish beat, if she listens with her ears she can just hear the hush and heave of the sea.

She wakes with a start. Wakes, so she must have slept. She wakes with a prickle. The room has gone dull and chilly, thick cloud pressing on the skylight. Her tongue feels thick and dry in her mouth, her teeth sticky. She forces her dry tongue between her teeth and the insides of her cheeks. Her head is dull as the cloud. What woke her? The photograph slides from her knee to the floor.

There really is somebody downstairs. Her heart beats its way up into her ears, almost drowns the sounds of the intruder. It must have been the door that woke her, someone banging the door. Someone is whistling softly. Whistling . . . she has not heard that for so long. The sensation of someone whistling and moving about below her as she works. But she is not working. Does not work. That is all so long ago. Someone is moving about below her. A stranger in her house. The whistling. She had forgotten how he used to whistle sometimes, sometimes hum, sometimes the words of a song breaking through, *Oh how we danced on the night we were wed*, something absurd, a kind of irony in the voice. The whistling is actual. Not just a sound in her ears. It is accompanied, under the din of her heart, by the opening and closing of the oven door, the clink of cutlery, the turning on and off of the tap – the stutter of reluctant water. All so familiar. Patrick. Within her flesh her bones are icy cold.

Old fool. Snap out of it. Now. *Not* Patrick. But who then, who? It would be so like him. Let her grieve for half a lifetime then appear, scare her out of her wits. But he is dead. Have you never heard of ghosts? But ghosts that cook up a stew and scour the cooker? Didn't he always play with her, play her like that, wait till she'd given him back to Sacha or to some other lover, wait till she'd given up on him and then return, awakening her desire? Seducing. Isn't that how he kept her? Oh what it is to be seduced. He knew the words to say all right. He knew how to turn her head and heart, tilt the whole world till she flowed back to him.

The sound of broken glass being swept into the metal dustpan, tipped into the bin. And then the voice:

'Are you up there, Miss Benson?'

The breath escapes from her lungs in a long sigh. Not Patrick's voice. Of course not. Not that she really thought that – but how the mind plays tricks! Exhaustion, that's what it is. Hard to find her voice, mouth moving idiotically before any sound will come.

'Miss Benson, Constance, are you ready for your meal?' It's a young man's voice, quite a nice voice, not frightening at all.

'I . . . I am here.'

She hears the creak of the ladder and then a head emerges. As it does so there is the first rattle of hail on the skylight, a cold scatter like the prickling of her scalp. It's a face she doesn't recognise. Long dark hair tied back.

'Pleased to meet you.' The young man has a sharp smile, his teeth very strong and white. 'Coming down?'

'Yes, yes.' He unnerves her with his unflinching stare. His

eyes are deepest dark and his eyebrows straight and glossy as two licks of wet paint. She puts her hands back against the arms of her chair to push herself up and his head disappears. The ladder creaks and the hail on the roof is like flung pebbles. She steps over the photographs and lowers herself down the ladder, conscious of his eyes on her as she descends. *You shouldn't live alone out here without even a phone*, she's been told over and over by visiting friends. *Miles from anyone else, anything could happen* and she's always snorted at their caution, never been scared, not for a second. This is her home. Not scared. Not her.

She turns slowly but he isn't looking, he's taking the casserole out of the oven, a tea-towel folded over his arm like a waiter. She crosses to the table and sits down at the place that has been set.

'Who?' she says.

He puts the casserole on the table and removes the lid. Thick brown sauce and white beans, a bay leaf sticking out. He stands back as if awaiting applause, as if about to bow.

'That looks nice,' she says because it does look nice. But she is not hungry at all, only thirsty and thirsty for solitude, too. Almost angry at this intrusion. She so much needs to be alone.

'Wine?' He puts a tumbler of wine in front of her.

'I was thinking more in terms of a cup of a tea,' she says, but reaches for the glass and takes a sip. He watches her drink, she doesn't like to be watched. The wine will blacken her dentures again. Who is this person? It is almost like a dream. Her own home but subtly different, a stranger treating her like a visitor. And the table only set for one.

'Aren't you . . .' she says.

'Aren't I who?'

'Aren't you eating?'

166

He throws back his head and laughs. He has creamy brown skin, maybe he is part Indian? Good-looking, there is no denying that. But who the hell does he think he is to laugh at her in her own kitchen? The tap drips. Must change that washer, she thinks. That drip familiar, at least.

'So who are you?'

'We'll come to that.'

'What do you want?'

'I wanted to welcome you home.'

She takes a deep exasperated breath. Really she is too old to be frightened by this boy. The few sips of wine have already started creeping into her bloodstream. Hits the spot quicker than tea, and that's the truth. The hail has turned to rain and the room would be almost dark if not for the single bulb that dangles above the table and carves hollows in the stranger's cheeks. His eyes are so dark there's no definition between iris and pupil. He will keep looking at her in that intense way, almost rude.

'That's very nice of you, dear, very nice,' she says. 'But unexpected . . . perhaps you could explain.'

'Eat first.' He comes round behind her.

'Not yet.' She holds her hand over her plate. He stands a bit too close, she looks sideways at the place where his shirt, white with a long dark stain, tucks into his jeans.

'Why don't you tell me your name,' she says. 'I always like to know a person's name.'

'I could say anything.'

'You could say anything. But why don't you tell me your name, dear?'

'Tony,' he says.

'Short for Anthony?'

'Yes.'

'With an H?'

'What the fuck does that matter?' He jerks away as if she's touched him. Quite a little tantrum. She'll have to tread carefully, she can see. What is the matter with the boy?

He walks to the door as if he will leave. There's something about his shoulders, tension in the dark muscles under the shirt, tension in the whole body. She closes her eyes and sees a bow pulled tight.

'You must forgive me,' she says. 'I find all this a little unnerving.'

He gives a harsh bark of laughter. 'A little unnerving,' he repeats mimicking the quaver in her voice.

Connie's fingers slide to the skin on her forearm and she pinches hard. It's not that she really thinks she might wake up, but that a sharp sensation might sharpen her wits. This is a predicament however you want to look at it.

'Have we met?' she says. Her mind is flocking. Perhaps he is familiar? So many faces lately, so many interviewers, photographers, all those people at the private view. She takes another steadying sip of wine. He has half turned towards her. He could kill her, of course.

FIVE

He could kill her, of course. Could wring her tiny neck, snap her tiny bones. It's all going wrong. He needs to puke. Goes out the door, slams it behind him so the window rattles, the whole dive shakes. Dark is seeping up from the ground, pressing down from the sky, not much left to breathe. He stumbles between the dunes, the wet spines of grass stinging his hands. The sea is a bleak shudder of light, the wet sand sucks his feet and the water streams down his face.

What the fuck is he doing here? It's not like it should be, she's not. What then? Leave. He puts his hands on his belly and leans over to retch. Nothing comes up but a sour string of drool.

Hey, stop that. Straighten up, scrub eyes, mouth with back of hand. Ask her for the stuff, Tony, you can ask her nicely and then fuck this misery that closes around you like a fist. You run to escape it, run out of the fingers into the dark, into the lonely lonely heart of the nothing. Patrick has led you here, Patrick with his trail of fucking whores with their eyes so open and their little flowery scrawls and skin so soft, the gifts clutched in their tender arms like babies.

His heart hammers with the fast run of it. Nothing is fixed, nothing is definite, can't think with the darkness hurtling past and that is the plan now, to get himself together and think. One moment a pale autumn day next a fucking tempest. What's a man to do? Water down his neck, through the cotton of his shirt, warmer than you might think.

He stops, panting, hands on his bent knees, cold clean air stinging his lungs. Crouches down and rolls a fag, stands to light it, draws hard on the skinny tube watching the end brighten in the dark. Somewhere distant a ship's lights. Sea sloshing and slurping as it drinks itself over and over. Some kind of hooter far out, a sound that wrenches the gut.

He stares out at the nothing that is the sea, hunches his shoulders and turns his back. Walks through the dunes towards the house, can't see it. Great, that's fucking great, lost now, lost in the dark of the wet of the night.

Hey, hey, hey, it's all right.

This is it. This is what his life has been pointing towards. What he has been waiting for, reading for, preparing for. And look, here, *not* lost, look, there is the window all lit up. A raindrop fizzes on his fag, another licks his cheek. Earlier he lost it but now it must be found. The point of all this. So stop, wait.

Earlier he did lose it looking at that photograph of Benson that made him think of Lisa that made him . . . No. No. Earlier, before the real Benson arrived, seeing her picture that made him think of Lisa, he ran, the sand shifting under his feet, the sky blowing rags. Knew that nothing was fixed but that a tender feeling would erupt into rage and that there was no control to be had. Does his head in, that eruption. Pelted, lungs searing, eyes burning thistles of light, ran until he left the anger behind, left it crouching somewhere between the wind and the sand. The brightness of those white foam edges joining and ripping, over and over again, like seams. That catching his eyes, over and over. His fucking mother and her jaw sharp above him, the shadow underneath a triangle. Eyes like beaks. 'In your room.' No touch. And the curtains like her hair and the glass between he thought – or was it dreamed – had her eyes, like a great mother's face pressed there, flattened, watching, and he didn't even dare to draw the curtains against her.

Between the breaking of the waves, had come a clear thought, painful but clean like a knife. How good it is to cook for another person. How that means, *could* mean love. The thought vibrated painfully like a fine blade quivering. How that could mean love. He'd thought to jack it in then. Cannot . . . ever . . . love. Not a living person. Yeah, jack it all in, what simpler? A few strides forward, a few swallows, gulps, the sensation of ice. Isn't it supposed to be pleasant, drowning? Don't you just relax? But a wave had lapped his trainer and he'd leapt back. No. He hasn't got the bottle.

He'd thought to go, then, quick, quick. Back to the shack to get his stuff, forget the elixirs, leg it back to civilization, back to Brixton, to Donna and all that. But as he'd got to the top of the dunes a cab had drawn up and it was her. He'd stood watching, stuck. Couldn't go forward or back. He'd come to the edge of his dream and there was nothing, no map, no plan, no dotted line to follow. He was alone. Was and is for ever more.

That feeling is the one he has to overcome and all he needs is the elixirs, the system, all he needs is that and some *time*.

Now he can feel himself calming down, and with the calming down he starts to shiver. If the elixirs cure? But there is no mention of cure. A cure for anger, is there such a thing? Don't hope for that, Tony, don't even hope. There is no cure but there might be rest. There might be all those things what what, what is the progression? Pleasure, Harmony, Happiness, Joy, Ecstasy, Euphoria, Bliss. Ecstasy, Euphoria, Bliss. Repeats it aloud to the rain that trickles in his mouth. Ecstasy, Euphoria, Bliss. And then what? That is a question that is not allowed to be asked.

He grinds the fag-end into the sand, approaches, stands in the trapezoid of window light and peers in. Thick light fuzz, breath, condensation, maybe steam. He pushes open the door. No air, fug, she is smoking a pipe, thick food smell. She meets his eyes, those bright eyes, a breathful of bluish smoke. The floor gives under his feet and he's afraid he'll fall, grabs the edge of the sink.

'What is it, dear?' she says. He closes his eyes as the room breaks into sparkling fragments. 'What is it that you want?' Can't fucking cry, can't. The edge of the sink is hard and real under his hands but the floor is soft. And her voice going on and on. Syllables and syllables hurling about with the colours in his eyes until he gets it together through the hard rim of the sink which is real and into his hands which must therefore be real and up his arms into his ears. Holds on to what she's saying as if it's a rope dragging him back to the edge of the sink, to the moment, back into some semblance of himself.

. . . obviously found the key well it's where you'd look I know, not a place for burglars what's to burgle . . . and the rain the rain . . . oh back after town but I liked the fridge I could get used to that the little bottles so generous they are just fill up that fridge day by day have what you fancy I could live like that and those nuts with hot spice on . . . room-service darling I should coco . . . that you are troubled . . . have you tried it . . . so what is it dear that you want? yes quite a turn if that's your object you achieved it . . . till I heard you whistling . . . *quite* a turn, just for a moment you'd laugh if you knew what I thought oh and you wet through . . . whisky that's the ticket and whisky I've got. A Scotch now there's a thought, sit down won't you by the fire . . .

He opens his eyes and the room spins and settles. Postcards, shells stuck round the window frames, table, ladder, old woman.

'OK.' The word like felt in his mouth.

'Sit down.'

He sits on a flimsy chair which she's positioned in front of the Calor gas heater. 'Your hair's wet,' she says. She picks up a towel from beside the sink. He'd thought it was a tea-towel, been drying dishes on it, can't use that on his hair, clean towel in his bag but somehow he can't speak or move. She lifts his wet ponytail and puts the towel round his shoulders. The gas heat gnaws his shins. 'Lovely hair,' she says. 'Why cut it short when it's so glorious? That's what I say. I do go for all this let it be, let it all hang out whatsit and piercing, yes, ears and noses, I do like that. You got that? Now.' She sloshes whisky into a cup and a glass, straight on top of the dregs of her wine. A fussiness rises in him but he takes the glass. 'Skoal!' she says. He stares at the gold fluid and the red wine beads still on the sides of the glass, lip smudges round the rim. When he drinks he tips the glass so that his lips don't touch it.

'Can I?' she says.

'What?'

'May I . . .' She has moved behind him, he looks up at her face. They bloat or shrivel, old women, he's noticed that and this one's shrivelled. She's grinning childishly, eyes bright in the leather face. 'Comb it for you?' He shrugs. 'Then it'll dry smooth.' She rummages through a drawer then stands behind him. His shoulders are slumped but he can't straighten them. She pulls out the rubber band, tearing some hairs at the nape of his neck, but he doesn't shout or even flinch. She combs the ends first, holding each lock so that it doesn't pull as she works out the snarls. Her breathing is loud with here and there a sigh. Little snappings of his hair. When she's done the ends she starts at the top of his head and combs down, not gently, the teeth of the comb dragging the back of his scalp.

He can't think who combed his hair last. Can't remember his mother touching it although she must have done. It was very short then, short as possible, so there wouldn't have been much touching. Now he never has it cut. The tap drips, the gas heater pops, the comb in his hair is a faint swish. There is her breath and there is the rain on the roof and below it all, a deep irregular bass, is the rhythm of the sea.

'Why don't you tell me what's up with you, dear?' Connie suggests. And he thinks, Why not? But then *what*? What could he say?

'Nothing's up.' Tips another swallow of whisky into his mouth, feels the hot gold settling him. She tut-tuts and carries on combing, pulling the hair from round the sides, combing above his ears.

'Beautiful hair,' she says, 'I haven't combed another person's hair for . . . for donkey's years.'

'Did you comb his hair?'

She sucks in her breath, pauses for a long moment between strokes. Then, 'We combed each other's. It was a kind of . . . a kind of soothing. Do you find it soothing?'

Tony says nothing but yes, that's just what he feels, just temporarily, superficially, amazingly, soothed. He closes his eyes and feels the comb travelling through his hair, the tiny passage of each tooth against the shape of his skull. Patrick sat here, felt just this. 'What was his hair like?' Tony asks.

Benson answers immediately as if she has been thinking of just that. 'White the last years, and thinning on top. He never realised that, because it was on top and he couldn't see. I never said, of course. Wavy hair. Black when he was young though already going white when I met him . . . he was a good deal older than me, you know.'

'I know.'

'You know about him?'

Tony feels an urge to laugh. Know about him? I know every fucking word he wrote. But he only nods.

'Some kind of journalist?' Connie pauses, the comb just above his ear, and then resumes.

'Me . . . no.'

'Then?'

'Black like mine?'

'No . . . quite a different type of hair. This rain! Yours is absolutely straight. Almost blue. Extraordinary that light in it. To paint it would be . . . yes, extraordinary. Paddy's was coarser and not, to tell the truth, *absolutely* black, more very deep brown, red lights rather than blue. There, all done.' She stands back.

He wants to ask her to continue. Wants to be sitting by the heater having his hair combed for ever, just to hang there, safe and soothed and never have to face what's next. She puts the comb on the table beside her dirty plate and he sees the long black hairs against the pale grain of the wood. The proximity of his own shed hairs and the sticky brown gravy, a bay leaf on the edge of the plate.

'I'll wash up,' he says.

'No need.' But he stands and picks up the plate.

'*De*licious,' she says, 'if not a journalist, perhaps a chef?'

He feels a crazy buzz of pleasure like a humming in his ribs.

'Not eating?' she says.

And maybe that is it, what he needs, food inside him to weigh him down. Good wholesome food cooked with love. Love! The word pops in him like a bubble of acid. Wine,

175

whisky, rain in his hair, smoke, adrenalin. All these things, no wonder he feels weird, his scalp tingling from all the combing.

'Use my plate, no sense dirtying two.'

He ignores that, turns on the tap, there is always a wait for the water, he's learning that already, the ways of this place, a wait, a judder of pipework and then a fierce surge of water that splashes your front if you're not careful and then slows to a reluctant trickle.

'If you'd just tell me what you want . . .'

He deflects the splash of water with the plate. Holds it under till the gravy is rinsed off. It'll have to be wet. Can't dry it with that tea-towel now it's been near his hair. Can't eat off a wet plate. He takes another from the cupboard, white painted with worn yellow flowers that look like specks of yolk. The food is no longer hot. He heaps it on the plate, stands by the sink with his back to her, shovelling it into his mouth. It's great, even luke-warm. Maybe he *should* have been a chef. He can just see his reflection in the steamy window. The light shining blue on his hair just like she said, what did she say? *Extraordinary to paint.* The idea gets to him, a new, big idea. He swallows, says nothing until the plate is empty and his belly full. He washes the plate, aware of her uneasy presence behind him. He's better now, back in control. Why is she hovering there behind him? What does she want of him? To comb his hair, to interrogate him? To think she's in control?

'You do have something I want,' he says.

'Well, of course I do. Else why would you be here?'

He turns. There is an expression of interest on her face. An at-last-we're-getting-to-it kind of expression. She sits down and takes a sip of whisky from the teacup which has no handle.

'I want . . .' he begins. She raises her hand and its shadow catches his eye, a soft crab sliding sideways on the table. 'I want the elixirs.'

'Aaaah.' She smiles. 'I should have guessed. People used to come . . . but not for years. I'd almost forgotten.'

'Well?'

'You've been reading Paddy's book. You must realise he was . . . prone to exaggeration.' Her smile is almost pitying. She will not dare to tell him the Seven Steps is a lie. She can't.

'Meaning?'

'Meaning don't believe all you read.'

Time swings loose. Again he's slipping. Oh Christ he needs a shower, his bed. Thinks longingly of his flat, Donna next door, his own bed-sheets so starchy tight. That life . . . it seems almost together now. But *then*, living that life then had seemed like nothing, just a waiting time, not a real life at all. Is there any way back?

'Meaning?' He imagines raising his fist, thumping the table, screaming it into her face – *meaning?* She is not frightened. She should be fucking frightened. If she knew. The girl he didn't mean to kill that he did kill, served time for. Served time, time the master. There was no intention. No guilt on that score. But the anger came and Christ, she was so soft, her voice in his ear, her skin silkier than silk, her armpit – his index finger slipping under her arm and the surprise of soft hair there, soft and damp where women should be shaved. Somehow that got to him, the sort of trust of it, giving him her body as it was, no make-up, perfume, a childish smell of soap, baby powder or something like. Tenderness and the backlash. How it is. Tenderness is danger. It has to be whores, the rougher the better but he can't trust them to be clean. Who could trust a whore? So he's stuck. Tenderness is the danger, oh yes that eruption of anger that screws his fists, his gut, floods his mouth with the taste of metal, that blinds him.

'Shall we have a cup of tea?' Benson says.

'Meaning?'

'Simply that he was far from perfecting . . .'

'But he got some way?'

'If you read you know . . .'

'And what . . . where are they . . . what there is?'

'Went with him.' He watches her run the horny edge of her thumbnail along the grain of the wooden table. He sits down on the chair that is frail as her bones, that feels like it will snap under his weight.

'With him where?'

'Wherever he went.'

'He went on the day I was born.' He waits but she says nothing. She is so fucking tiny, her head about the size of a grapefruit. 'So you don't have anything?'

'If I did?'

'I would ask you to give them to me. I need . . .'

'*Need*?'

'I would ask you.'

'And do you suppose I would give?'

He stares at her. *I'd fucking take them*, he says with his eyes but he can't stare her out, those bright eyes, maybe they can't see, maybe he's out of focus to her. Maybe to himself he is out of focus. It's sinking in that he has come to the end of the trail, lost the scent. Needs to think, to get this sorted in his head, *what* then? what *now*? From behind the table Patrick smirks. The portrait of Patrick that she painted, this woman, famous painter. If this is famous! Living like this in a sink hole. Which he will leave. Leave her, leave her to rot and crumble and fall through the floor. Done nothing wrong, he can leave now. Stop this.

Must get clear. For years there's been the plan, dream, *trust* – that is the worst of it – that he will find the elixirs, that in this way Patrick will save him from himself. But no. Patrick fucked off out of it and took whatever there was with him. So now what? Nothing. Nothing to keep him, nothing to . . . head for. He loved Patrick. Patrick has let him down. Smirking down there in the shadow.

'Would you carry him up for me?' Benson has followed his eyes. 'Only I'd like to get him settled back.'

He shrugs. Gets up. 'OK.' Lifts the painting, averting his eyes from Patrick's that surely are taking the piss.

'I'll go up first and switch on the lamp,' she says. 'No big light up there.' She climbs up the ladder, kind of like a child, putting both feet carefully on each rung. He waits at the bottom looking at her stupid shoes, like kids' party shoes, watching those thin shins that disappear inside a green dress, thinking once *he* must have watched those legs and lusted. Thinking very dully. No anger, that is good, odd, but good, no anger no, just a kind of letdown, like a scaffolding's gone.

The light comes on up there and he goes up after her. Hangs the painting on the hook she indicates.

'Welcome back, darling,' she says. The light is just a pool on the floor so Patrick still looks shadowy. Shady. Tony almost trips on something.

'Mind,' Connie snaps.

He looks down at the brown-paper parcel, an actual brown-paper parcel tied with string. 'Paints,' she says, 'new paints.'

It reminds him.

'Would you paint me?' For maybe that is it. Yes, that's it. She paints him, immortalises him in the way Patrick is immortalised. The portraits can hang side by side. Someone would pay a lot of money for a new portrait by Constance

Benson. A portrait of Tony. Next exhibition there he'd be, at
the view, up there in the light, never mind shut out in the cold
and the rain. He'd be up there, he'd be someone, someone
among all the Patricks. It's as if all the particles of him jump
together at the thought. Yes, that's it. And the elixirs, she
could be lying about the elixirs for all he knows but if he
sticks around . . . Who knows? Maybe the truth will out.

'No,' she says.

'What?'

'No.'

A long pause. 'What are you saying?'

'I'm saying no.' The light shines up from the floor so that
her face is a dark mess of angled shadows, lines, eyes gone.

'No?'

'I don't paint, dear. Not for a long time.'

'You do paint. These are paints.' He kicks the brown-
paper parcel.

'I buy paints because I love paints. I can't not buy them, all
the colours. But I don't paint. I'm going down.'

Tony watches her. His hands hang by his sides, loose fists
that could beat the shit out of her no trouble, but he lets her
go, the thin wisps of the top of her head disappearing last.
When she's gone he turns to look at Patrick. It's only paint
on a flat canvas but his head seems to turn slightly, can't, and
the eyes seem to blink. Is that a wink? No. Come *on*, Tony,
get a grip. She says no. But nevertheless she will paint him.
That is the new idea. He will stick around and she will paint
him and maybe the elixirs will come to light, the truth will
come to light.

He kneels and unties the string, unfolds the brown paper.
In a wooden box are tubes and tubes of paint. In the dim
light he holds them close to his eyes: cadmium yellow,
ultramarine, veridian. He presses between his finger and

thumb, unscrews the lid of one tube and squeezes. The colour that comes out looks blackish in the poor light, a worm of black on his hand, an oily rich smell. He rubs it round his palm, a wet dark hollow. The paint on his hand is fine at first but then it starts to feel like mud or shit. It's dirt and he needs to wash it off, quick, quick, to get that feeling off his skin. He goes down the ladder and to the sink.

'You been messing with my paints?' she says, she's sitting at the table swigging whisky. It makes a kind of creaky gulp as it passes down her throat. He turns on the tap. 'You won't get it off with water.'

'What then?' She takes her time, wipes her mouth on the back of her hand. He splays out his own fingers, can't bear the sticky feel of them pressing together. 'What?'

'Turps, under the sink.'

It makes him almost want to get rid of his hand, the feel of that paint clinging. He pulls back the bit of raggedy curtain, soggy cardboard cartons and cylinders of Dreft, Ajax, Flash, a bad damp smell of clean gone wrong. But there is a plastic bottle of turps, he pulls it out, unscrews it and splashes some on his palm, rubs his hands together so the paint thins to a stinking runny brown. He puts his hands under the cold water, squirts Squeezy on them, making shit-coloured suds in the sink.

'Raw sienna,' she remarks.

He rubs and rubs in the water that feels icy until the stain has gone, until his hands are raw and red.

'Finished?' she says.

Don't laugh at me. Tony sits down opposite her, reaches for the whisky, pours himself a drop, just a drop. Tosses it down his throat without touching the glass to his lips. Waits for her to say more but she says nothing, stares into her cup with a far-away kind of smile, makes some awful clicking swallowing sounds.

'I want you to paint me,' he says. A clear and reasonable enough request. After a pause he even adds, 'Please.'

She shakes her head. 'Oh no. No question of that.'

'You don't understand,' he says, staring at her face wondering *does* she, *does* she understand? 'I'm not asking, as such.' He pauses. 'I'm telling.

She snorts. 'Let me get this straight. You, *you* are *telling* me to paint you?'

'Yes.'

There is a long silence. Not silence of course, it rarely is, there are all the sounds of the sea and sky and room and the two living bodies inside it. But still, the not speaking has a resonance all of its own.

'And I am saying no.'

He rubs his cold hands on his thighs. He shrugs, smooths his hair back, feeling the blue light in it crackle against his hand. It's nearly dry now. He picks the rubber band, all stuck with broken-off hairs off the table, and snaps it on his hair.

'We'll start tomorrow.'

'I'm off to bed,' she says.

'And we'll start tomorrow at . . . nine?'

She goes to the sink, picks a foul discoloured toothbrush from the windowsill and fishes in the drawer for some toothpaste. She puts a finger in her mouth and flips out her dentures. He shudders. She runs the tap, scrubs at the pink gums and ivory teeth and plops the whole denture in a cup with a fizzing tablet. She scrubs the same toothbrush round in her mouth and spits in the sink. She lights the gas under the kettle again then she goes out of the door letting in a fresh blast of rainy air. While she's gone he listens to the fizzing of the dissolving tablet, the dripping of the tap, the racing of water approaching the boil, the far-off rush of the toilet flushing. She comes back in acting like he's not there which he fucking is. She stoops down and from under the sink, brings out a pink hot-water bottle. She fills it from the kettle and, holding it against her chest, goes to the bottom of the ladder.

'I'm sleeping up there,' Tony says.

She opens her mouth at him, no teeth, her little face folded even smaller now, her mouth a ragged O. She looks at him for a moment, but says nothing, turns and shuffles off into the bedroom. The door closes behind her with a hard click.

'Good-night,' he calls. But he doesn't climb the ladder. He opens the outside door and steps out, rubbing his cold hands on his jeans and looking at the rips in the cloud through which the stars sing, icy-clean and unimaginably far away.

SIX

The bed is damp, of course it is, not slept in since . . . Connie hates to come into this room. The memory of Patrick, not the painted Patrick but the real physical Patrick, the flesh and the bones, is so strong in here that it makes her cold. Not ordinary cold, but as if the air around her clings wetly, condenses on her warm live flesh and trickles down. *Stop it.* The bulb is dead and she stumbles to the dressing-table and wrenches at the sticking drawer, pulls out a damp tangle of woollen underwear, frowsty with her own smell. She fumbles at her clothes, takes some off, pulls on the long-johns and a cardigan, some socks that are his woollen socks knitted by Sacha and still good. A sudden memory of Sacha asleep in the conservatory, sun on her lined face, knitting dangling from her lap. Hard in the darkness to dress but she's not having that door open with him out there.

The hot-water bottle has warmed a space on one side of the bed. She curls round it, stomach burning through all the wool. Movement outside, the outside door opening, him in or out. No lock on this door, if only he would leave . . . oh Patrick who she needs, bloody bugger that he is, was, is. Paint him indeed! Paint him. As if he can threaten her. As if she's anything to lose. Not asking but telling!

The blankets on top of the sheets are heavy with damp, an awful smell. Last time she slept in this bed it was with him, his long body angled round hers, warm, warm. And now he is only bones. She is uneasy in this room, hates to think of the cold under the floorboards, that deep cold sand.

And sheets not changed for thirty years! Thirty years! She finds that she is sniggering. Sniggering! With that lunatic at large. *Stop it*. These sheets almost stuck together at the edges with the damp, mould probably. There must be some of Patrick left in this bed, some old skin cells, hairs. She can almost feel the arthritis starting up again in this damp. The floor nearly as soft as the bed itself. Face facts, Connie, the place is deteriorating faster than you are. Built as temporary in 1945, lived in for over fifty years, not bad, not bad at all. Patrick and his improvements. Crazy when he built the studio. Impossible said the architect who used to come and bring a different woman every time only they were all practically identical: slim, dark, wavy hair, you couldn't risk calling them by name – Sue, Lou, Pru – whatever it was he was searching for in them he never found. Patrick going ahead, hardly a one to take advice, she grins in the dark at the idea of it, built a floor, a window in the roof and he was right, it worked, and if the place is starting to lurch now well, who's to say it wouldn't be lurching in any case?

Hard edge of the rubber bottle against her, slosh of water as she moves. Someone moving in her home, some other mind thinking what? Planning what? Is this fear? A heart that she can hear and feel beating, a body curled round a rubber bottle, head under the mouldy sheets, smell of rubber, the heating of damp cloth, almost a kind of steam and her own whisky breath rebreathed. Her back is to the door but she doesn't dare turn over. Aware of the door through the blankets and the sheet and the slab of dark behind her, but her body is locked now in position, can't move. It's as if the hot-water bottle is beating like her own huge heart ripped out to which she clings. He could open the door and come in with a knife, an axe, a brick, and the light within her would be smashed. Would there be pain . . . that is almost of more concern . . . not afraid to be dead, only of dying, afraid only of the knowing and the pain.

How will she sleep and how will the night ever pass? The moment returns when she thought, crazy for a second, that he was Patrick. No, she never really could have thought . . . Patrick, Paddy, my love, take me. Oh that would be a joke if she could go tonight, float off, of natural causes they would say. Is fear a natural cause? What a turn it would give whatsisface, waiting for his nine o'clock *appointment*, if she didn't emerge. What would he do, bring her tea in bed, kick open the door and yell? And there she'd be, stone cold.

If this is fear, it's not as terrible as she thought it would be. Or is this not full fear yet, if fear is a mountain is this only the foothills? The tiredness, Lord she's bone tired from all the excitement of the week, the travel, the blast of life. And now this shock of . . . of invasion. And alcohol, she's had her fill of that. Perhaps, tomorrow, if she's spared, in the light of day it will all seem different. Maybe then she'll be paralysed with fear. She snorts, suddenly aware that what she feels most strongly right now is affronted. Is that the way to feel in this predicament? What is the right procedure, etiquette? God, her face is grinning now, gums clamped together in the slidy way that's become a comfort. If Patrick was here they would be, surely, the two of them sniggering, stuffing the blankets into their mouths for fear the lunatic potential mad knife-man outside the door might hear and be enraged by their mirth.

Oh yes, Patrick might be gone but he is still her solace. They just did get on like that, laugh at the same awful things.

Eccentric so he was but she did love him. Back to the wood then, to that first touch. Memories of the beginning still the sharpest, the colours faded through the years so that recent things, even the gaudy London stay, is muted. But bright that sixteenth birthday. May flowers gathered on the way back from the dawn walk. Sacha greeting her with a kiss. Happy Birthday, did Patrick find you in the wood? Connie awkward then not knowing what Sacha thought, whether, knowing Patrick, she would have assumed an attempt at intimacy.

She spent most of the day alone, painting the flowers she'd gathered – campion, cranesbill, cornflowers and red and white clover – the studio windows wide open to the sound of birds; the swallows feeding their squealing chicks; an occasional visit from a butterfly or bee; now and then a breeze stirring the flowers in the jar, the smell of paint and swallow dung and pollen all combined.

Then there was the tea-party. Sacha had invited a couple of critics, friends, people they thought Connie should meet. And there was Martin Redmartin. Oh yes, Red. It could have been a different life.

She had painted all that day, pressing the thought of the party from her mind. So full of feelings, she could hardly contain herself, hardly lose herself in the colours, hardly keep herself away from the window or the mirror. There was excitement and fear, too, she'd grown shy during her time in the country, most of it spent alone or with Sacha and Patrick. Visitors came to see Patrick sometimes, to listen to his ideas, but Connie stayed out of the way as much as she could. Many of the people were strange in the way they dressed and behaved, her parents would not have approved. Most of them were women who Patrick often entertained in his shed. Patrick attracted women all through his life. It was one of the mysteries about him – he was not obviously attractive, he was eccentric, obsessive, quite idiotic sometimes. But they fell at his feet. Loved him. And Connie loved him, too, despite everything. But there could have been another life, there could have been Red. Does she regret her life, does she?

Oh but that day, it was almost sultry, she felt guilty that she could be so . . . taken up with things – joy in the flowers, the paint, in a feeling that she really was stepping through the girl door into the woman world – guilty that she could be so happy when Mother and Father and Alfie were gone. Happy in a way, and about things, they would never have understood, would have found shocking. And she was frightened, too, because new people were coming to look at her work, so fearful that the brush trembled between her fingers when she let herself think of it.

And conscious of a strange full feeling in her chest and belly when she thought of Patrick in the dawn, a scene that had quickly gone like a dream in her memory, all dew and sparkle and the strange heat of that new touch. And more guilt at her fascination, guilt because of Sacha, because anyway, all that, it is not *nice*, it is not – surely not – *right* . . .

And later, bathed and dressed in the new blue dress Sacha had made her, a very grown-up dress, nipped in at the waist, silky stuff that clung to her small breasts, swished silkily against her thighs as she walked. Watching people arriving from the studio, the tops of their heads, not so many people, four or five. The first glimpse of Red's head, dark shiny brown. Cora Mansfield with a voice that could carry for miles, in a mad green dress, not even clean, her long white hair loose around her shoulders. Alex Waverley, quite an honour that he should have come, respected artist, critic, and Duffield, too, collar, tie, even a monocle or is she fabricating now? The two of them surely were a couple, homosexuals, although at the time Connie had no idea that such a thing was possible. Connie hid upstairs until Sacha came to lead her down to meet the guests.

Red was not expected, some sudden chance of leave, what a coincidence that it had been her birthday, that he had arrived just in time for the party. She had been so curious to meet him, seen the photographs and Sacha's paintings of him, a tousled brown-haired boy, sturdy in woollen sweaters that Sacha had knitted. In one he had such a frank stare, hair in his eyes, smudge on his cheek, sleeve of his sweater unravelling that she could hardly bear to look at him, such a *boy*, reminding her of Alfie. Sacha said little about Red, but on the rare occasions when she received a letter from him she wore it inside her clothes against the skin of her bosom so that Connie could hear it crackle when she moved. And then there he was, on her birthday, home on leave.

He was stocky, like Sacha, and not tall and his eyes were an unexpectedly vivid blue in an olive complexion. The skin on his neck looked so very tender above the collar of his uniform that she could not take her eyes off it. Odd to fix on such a place – but such tender tender skin it made her want to touch. He shook her hand and his fingers were firm and dry. Hands always important, could never love a man with clumsy hands, even the intruder's hands are . . . no, no, don't let him into this, cling to this treasure and do not let him spoil. Red's hands, the fingers slightly tilted back at the tips, small nails cut square, purposeful hands that held on to hers so firmly.

Praise for her work. Before tea they all came up to the studio and she waited, back to the door, heart in her mouth, for their verdict though she didn't *care*, she told herself, liar that she was. But they liked, enthused, praised. Red gave her a slow smile and raised a finger to his brow, in a sort of salute. His mouth was slightly crooked, she noticed, tilted up more one side than the other, and his smile got inside her and made her smile. Then there was the beer that Patrick brewed that was so odd and strong that if you drank too much you hallucinated. Something to do with the yeasts or moulds, something that he cultivated, refined later in his elixirs. Splendid beer, unique and almost worth getting sick on, she used to think.

It was such a beautiful evening that at the last moment Patrick and Red lugged the dining table out on to the lawn, everyone else following with the plates and glasses and food. Sacha lit candles that kept blowing out in the warmth of the evening breeze. Red sat beside Connie – a little closer than necessary – but the beer made her smile and perhaps rest her thigh against his under the table? Perhaps she even increased the pressure? Or not . . . She snorts at her own memory, startling herself, remembering where she is, breathing in the rubbery, whisky, mouldy air of the bed. She snuggles away from what's behind her and up to the bottle, the comforting slosh of warmth.

Patrick in his absolute element held forth from the head of the table, splendid in a shirt dyed purple, his hair brushed out, his eyes bright. They were eating corn on the cob, it all comes back to her, the slippery beaded yellow butteryness of it and threads getting jammed between her teeth. Each of them held a hot cob with a linen napkin and dug their teeth in, suddenly savage like a pack of well-dressed wolves. Patrick, his mouth half full, suddenly looked up and posed a question:

'What does stigma mean?' One of his trick questions, of course, the answer would prove some point or other. Sacha smiled at Red and shrugged as she gnawed at her corn.

'Some stain on character?' Red tried. 'To stigmatize – to

criticize – to brand as unworthy?' He darted a look at Connie. Approval? Sacha certainly looked proud.

'Precisely.' Patrick put down his corn and steepled his buttery fingers, eyes mischievous above them.

'Come on, darling, get to the point.' Cora leant forward and wagged a grubbily elegant finger.

'Also places that bleed . . . the stigma of the cross . . . or the stigmata is that?' Duffield spoke diffidently, a spot of melted butter on his chin.

'Stigmata's the plural, darling. A morbid spot that bleeds. Disease,' Alex Waverley said, relighting a candle with his silver lighter.

'Yes, yes,' Patrick eager, coming to the point now, almost as if coming to the boil. 'What else?'

Sacha put down her cob and wiped her mouth on her napkin. 'Part of the female genitalia of a plant,' she said looking apologetically at Red. 'The vulva, to be exact.'

'Isn't that illuminating?' Patrick netted them all in his gaze. 'Same word for the vulva and for such opprobrium. To stigmatize. Ha!' He took a swig of beer and froth hung creamily from his whiskers. 'What are flowers but sexual organs?'

Red flicked Connie a look but she was used to Patrick and only smiled, noticing the heat along the length of his thigh where it touched hers.

'They have been desexualised. That's what botany has done. What must be undone.' Patrick banged the flat of his hand on the table and made the glasses jump.

'*Really*, darling,' said Cora giving him her long red smile.

'Flowers are just great glorious erotic *blurts*. Great fragrant open beckoning cunts and erect cocks shooting sperm. Pollen! Pollen? And *filament*, can you imagine a word more . . . more flimsy for what it is? Oh!' Patrick leant back and ran his hand down his body and around his genitals.

'I say,' said Alex Waverley, putting down his corncob.

Connie sneaked a look at Red. 'It's all right,' she whispered, 'he goes off like this. It's the beer.'

'Patrick, do calm down,' said Sacha. 'You're putting us off our food.'

'Hear, hear,' said Duffield, and Waverley nodded.

'What's the matter with you all? After all, what are you eating?' Patrick looked from one of them to the other, his eyes resting on Cora whose smile was drunken, fond. She must have been one of his lovers, Connie realised, just from that knowing look.

'I'm sure you're going to tell us, darling,' Cora said.

Patrick picked up his half-eaten cob. 'Each one of these,' he pointed to the kernels, 'is a separate ovule. Each strand of the silk you tear off before you cook this – you know, the silky pubic stuff – each strand is in actual fact a vagina,' his eyes went dreamy, 'a long, sinuous, silky vagina.' Red dropped his cob and Connie, dizzy with the drink, had to bite her knuckle in order not to laugh.

Duffield changed the subject, mentioning Jacob Epstein's sculpture that he and Waverley had seen in London and the talk slipped into war talk, the situation for the Jews which made Connie shudder though she couldn't quite believe it could be true. She looked sideways at Red, flushed from the beer and conversation, the only one at the table who had taken part in the war that still seemed, despite everything, despite even her loss, an abstract thing. His uniform beside her, the material of his trousers, rough through the thin stuff of her dress, the only bit of war that she had touched.

'He's a bully,' Red said to her later. Only the two of them were left sitting at the table. The shrubs and lawn were dark, the sky a clear turquoise glass upturned. One big low star pricked the sky. A splash of laughter spilled from the house which was all in darkness, the blackout being observed for once, for the benefit of the guests.

'No he's not.'

'You don't like it, the way he humiliates people?'

'No, but he truly doesn't mean it.'

'How Mother puts up with it . . .'

'She understands like I do, it's not bullying, Red, it's, it's . . . enthusiasm. He's really very . . . lovable.'

'Hmmm.'

'Want to walk?' Connie stood up.

'Yes. Warm enough? Why not fetch a cardigan or something?'

Connie's arms were cold but she didn't want to spoil the effect of her dress. She slid her palms up her arms, the skin cool.

They walked across the lawn and Connie led the way between the trees, the same path she'd trodden at dawn. 'He doesn't mean to upset individuals,' she said, 'he means to upset ideas. Do you see the difference?'

'He could be more sensitive about it.'

'He *could* be.'

Between the trunks the shadows whispered and rustled with settling life. Connie slowed down and took his arm, felt him stiffen and then relax.

'You know I've never much liked Patrick,' Red said. 'I was pleased for Mother of course that they met. *She* seems to like him. I was seventeen, old enough to leave, when they . . . when they set up together. It is a funny set-up, isn't it? For a girl I mean.'

'Perhaps.'

'With his well-known . . . proclivities.'

'Well . . . this is all I've got now,' Connie said.

'Yes, I know, you poor girl . . . it must have been . . .'

193

'Don't.'

'You don't want to talk?'

'They are dead. What is there to say?' Connie pulled away
and walked fast. Her dress rustled about her legs. His footsteps thudded behind her.

'Sorry, Connie. Can we just scrub that?'

She walked without speaking, counted ten steps. 'Yes,' she
said and slowed and this time his arm went round her, warm
dry hand against the chill skin of her upper arm.

'Did you hear that?' Red stopped.

'An owl,' Connie said. 'No, two owls. One calls toowit
and the other answers toowoo.'

'I never knew that.'

'Well, that's what Patrick says.'

'Hmmm.'

They laughed. Red pulled her against him. His chin was
rough against her cheek and she could feel the heat of him
through his tunic. 'What will become of you, little one?' he
murmured into her hair.

'I'm all right.'

'Patrick's reputation with women . . .'

'It's not just Patrick, you know,' Connie said, 'your
mother, too . . . she has her . . . adventures. Apparently.'

'Well, that's up to her. There could even be doubt cast
upon the proximity of . . .'

'Of?'

'Speculation about *you*, do you realise that, Connie?' She
heard a pause in his breathing: he was waiting for a clue. She
pulled away again and walked forward into the darkness,
very dark between the trees now, too dark to walk without
stumbling.

'Your own speculation is this?'

'Would that be so strange? Connie, wait, wait . . .' She

waited half because the dark was starting to scare her, the snapping of invisible twigs under her feet, the soft scratch of leaves against her face. The beer made her dizzy, made flickers of light in her eyes as if there were fire-flies everywhere. He held her again and this time she could clearly hear his heart beating and smell his skin. She reached her face up and put her lips on the tender place above his collar. She remembered Patrick in the wood, that stiff slant under his pyjama trousers, tried to push that image away, the memory of hot silk in her hand. Found that she was breathless.

'Perhaps you do right to wonder.'

'Are you . . . ?'

'Is this to be an impertinent question?'

'Yes, extremely.'

'Do you think it proper to continue?'

'Of course not, but to hell with propriety.'

Connie gave a mock gasp. And waited. But he said nothing. 'Go on then.'

'Are you a . . .'

'A?'

'Are you a virgin?'

'Yes.' Another owl cry, or two owls. Remember those soft white wings in the dawn.

'Patrick hasn't . . . then.'

'No.' Which was almost the truth.

'I think I'd murder him if he did.' And then he kissed her, his mouth strange on hers, the shape of his open lips, the beery taste, the sharpness of the stubble around them, the tip of his tongue flickering between her own lips that opened and made her think of flowers opening, fat wet petals. They stumbled together and held up. Oh, Patrick and all his shocking talk.

'Have you been kissed before?'

'No, no.' She reached her mouth to his again, her legs weakening, hanging on him almost to keep her up. 'Not kissed like this.'

He stopped. 'Did you hear?'

'What?' But then she heard Sacha's voice carrying between the trees calling first Red's name and then her own.

'We'd best go back,' he said. 'But tomorrow? My last day. I'd like to spend it with you.'

She paused, warmed suddenly, grinned into the darkness. 'Yes.'

'I do like you very much, Connie.'

'Yes, yes, me too.'

He held her away from him by the tops of her arms and looked down at her although it was too dark to see his face. 'Not as a brother, do you understand.'

'Well, you're not my brother.'

'Understand?'

'Yes.' She wanted him to kiss her again then, but he turned and drew her back along the path towards Sacha's voice.

SEVEN

Tony wakes, hot light pressing on his face. He keeps his eyes closed. There's a red glow inside his lids. Where the fuck is he and why so bright and hot? In a sleeping bag stretched out on a hard floor. Christ. He turns over and opens his eyes to the huge shadow of a dead wasp. Can't bear the filth, can't bear the nylon. Gets out of the sleeping bag quick, staggers a bit, bones stiff. Not getting old, Tony, not at thirty? It's being here with an old woman, that's all. Old age rubbing off like a contagion.

Not how it should be. Nothing is. His armpits itch. He scratches his chin, needs a shave, needs a shower, needs clean sheets to bring a proper rest, last night all tossing and turning, sweat, sore bones, bad dreams. Burned out. Can't put his unwashed body back in his unwashed clothes. There should be a washing machine or a launderette close by. How does she wash her clothes? There should at least be a shower.

You can't even stand straight in this dwarf space. Sun bright on Patrick's painted face. One day someone will wake to Tony's face on canvas, stare into his painted eyes and read some expression. And then he will exist, other than in this self, he will exist. Yes, there's that.

He pushes open the skylight. Cool dawn, can't see the sea from here, wrong side, just a scrub of bushes with berries on, straggling trees turning brown – but you can hear the sea. A swim? That would wash away the sweat at least, the reek of hot, stale skin. He kneels at the edge of the trap-door and looks down. Darker down there, except for the bright rectangle that contains his own shadow. Her door still shut. Twenty-five-past seven by his watch.

He gets a pair of clean underpants from his rucksack, but yesterday's shirt and jeans and, bollock naked, climbs down the ladder. No one to see, straight out the door. First time he's been naked outside? Yes? Shivers, but the cool air is at least clean against his skin. Through the dunes, cold sand forced between his toes, sharp prickle of grass against his legs and on to the firm ripples of wet sand. He drops his clothes at the last dune and runs, feet smacking and into the shallow cold of the sea that is milky in the early light and sooo cold. Strides in over a ridge of pebbles, gasping, water up to his thighs, balls burrowing up inside him, the cold lick of water meeting round his waist making him shout and then he plunges. It almost makes his heart stop, *icy, icy*, but then he's swimming and it's fanfuckingtastic, arms parting the water ahead. He wants someone to have seen him, some woman, perhaps. Squints through wet lashes at the beach but there's no one. Swims just a few breast strokes, crawls a bit, too bleeding cold for more but it's great. It's *great*.

Suddenly so wide awake, his body all at one. Exhilarated, that's the word. And clean, clean in the cold of it. And then he's out, legging it up the beach, teeth chattering, hair like wet weed clinging round his shoulders. Too wet to dress he makes himself run. Christ, early morning swim and run, this would impress them. Impress who, Tony? Who cares? Runs until his skin burns as it heats under the cold skim of water.

A sharp stab in his foot stops him. Christ. A broken bottle in the sand. He lifts his foot to look at bright blood leaking from behind a sandy flap of skin. Stares at it. No. He hobbles, shivering, back to his clothes and tries to pull his shirt on but the material sticks to his damp skin and it won't go on.

And then he starts to cry. To *bawl* like a great fucking baby, tears and a string of hot snot stretching from his nose. Hops into his pants, sobbing all the time, sand from his foot sticking to the cotton, smear of blood on the white, jeans sticking to his legs.

Dressed, he sits in sand-dunes, holds his foot in his lap and waits for the crying to stop. Sees himself like someone else would, twisted leg, the sole pulled upwards, shuddering shoulders, pale damp shirt with the wet of his black hair spread over it, twisted face.

He sat on a single bed like this at home once, not allowed to sit on the bed but sitting there all the same and crying. How it hurt to cry. How old was he . . . young. And she had caught him wanking. Something that made him sick with himself even that early but he couldn't help it, sometimes it just came over him this kind of itch and heat till he couldn't be still or think of anything else and he did it just to get it out of the way but then she came into the bathroom – forgotten to lock the door, how could that have been? – and . . . the memory scrubbed out after that . . . the utter horror is all he remembers. The utter sickening, shocking, shame. The look on her face. Night after night he had known *she* was shagging men whose names he never knew. But the look on her face. She never touched him again. He remembers no touch ever just her face white between the black wings of hair: nothing warm, cold food cling-wrapped in the fridge, starchy piles of clothes delivered by a laundry service.

Blood so red against the white flap of skin, skin thickened and withered by the wet and cold. He prods it, can't feel a thing. Still the fucking tears coming from somewhere, it hurts like someone's wrenching something from his gut. All the crying coming together. Another bed, hard stinking bunk, crying there, the Prison Chaplain: 'Have faith,' as he *would* say. And Tony getting himself together enough to say, 'Faith in what?' 'Whatever you believe in.' 'I believe in nothing.' 'Then believe in yourself.' Hadn't answered, not worth an answer. But later, lying on the bunk staring at the ceiling pocked with little bits of paper chewed and spat there by inmates before him, he had found himself thinking about that. Believe in himself. What is there, body, mind – almost managed to get a degree for Christ's sake before – and surely that must prove he has a mind. And he feels hunger, pain and loneliness. He eats and sleeps and shits and cries. He is someone. To believe in? Why not?

So the Chaplain's trite crap cheered him enough to borrow a book from the library, to use the mind that was knackered by boredom, guilt, anger, the stupidity of those around him. And the book was Patrick's Memoir. The stuff about plants that grabbed him somehow, the stuff about the elixirs, the Seven Steps to Bliss that he thought would save him. Like a message that book then. There is hope. Maybe there is still. That's why he's here, for Christ's sake.

He wipes his face on his sleeve. He's stopped crying now, just a judder in his chest with every in-breath and soon that will stop. And nobody saw him and nobody knows. Come on, Tony man. There may still be hope. Fucking freezing, teeth chattering now. He gets up, limps between the dunes, grains of sand forcing themselves up into his cut. Thinks, This is where Patrick lived. Patrick knew here. *Was* here. That is why I'm here, because of Patrick, and that idea returns to him like an embrace. *It's all right*.

And the woman that Patrick loved when she was young is going to paint him and he will find the elixirs, he's sure of that, suddenly, because that is the meaning of all this. There is meaning and living in Benson's squalor may just be the price he'll have to pay. Everything has a price, of course it does, how could it not? In the end you always have to pay.

She's up when he gets back sitting at the table, a cup of tea in front of her. She doesn't look up, doesn't speak, so the Coventry treatment, is it? But then she says, 'Tea in the pot if you want it.' She looks like someone who hasn't slept not just for one night but for several.

He goes to pour a cup of tea, recognising, just in time, the cup the dentures went in last night. Sun shines straight through the window on to her sparse hair, black at the ends, white at the top, showing how pink her skull is, the scalp-skin tight while the skin of her face is wrinkled like an old apple, lines like long stitches all around her lips.

'What do you think I've got to lose?' she asks. 'I mean what are you threatening me with if I fail to comply with your . . . hardly a request, is it, dear?' He finds another cup, pours the tea, sips it staring at her. She still hasn't raised her eyes to him. Is this rudeness, is this fear? 'Murder, would it be?'

What is the time? They agreed to start at nine. He looks at his watch. Glass gone misted. Stupid pillock, wore it in the sea. Not waterproof, not at a tenner from Brixton market, might have been called a diver's watch but now it's buggered. Holds it to his ear to hear the faint battery tick, but there's nothing.

'Been for a dip?' She looks up at him.

'What's the time?'

'Wet hair again, tut tut, you'll catch your death.' She shrugs her shoulders. 'Search me, dear.'

'Stop calling me dear. Where's your clock?'

'What clock?'

His foot is starting to ache. He holds it clear of the filthy floor. Keeps his temper. 'So how do you tell the time?'

'Why would I want to do that?' she says, and there is triumph in her voice, she's having him on. She must have a way of telling the time. It will become apparent if he just waits. Not a big deal, he can manage for now, he can manage.

'It's nearly nine,' he says, 'by my reckoning.'

'So?'

'We said nine.'

'*We*? I think I could fancy some nuts.' She gets up to fetch a packet of salted peanuts from the cupboard. He stares at her until she turns and meets his eyes at last. 'And you actually believe I'm going to paint you?'

'I'll have a fag, then, yes.'

'And if I don't?'

'Well, I'm the stronger of the two of us, wouldn't you say?'

He sits down at the table. Must do something about his foot, hurts like hell. Takes a pinch of tobacco and rolls up, looking at her as he licks the edge of the paper.

She scoffs a handful of nuts. 'So, you'll beat me till I paint you?'

'You'll paint me.' Lighter run out, has to get up to fetch the matches. She notices his limp.

'Hurt your foot? Is that blood?'

There's a smear of blood on the floor, might be dirt in the cut, dirt in his bloodstream. Stop it. Don't panic. He sits down again, lights his fag, inhales, shuts his eyes, awaits the first buzz of nicotine, best of the day. Breathes out. 'Got any TCP or plasters?' he asks, as if she would. But she gets up and rustles through a drawer, brings out a cracked old tube of something, throws it on the table. She goes off outside.

He tries to read what's in the tube but the name's worn off.

He unscrews the lid, squeezes out a bit of pinkish stuff, sniffs it, smells antiseptic, kind of familiar. He hops to the sink, lifts his leg and puts his foot under the tap. Waits for the rush of cold water that rinses the cut, rinses off the sand. He watches the water marbling with his blood against the enamel. Stands with his foot in the sink for a long time, feeling like a complete prat, till his foot aches with the cold, till the water must have washed it clean.

She comes back in, gives him a look. 'If I was to paint you,' she says, 'just as a matter of interest, if I was to paint you, then what?'

He removes his foot from the sink, hops back to the chair, holds it in front of the gas fire to dry. 'Then we'd all be happy,' he says.

'If you do have murderous tendencies, dear,' she says, 'then who's to say you wouldn't let me paint you and then . . .'

'I'm to say,' Tony says. 'I wouldn't.'

'Your word of honour?' Sarcasm or not? Can't tell so doesn't answer. He lifts his foot into his lap to examine it. Very pink and clean, the flap over the cut pale, still a few grains of sand in there, but still. He smears on some ointment. It stings.

'How long would it take?'

'Hard to say.'

'A week?'

'I could do it in less than a week. And then?'

'And then you sign the picture, give it to me and I go.'

'If not? I say no?'

'Then I stay. You stay.'

'A hostage, would you say?'

'What?'

'Just like to get these things straight. Am I to think of myself as a hostage?'

Tony considers. 'If you like. What's the difference?'

She eats another handful of peanuts. Then she goes to the kettle. 'I'm making another cup to take upstairs and have with my pipe,' she says. 'It's what I do of a morning. Now, if I *did* paint you it wouldn't be out of compulsion. No, no, I don't feel myself compelled. Your execrable manners could only have the opposite effect on *me*. If I paint you it's because I am tickled by the idea, intrigued. If I paint you . . . the colour of your hair.'

To his own surprise, Tony smiles. 'If that's how you want to look at it,' he says. 'I'll have a shave.'

He sits staring past her at Patrick as she sketches. The skylight is open. It's cool but not cold and the sun is pale on the dusty floor. One patch, that he brushed before he lay down in his sleeping bag, is cleaner but there are so many cobwebs and dead things, dried-out little wings everywhere. She sketches rapidly. Patrick gives Tony a strange look and Tony tries to mimic his expression. Such a weird light in those eyes today. He sets his jaw in the same way. An immortal expression. He likes this, being studied, being sketched. Feels better now he's shaved, skin smooth, the nice scent of his shaving soap clinging to his hands. Horrible shaving in the kitchen sink but better than not and he knows he looks good. He watches the way she draws, appraising him quite impersonally, holding up her pencil, working her jaw so he can see all the stringy old sinews in her throat. Sucking and sucking on those disgusting Fisherman's Friends.

Patrick shouldn't look younger in this last portrait. He was an old man. Yet in it he looks younger than in any other. Unbelievable that he loved this old woman, *old* woman with thin hair, humpy-shouldered in an old brown cardigan stretched down at the front, up at the back. And the stupid party shoes with sparkly bits on. *He* thought this was the sexiest woman alive. Had hundreds, thousands possibly, yet he preferred *her*. She must have been . . . something.

'You must have been gutted when he . . .' Tony nods towards Patrick and Benson jumps. Her face goes all loose then tight again, composing itself. Tony's never seen a face do that before, like a mask going off and on. Knows the feeling though.

'Sorry, dear, miles away,' she says. 'Just turn your head a bit, no, other way. God, I'm rusty. Just a mo . . . there. Let's stop for a smoke, shall we?' She puts down her sketch pad and picks up her pipe. 'Wouldn't fetch me a cup of tea, would you?'

He goes down the ladder to make tea. While he waits for the kettle he gets Patrick's Memoir from his bag, pages coming loose with so much reading. Opens it at the end where it finishes quite suddenly mid-sentence.

So we experienced once more the cellular unanimity of all creation. I could hear the blood flowing in Con's veins, the sap flowing in the cabbage leaves, we could hear the vibrations of those squat green creatures so healthful to be near. In love with creation this day, expressing that love of all creation through our bodies. Moment of climax a fusion of all there was and is and ever can be. Con spoke wisely of

On the 18th July 1965, the day after conducting this experiment, Patrick Mount left the home he shared with Constance Benson. He left no explanation of his disappearance, and made only a casual farewell. Benson assumed he had gone for a walk. Because of his irregular habits and refusal to be accountable for his whereabouts,

Benson was not unduly concerned when he failed to return that night. On the third day she became anxious and contacted friends to try and ascertain his whereabouts. Several weeks after his disappearance he was listed as a missing person. Patrick Mount has never been seen or heard of since.

Editor

Tony carries the tea up the ladder. Benson still sits on the little chair, puffing smoke from her pipe, some ratty old cushion clutched on her lap. So fucking *tiny*. Despite the open window the room is thick with pipe smoke. 'What were your words of wisdom?' Tony asks. She looks at him blankly. 'At the end of the Memoir . . .'

'Oh! That!' She smiles. 'The times I've been asked that! The things I've been tempted to say.' She breathes out a plume of grey and the smile fades. 'The truth is I can't quite remember. It was something about it being more than the human frame could bear. I was afraid of the experiments – the effects getting stronger, more intense.'

'You took many of the elixirs?'

'Like it says in the book, I helped.' She sucks on her pipe till it gurgles. It has tiny white hands carved into the clay, small as mouse paws. She plucks at the material of the cushion. 'You want me to tell you what it was like.'

Tony sits down, puts his cup on the floor and rolls a fag as she speaks. 'I didn't like it. To tell you the truth I didn't . . . I do like to stay in control. Those elixirs made me feel like . . . well, I wasn't quite me. Oh it felt glorious sometimes, soaring and light and this sense of . . . of a kind of stunning peace . . . unity. Like God, dear. Or sex.' She gives an oddly throaty laugh, then coughs. 'But I . . . I prefer to be me, feel what I really feel.'

206

'But you really felt *that*.'

'But . . . well, each to his own. Patrick certainly liked it.'

'You have none of them left?' He watches for a flicker, hopes to find her out. She might have a little stash here or there.

'Shall we get on?'

'How far had he got . . . the final elixir. Bliss, did he make that one?'

'It's all in the Memoir,' she says. 'I don't know no more than that. Any more, rather. I never did know the details. His thing, it was, not mine. Crazy idea that you can solve anything with drugs.'

'Course you can. Antibiotics, they cure . . .'

'No, I don't mean, he didn't mean. More universal things, he meant, abstract things. Like war. By making the need for war . . . well, unnecessary. Irrelevant.'

'But . . .'

'You don't understand, dear?' She laughs again. 'You aren't the only one, believe me. Now if you want this thing done we better get on.' She knocks out her pipe and picks up her pencil.

To solve *war*? That isn't in the Memoir, it's more individual what Patrick says, more for individual . . . improvement. He wants to argue with her but she is shut in with concentration. Her head bobs over her pad, her hand makes scuffing sound on the paper. There's a bit of drool at the corner of her mouth which she wipes away with a finger, then wipes her finger on her dress. Old. Patrick looking over her shoulder does look so young.

'How old is he?' Tony nods at the portrait.

She starts. 'I was just thinking of that . . . the last portrait I did, apart from . . .' She waves her hand over the sketches that are scattered round her chair. 'I did it after he'd gone.'

'Can you call it a portrait if he wasn't there?'

'He was there.'

'You said . . .'

'Don't take any notice of me. And call it what you like.'

'He looks so young.'

'It's just how he looked when, when I last saw him.' Her voice has gone small like a lost little girl's. She clutches at the cushion like a baby at a blanket. Makes him feel . . . something. Christ, he's getting soft, must not. It's just the smoke in her throat making her voice go like that. It's nothing.

Tony takes a scalding swallow of tea. 'He looks so different. From how he does in all the others.' Getting used to drinking it without milk. Maybe he'll stick with it black from now on, tastes cleaner, thin and hot.

'Yes, well . . . a portrait is as much a portrait of the painter as the sitter. Now.' *But it doesn't look like you*, he wants to say. *What do you mean?* She waits for him to resume his pose. 'You don't need to be here all the time, just get the composition sorted. You going to tell me what your interest in Paddy is?'

'Just . . . interest.'

'The drawings are not considered good.'

'Not the drawing, the ideas.'

'Oh he would have liked *you* – and the elixirs, yes. Lots of hippy types liked the thought of them. Not Patrick's idea at all. Not for fun, not recreational, not that. His intention was serious. Very high-minded, Patrick, though he did laugh, too, he had a sense of humour.'

'I don't understand what you said about war. But if someone had . . . I don't know, kind of a mental problem, if someone came to him with a mental problem would he think the elixirs could help?'

'Aaah.' She peers at him and nods. 'Aaah.'

She makes him feel naked, naked and stupid looking at him like that with that kind of *understanding*.

'He wasn't a doctor,' she says, then grins at the idea.

'I'm not saying . . . I'm just saying *if*. Like I said I'm interested in his ideas. And in what happened to him.'

'Nobody knows,' she says, sharply. 'And nobody ever will.' She pinches her lips together in a thin line and starts sketching, gestures to him to arrange himself. *Mental problems. Christ, how could he have said that?* He looks down at his knees, at his hands on his knees, the black hairs on their backs. Patrick is supposed to help him, that's why he's here. Must wait, must be patient, don't blow it now. He really wants this portrait, wants it. He sits for a while, questions building up in him. Christ, he feels so *near*. But he wants this. Wants to be concentrated on like this by Patrick's woman. If she was young maybe he'd . . . No. For a minute there he caught a bit of . . . something about her, something that made him feel . . . what? Pity? Liking? NO. Stop. And she's probably lying to him, even now, probably thinking, *Mental problems, eh?* She better not fucking laugh. Stop. Look at Patrick, keep your eyes on Patrick's eyes. On that wild shine.

'Or cares,' she says, making him jump.

'What?'

'Nobody knows or cares.'

'I do.'

'Care? You mean you want something.' Stares her out. Something strange, must be the light, or staring too hard at Patrick or something but for a moment there he thought he saw . . . not saw but *sensed* something like a girl, something that might make him want . . . no. Not to want to touch. Not to feel it, not tender, no. The feel of Lisa's body in the toy fur coat. No. Those open eyes. No. No. Something behind the lines, face screwed up like some old brown-paper bag, see behind all that to something soft. Something Patrick loved and he can almost see it. NO.

A seagull flies low over the skylight casting a shadow. The room suddenly goes cold. Patrick's eyes cold now. Oh please! This is a painting we're on about here. A painting of a dead man. Flat canvas you could put your fist through.

Benson sketches on, both profiles, different angles, the light falling on him this way and that.

'You could tell me your shady past,' she suggests, looking up at him, eyes all bright. 'Assuming it is shady. Say if I'm wrong.'

He could say anything. Could say everything – or nothing. He's the one in control here whatever little games she wants to play. She's doing what she was told, isn't she? *Isn't she?* Think what she likes.

'Not telling? Let me ask you something then. Whatever possessed you to read Patrick's book? I mean, you're young, it's considered nothing but a curiosity piece nowadays – always was for that matter. Wherever did you find it? Out of print for donkey's years.'

OK. Right that she knows who she's dealing with. What. Mental case. Yeah. Take that kind of monkey twinkle out of her eyes. 'Inside.' He watches for her reaction.

'Inside what, dear?'

'Prison.'

'Ha!' She drops the paper and stands up. 'You found it in prison. Oh glorious! Patrick, did you hear that? Priceless!'

Who's insane? *Laughing*. She walks about the room cackling, those green shoes crushing the dead bees and wasps. Isn't she going to ask? She goes back to her chair in the end, sits down, though still flicking stupid smiles at the portrait. 'I'm getting tired,' she announces suddenly. 'Can't work when I'm tired. Usually have a nap round now, after lunch. Do you think it might be lunchtime?'

'Don't know.' Tony looks at his useless watch. Taking the piss, that's what she's doing. Still thinks she's one up on him. She knows he wants her to ask, why, why he was inside, what he did, and she won't. As if she's in control. See how she kept Patrick on a leash, wiles, that's what they're called, female wiles.

'Tell me if you like,' she says. 'It's your business. I won't ask.' See there she goes, putting the ball into his court. Making it be up to him. Making as if she doesn't care what he might have done.

She goes to the trap-door and sits on the edge, stiff and old, as soon as she turns her face away from him he can see what a decrepit old bitch she really is. She pushes her feet in the stupid shoes or to the rungs of the ladder. Could shove her down and no one would be any the wiser. Misadventure. Stands over her looking at the pink scalp under the thin puff of hair. 'I killed someone,' he says. She doesn't answer or look at him, manoeuvres herself round to descend the ladder.

Tony needs to see her face to see what she's thinking. Goes down after her, too quickly, feet almost in her face. They stand at the bottom of the ladder, she looks down at the floor, he at her bowed head. So she is scared then, scared to meet his eyes.

'I don't eat much as a rule,' she says. 'Oh . . . but there's still your stew. You have more stew, that'll last for days at this rate. I'll have a bag of crisps.' She rummages in the cupboard and brings out a pink bag. 'Prawn Cocktail, good,' she says. 'Incidentally, dear, did you like them?'

'What?'

'This person that you killed. Did you like . . . or love? I can't see the point of killing someone otherwise.' Tony turns to the stove, flicks his lighter at the gas. A swoosh as it lights, a big blue flower of flame squashed by the pan. Benson is stuffing crisps, crackling, munching, Christ. Doesn't see the point? The *point*? There is no point. She's completely fucking barking. 'Or hate?' she suggests. 'Do you want to talk about it?'

He watches the cassoulet heat. The greasy skin of the top goes glossy and it starts to bubble, lazy heaves of vegetable and meat. He tries to block out the crunching of the crisps, that horrible swallowing sound she makes like she's got some kind of mechanism in her throat. 'Tea?' she says, and he refills the kettle – still warm from last time. Spoons some food on to a plate and switches off the gas. He waits till she's finished the crisps and sits down at the table. She has salt and bits of crisp all stuck in the hairs and wrinkles round her mouth.

'Manslaughter,' he says, 'a girl.' She does miss a beat then, surely she does miss a beat.

She screws up her crisp bag. 'Funny word, I've always thought. Manslaughter. Split it up and you get man's laughter. Funny that.'

'*What?*'

'But anyway, dear, it means not deliberate?'

'Not premeditated.' Tony takes a mouthful of the cassoulet. Swallows. Good, even better than it was, the flavour rich, not quite hot enough, not warmed through, but good. Cooking is something he can do. She keeps her eyes on him, head on one side.

'I suppose not. And why do you want yourself painted?' He won't reply. What is this? Why will this woman not react properly? Must have driven Patrick mad, no wonder he pissed off out of it.

'Rather than a photo?' she says.

He won't answer.

'Photographs are quicker. More the thing, I'd have thought.' He finishes the food and gets up to wash his plate. 'I'll take a cup of tea and have a nap now,' she says, 'just forty winks. And I'll have them upstairs in my chair if you don't mind. Not that dreadful bed.'

He watches her make tea and pour herself, not him, a cup. She climbs up the ladder with it. Watches the thin legs, the twinkling shoes disappear. His mother had shoes that shape but never green, always black or brown and smelling of Cherry Blossom polish, a smell that makes him want to puke, even the thought of it. Every Sunday evening that was his job – to clean the shoes. He had one or two pairs but she had several and he had to do them every week, shoes and boots, even if she hadn't worn them. She'd stand them in a line by the back door on a sheet of newspaper and the tin with the brushes and the tins of polish – dark tan, light tan, black. He had to polish till she said they were shiny enough, brushing and brushing, little lumps of polish getting under his nails, staining his fingers, the smell of it getting into his skin. She said you should be able to see your face in them, she'd hold them up to her face and frown, black lines across her white forehead. But even when they really shone his own face was just a smear in the leather, you never could have told it was a face. Then in the bath scrubbing and scrubbing with the sharp nail brush to make that smell go away, staying in the bath till his fingers crinkled and the water got colder than the air.

EIGHT

Connie settles herself with her tea. The door downstairs opens and bangs shut. Gone out then. Good. She sags. Good to be alone, even just for a moment. That blasted boy is no danger, not really, not if she handles him right. Later she'll go down to the sea, just for a while, just for a breath of it. But what to make of *him*? Manslaughter, a girl, what to make of that? True? Murder you might fantasise, but manslaughter?

Just a boy with a screw loose who thinks the elixirs would help him. That's all. Nothing to fear. She told him a lie, but sometimes lies are good not bad, sometimes lies are the very best, the safest thing. Just keep a step ahead, just keep your head. What this manslaughter business is about . . . should know more, doesn't want the detail, just the bare bones. Like how long ago. Thinking of bones: the bones in his face, good, cheeks, aquiline nose – Patrick must be bones by now, loosened and sprawled – her own bones ache with tired, but nice to be in the chair, in her place, Patrick back in his rightful place.

Oh if only Tony would go. It could be all right, she could be. Think of something that will make you warm. So sleepy with the upheaval. But it isn't anything much, it isn't. It isn't anything to be frightened of. Just bear with it, just go along, make the best of it.

Funny how life happens. How she's here, stuck here, like a

214

prisoner, forced to do the thing she used to love, that *was* the point of her. Funny how life happens, the hinges that bend you this way and that. If this had been different, so would that. If not for this, if not for that. Useless to regret because who knows what else there was? If not for the war, what? No Patrick, no Sacha, no Red. Maybe no painting? That is hard to believe. Other lovers – a husband – babies? Certainly another life. But she's had this one, this life. And here she is, stuck in her studio with him down there. Oh well. Useless to regret, the only regret allowed is Red. Let's think then, let's think of that.

The day after her birthday she woke with a headache. They had sat up late drinking beer: Patrick being outrageous, Sacha long-suffering, Cora flirtatious, Duffield and Waverley by turns shocked and provoking. Connie and Red had sat a little apart from the rest, said little to each other but touched each other with their eyes and with sideways smiles. And when Connie went to bed he had followed her to the door and kissed her good-night, just a kiss on the cheek, but in front of everyone, and said, 'See you tomorrow,' sending a thrill right through her.

But the next day was thick grey streaming rain. Everyone was out of sorts and the house was cold. It was too wet for walking. Connie had imagined sunshine, thought that she and Red would lie in a field and listen to the birds and that he would kiss her again. She wanted to touch and to be touched. The rain upset her and the pain in her head. Patrick gave her a drop of one of his prototype elixirs. Red complained of a headache, too, he appeared in the kitchen just after her, looking pale, in need of a shave, not so . . . attractive, not like he'd been in her mind all night. She was disappointed. Patrick gave Red a drop, too. She'd watched him stick his tongue out and Patrick drip the stuff on it and she had turned away.

What a dull, dull headache of a day. If she couldn't walk, if there wasn't going to be some kind of love – and oh she did want some kind of love – then she may as well be painting. She could try and catch the watery grey of the light, but it seemed rude to go off alone when she'd said she'd spend the day with Red. Until Sacha said, 'Connie, why not paint Red?'

'Well?' He looked at her and she caught the warmth in his eyes. Oh yes, it was still there that feeling.

'I've never done an actual portrait.'

'There's a first time for everything,' Sacha said, smiling from one of them to the other.

'I'd be most honoured,' Red said.

'All right then.' She led the way upstairs. She felt him pause on the landing and turned, knowing why he had paused, what he would be looking at. And she was right. He was gazing at Sacha's painting of herself standing before the window, her long pigtail snaking down her naked back. 'Come on,' she said and he looked away from the painting and met her eyes and flushed.

It was so chilly in the studio that she lit the fire. He wandered about looking at her paintings. 'I know nothing,' he said, 'but the colours are so superb. Are you excited about what Duffield said?'

'Of course.'

'Will you go to Goldsmiths'?'

'I don't know. I don't know if I want to study. I just want to paint.'

'But you would get better. You would get stimulated.'

'Perhaps.' Pale flames licked the log in the grate. 'Good,' she said, 'that's caught.' He knelt down beside her, took her hands. His were cold but she liked the firm way he held hers between them.

'Would you not like to be stimulated?' he said. She could

216

not believe he really meant what he seemed to mean, but his face was warm and close to hers and she opened her mouth to his kiss. It was so easy and natural and there was no shame in what followed. There was only one day before he went back or maybe they would have waited, maybe they would have taken time to flirt and court. Maybe the drops of elixir that Patrick had given them had some effect other than curing their headaches. Because there was no shame or inhibition. He kissed her and she kissed back, feeling a new sort of thirst and a new sort of hunger, too, as they lay down on the rug by the fire and he touched her under her clothes, his hands heating now, discovering all her curves, hollows, finding a kind of rhythm in her that she never knew she had. She ran her fingers down the warm skin of his back, round his waist, and when she touched his cock she found it smaller than Patrick's, or shorter, but maybe thicker, she could hardly meet her fingers round it. The hot sliding silk of the skin fascinated her. She sat up to look closely at the sheeny rose colour of the tip, the tawny skin that slid up and down, the black hairs that curled around. 'It's beautiful,' she said.

'My filament,' he said in a good imitation of Patrick's voice. She laughed but closed her eyes to try to banish thought of Patrick from her mind. She opened them to see that Red was staring at her, his eyes so hot she shivered. Then she took him in her mouth, without planning or thinking, or meaning to. A shocking thing, she had never even thought of, and when she took her mouth away she saw that he looked startled, but also very pleased. He laid her down and touched her where she had grown moist and aching: 'The stigma,' he murmured, 'oh Connie, *you* are beautiful.' They lay and kissed and caressed until the log had burned half away. She wanted him to make love to her but he would not. 'It's too dangerous,' he said. The rain stopped and weak sunshine shone through the running glass casting watery reflections on the floor and in the hearth, quenching the brightness of the flames.

'In that case,' Connie said, standing up and fastening her clothes, 'I'd better paint you.'

'Connie.' Red's voice was suddenly serious.

'What?'

He stood up and grasped her by the shoulders so hard it almost hurt, looked down at her, his eyes fiercely bright. 'Watch Patrick.'

'What?'

'If he ever touched you, so much as laid a finger on you, I'd kill him.'

Connie shivered, pulled away, laughed. 'Don't be silly,' she said. 'Come on, let me draw you.'

She did a quick charcoal sketch and mixed the palette of colours, the olives of his skin, almost cobalt of his eyes and the rich umbers and sienna of his hair. 'So I remember,' she explained, because there was not time on that afternoon to begin the painting.

'I love you,' he said as he watched her at work. 'So much that I'd like to marry you. What do you think?'

She was quiet, dabbed her finger on the red-brown paint. It was so simple, the way he said that. *I love you. I'd like to marry you.* It did sound so simple.

He came across and kissed her. 'Hey?'

'I don't know.' She grinned at him, feeling a rush of things, happiness, pride, confusion. Love, too? 'Ask me next time.'

And if there had been a next time . . . Connie feels her head nod, wakes her up, a sudden jarring in her neck. It's not then, it's now and it's cold and there's his sleeping bag spread out on the floor to remind her. She shivers. It's too cold and

218

she is too old, simply too old for this nonsense. Can't paint his portrait, won't. Why should she? She won't be bullied. You can't be forced to paint.

Her neck hurts, the arthritis starting up again after a rest, the prospect of it bringing tears to her stupid old eyes. She dashes them away. He won't hurt her. He's just a boy with problems. She must be bright and she must be kind, soon he will get tired of this and leave, or someone will come. Barry or his mum call sometimes if she hasn't called at the shop lately. The Calor-gas man . . . only she's well off for gas just now, the canisters refilled before she went away. She was one step ahead this morning, that's for sure, her wits about her. Oh the body might be failing but her mind, her mind is sharp as ever. But she will stop wearing these cruel shoes that pinch her toes so. What is she about? Surely not *vanity*?

She starts to get up from the chair and lets herself fall back. There are painkillers in a bottle in the kitchen drawer. The arthritis let up this summer, because of the sun maybe. But now it is back. She knows the speed with which this first ache gets its teeth in, gets a hold till she can scarcely turn her head. She can't go on with this, can't. When he calls her she will just say no. If he kills her . . . he won't of course, but still she should face the possibility, be prepared for all eventualities. People do kill people after all, and she has no defence. Her own death she has planned for when the time is right. She doesn't want to be cheated of that. Of that decision.

The door bangs. 'Still up there?' She doesn't answer, hears him moving about running the tap, drinking water perhaps or washing his hands. She will not be bullied. His feet on the ladder, his head appearing through the hole. He smiles almost as if he's pleased to see her. Unexpected, that's what he is, unpredictable, like someone else.

'Ready?' he says. 'It's great out there. You ought to get out later. Did you rest?'

'Yes,' she says, 'only I don't feel rested.'

'Shall we get started?' He steps up into the room and the floor tilts towards him. 'It's doing me good, all this fresh air,' he says. He rubs his hands together just like someone else, yes, just like Patrick.

This is a delusion. Look again. This is not Patrick, nor nothing like. This is old age and exhaustion and yes, maybe it is fear. It is there in her belly clutching. She strokes the little cushion, her nail catching in the shiny stuff, a hair catching in her nail.

'I can't work this afternoon,' she says. The way he is standing she can't quite see his face. He's looming above her against the skylight, shoulders bent because he's too tall for the room, the light shining blue on his hair.

'But we must.'

'I said I can't and I can't.' She sucks in her breath and waits.

'What does that mean?'

'It means I can't and I won't.'

'Sorry.'

'I won't paint you, Patrick.'

'What?'

'I won't.'

'Did you call me?'

'Oh oh, it's my neck and . . .'

'My name is Tony.'

'You never said.'

'I did say. You called me.'

'I am old, *old*.' Connie's voice cracks as it rises. 'I am too old for this. I am not well.'

'I'm sorry but you have to. You said.'

220

'I never said.' He takes a step towards her. His shadow falls across her and she stops herself cringing, only grips the cushion between her hands more tightly. 'You can't make me paint you,' she says, keeping her voice even, reasonable. He lifts a hand. 'If you kill me then I most *certainly* can't paint you.'

He turns suddenly, the movement sharp enough to make her gasp, and he goes down the stairs without a word. It is very cold. Her heart resumes beating. She hadn't known it had stopped. The skylight lets in the salty stiffening breeze. The sky is grey. Soon it will rain again, that is the pattern the weather is set in, fine mornings, dull afternoons, stormy nights. Is he leaving, simple as that? *Please*. He is opening cupboards, drawers, as if he is searching for something. The kitchen drawer opens, she recognises the scrape of it and the slam shut. No good slamming it it only slides back you have to be gentle with that drawer, you have to know the little ways of a house to make it work for you. Like a person, yes yes, like Patrick you had to know his ways. No one else knew his ways, no one else understood him.

Please go, just leave.

Pain is reaching tentacles down her spine and into her arms. If he left would she ever be calm again? Ever? Yes. Of course. Come on now. A small bird hops on the roof, she hears the scritch-scratch of its claws. Life would resume, she knows it, it would resume. Until the time when she's ready for stop. Which she will choose when it hurts too much, when there's no more point.

He's back up the ladder, something in his hand. A roll of brown-parcel tape. 'Hold out your hands.' She hesitates then lets go the cushion and holds them out in front of her, palms down. Obey, that's all you can do, obey. She can't prevent the tremble. Her stomach shrivels. So this is it then, this is it, how it will be.

'Like this.' He puts the tape under his arm and his palms together as if praying. She copies the gesture. He kneels in front of her, pushes up the sleeves of her cardigan and wraps the tape round her wrists, one, two, three times. He bends his head to tear it with his teeth. She feels his breath on her skin, a tickle of hair. The tape feels tight and stiff.

'Feet,' he says. She stretches out her feet. All she can do is this. It is ridiculous. Why tie her up? But she can't fight or argue and if she does everything right then he'll calm down no doubt, he'll get over this . . . stuff and nonsense. He pulls off the shoes, starts to put his hands up her skirt to remove her tights and stops, wraps the tape round her ankles over her tights, the sharp bones pressing together, winds round and round and tears with his teeth.

'Why?' she says.

There is no particular expression on Patrick's face as he watches Connie being taped up. The eyes are just flat areas of paint. Connie is shrinking and shrivelling with fear, and this *is* fear now, full on. All the animation is in the boy, in Tony, all the light in the room has collected round him.

'Can you get up?' he asks. She moves her head a little side to side. Hard enough to get up before with the exhaustion and the ache, now she would not even try. He rips another length of tape from the roll and approaches her mouth with it. 'No . . . please . . .' She could not bear it, please no.

'Can't have you shouting.'

'I won't shout. I promise. Who if I shouted would hear me?'

'I would. I would hear you and I don't want to hear you. Understand?' His face is so close now, young sheeny skin, the irises of his dark eyes clear against the whites.

'First, could you fetch me my pills, painkillers, arthritis, and a drink. Grouse.' He stands back and regards her for a moment. 'Please,' she adds. His eyes travel slowly from the top of her head to her poor stiff feet. He says nothing but goes down the ladder. 'In the drawer,' she calls and can't stop the quaver in her voice. To be pleading with him. She has never pleaded, never once in her life. He comes back up the ladder with the pills and the whisky bottle.

'How many?'

'Three.' They are strong pills and it should only be one but she can't bear this. They might help her bear this. They might even kill her. He tips out three. She opens her mouth. He hesitates but leans forward and delicately so as not to touch her lips, he places one of the pills on her tongue. He opens the bottle and holds it to her lips. It comes too fast and spills down her chin but she gets the burn of it, the lump of the pill in her tight throat. He is gentle in the way he does it, almost tender in the midst of this . . . this outrage. The last pill swallowed, he presses the tape over her mouth. Runs his thumb across it, across her lips, hard through the tape.

'We'll try again tomorrow,' he says. She opens her eyes at him, tears swelling in them. Nothing else she can do. Nothing left to communicate with except her eyes but he's not looking, looks at the skylight instead. 'Don't want hypothermia, do we?' he says and bangs the window shut. He picks up his sleeping bag and tucks it round her, over her knees, folds it under her feet, snugly round her shoulders. Again almost a gentleness before he goes down, leaving her alone and bound in the cold and darkening room.

NINE

It hurts. The bones in her ankles hurt most. She can't get into a comfortable position and her neck aches more and more. The tape on her face pulls at her skin, tight, cold. She has to breathe carefully and slowly through her nose because she *can* breathe though her nose. There is no need to panic. She will not suffocate. Her wrists pulled together like this are dragging at her shoulders and that is growing more and more uncomfortable already. How will it feel by morning if this really lasts till morning? He can't really leave her, surely not. She should have said while she had the chance that she had reconsidered. Why so stupid? Why that sudden stubbornness? She could have stalled and had a better night than this in that horrible bed but able to move at least. *But I won't be bullied*, cries a voice inside, a voice that is separate from the physical pain or doesn't care.

She hits a sudden wall of warmth and fuzz, a kind of giddiness that would take her horizontal if that was possible. It's the painkillers of course, bless them. Surely he won't leave her all night? She is starting to float just above the chair and it is raining now, rivulets of grey light, a soft drumming, impatient fingers tapping on soft flesh. *Wake, wake.* Patrick roaming about downstairs – oh stop it not Patrick but still roaming, the smell of tobacco the sound of the kettle. He says he's killed. Man's laughter is what she hears, not Patrick's because Patrick is dead no matter how you poke him or try to breathe your breath into his mouth. Kissing his mouth, how it happened, how it turned to love.

A month after her birthday, was it, or sooner or later, well, it hardly matters when. Sitting in the conservatory eating salad, big vivid salad grown by Patrick. Patrick drinking beer, God he was better after he gave up brewing that beer, saying, 'The sexual organs of plants are renewed, they do not age, not like the womb of a woman withering, the ovaries emptying its last stale eggs.'

Sacha flinched at that and pulled a face at Connie. 'Each flower new and fresh and temporary. Each time a flower fucks it is with new equipment, fresh, young equipment.' Patrick's eyes scorching Connie's face deep red as she bent over her food, trying to avoid the eyes of them both. 'Each flower a virgin, even on an ancient plant – think of that old magnolia – think, the branches, trunk, old and gnarled, and yet the flowers new-born every year, sex-organs, new-born.'

'All right, Paddy, that's enough.' Sacha almost snapped, most unSacha-like.

'Red asked me to marry him,' Connie said, surprising herself as much as them. She had not meant to say, had kept this to herself sucking on the memory of his words, sweet as a secret lozenge in her mouth.

'Connie!'

'And what was your reply?' Patrick asked, pulling at his beard.

'I said I might.'

'Oh.'

'Well, that's . . . it's good news, isn't it, Paddy?' Sacha gave him a long, almost warning, look. 'You're so young though, Connie.'

'Young is good according to Patrick,' Connie said, the words jumping spitefully from her mouth.

'But your painting?' Sacha said.

'It won't stop me painting. It hasn't stopped *you* painting.'

'No, you're quite right.'

Patrick, gone unusually quiet, went out then, left Connie and Sacha drinking tea. Sacha seemed embarrassed. 'That's upset him,' she said.

'But why?'

'If you marry you'll leave.'

'Well, yes, but it won't be for a while. Of course I'll leave one day anyway, won't I?'

Sacha put down her cup and knitted her fingers together. 'He would have liked you to stay.'

'What, for ever?' A spider ran down the ivy leaves and across the floor. The floor was littered with dead leaves and the things that live in dead leaves. Sometimes Connie thought she'd sweep it but she never did.

'Do you think you love Red?'

'I don't just think it, I do,' Connie said, sounding much more certain than she was. 'Of course, we need more time.'

'This blessed war,' Sacha said, then smiled. 'Well, good. I want you both to be happy. You are . . . I care more for you two than for anyone. If you are to be happy, then what more can I ask?'

'You care about *Patrick*, too.'

'Of course. More tea?' Sacha picked up the pot. Something strange about her, a flush on her cheeks, a fidget in her.

'What is it, Sacha?'

She finished fussing with the tea and sat back, took a deep breath, sighed. 'Well, all right then. Patrick had . . . hopes.'

'I don't understand,' Connie said, though she could feel the slow drip of understanding.

226

'He wanted you to come to him.' Yes, Sacha's face was definitely flushed, her gaze, usually so calm and brown, quivered as if she could hardly look Connie straight in the eye. 'He thought, he was beginning to think you would.'

'Come to him . . . ?'

'Yes.' The memory of her birthday dawn came to her, Patrick's cock rising under the cotton of his trousers, the delighted way he laughed when she asked if she could touch. She felt a sudden twinge, low in her belly. But it was Red who had touched her and brought her alive, Red.

'Oh. But he's *old*.'

'He wouldn't thank you for saying that!'

'And, and he's yours.'

'Don't let that worry you.' Sacha looked down into her cup, her lips twitched.

'You wouldn't mind?'

'I *would* mind if anything happened that you didn't want to happen. Understand?'

'I think so. But anyway, I love Red.'

'Yes, that's good, that's better. Yes.' Sacha got up suddenly.

'And isn't Patrick supposed to be more of a father to me?'

Sacha gathered together the plates, ate a left-over circle of cucumber that Patrick had left. 'Don't worry.' She suddenly bent and kissed Connie on top of the head. 'Really, forget about it. Don't worry. I'm so glad for you, and Paddy *will* be. I promise, he'll come round in the end.'

And what happened to the love for Red? What did happen? The thick fuzz of the pills makes her feel nauseous, but she can't be sick with tape on her mouth and she will not panic. Not *too* nauseous and at least there's warmth, coming from inside or out she doesn't know, can't tell. A flush on her cheeks that is a sort of shame at her own, what? Wantonness, is probably what it was, she was probably just a wanton little hussy, trollop, tart. Because what did she do a few mornings later? She lay in her bed remembering Red, her legs pressed together, her hands on her breasts. She lay with the morning sun slipping through the open curtains and on to her skin and imagined Red's fingers and how they roused her, his lips and his stubby cock. And then she got up and went downstairs. She put a jacket over her nightdress and Sacha's boots and went out, leaving the door open like before, leaving a trail of footprints on the lawn. Was she meaning Patrick to follow? Impossible to say, but he did follow. He found her by the beech tree. She was thinking of Red, surely it was Red she was thinking of, wanted? But it was Patrick who was there. She was sitting cross-legged beneath the tree, her back against its bark. Was she waiting? He came striding towards her. 'It will be ordinary love,' he said, anger in his voice.

'What?'

'If you marry him you'll buy a little house and have four children, I can see you. You will be the little wife and mother and your painting will die.'

'Why should it?' She was taken aback by his anger. 'Ordinary love, what does that mean?'

'With me it would be extraordinary.'

'But you're supposed to be . . . a sort of guardian.'

'That's just a *word*. Let me show you, Con, let me at least show you what it can be like.'

'No.' She pulled her knees up and hugged them to her chest, feeling shocked, feeling thrilled, feeling ashamed of the way she heated at his words. He wanted her, he really wanted her.

'Did he take your virginity?'

'Not . . . we didn't actually.'

'You are not deflowered.' She wanted to laugh at the way

he said that. But he laughed first and took her in his arms, pressed her face against his chest. Was that when she started to love him? There was so much that was ridiculous about Patrick, but he did know that. He deliberately made himself more ridiculous than he really was as if he was playing up to some caricature of himself. Like a sort of defence, making more fun of himself than anyone else ever could. And looking into his eyes you felt stirred. So much brightness, excitement, so much electricity in him. And something vulnerable. You didn't want him to be hurt, or disillusioned. You wanted him to make love to you, he was such a lover, *such* a lover, and all through your life you still wanted that. It didn't stop even after he was gone.

'I am jealous,' he mumbled into her hair. 'I don't believe myself, I don't believe in jealousy but I am jealous. I don't want anyone else to touch you.' There was a kind of astonishment in his voice. She didn't know how to reply, just let herself be pulled against him, feeling the heat of him, the pressing of his groin against her, the thumping of his heart. His beard tickled her cheek. 'You make me weak,' he said. 'I stopped myself because you were a child, in some ways a child but . . . I can see the woman in you. No one has made me weak with longing like you. No one ever.' And as he talked like that, fast and breathy, his hands slid her nightdress up and she let them.

She let him lie her down on the ground and stroke her legs open. He knelt beside her, ran his hands over her, looking at her, touching her almost reverently. And he did amazing things to her with his fingers. He made her fly till she was almost scared at the way she rose and fell under his fingers and his tongue, over and again like a new bird swooping till she forgot herself, who she was or where, and became only scattering light and a high thin wail.

Only when she was completely lost did he lie on top of her and press himself inside. It hurt and brought her back to where she was, but he murmured so tenderly, 'All right, all right, just relax, just open to me,' and she was so proud to be a woman for him, such a lover and such a man. And soon the hurting stopped and she felt complete with him on her and inside her like that, that weight the thing that earthed her, made her whole. With his weight on his hands he raised himself to look into her eyes and then kissed her very tenderly on the lips.

She did love him she *did*. Red was eclipsed at that moment. She loved Patrick from that morning to the day of his death. They became lovers, regular lovers. Soon he took to sharing her bed on the nights he didn't stay up working on his elixirs. She'd lie and listen for his feet on the stairs, the landing, and she would hold her breath until the door gently opened and he'd enter the room, a tall shadow. She'd hear the soft sliding and crumpling sounds of his clothes as he dropped them, feel the cool of the air as he lifted the blankets and slid in beside her, warm, warm skin all along her length. It was so gorgeous, luxurious, the warmth of him, the softness of his hair and beard and lips, the way he held her as if she belonged not just to him but to the world.

In the dark she could not resist but in the light she worried about Sacha. Whatever she had said surely she didn't want this? Connie studied her for a change but she didn't seem different, not cold or sarcastic. Maybe a little more distant, more involved in her painting. But not bad-tempered or unkind.

One morning, still bleary and musky from bed with Patrick, Connie went into the kitchen. Sacha was at her easel painting. The painting was of the kitchen window, a clutter of dishes, a jug of grasses, the leafy movement of outside through glass. Since the beginning Sacha had given up her studio.

'It's not fair,' Connie said, 'it's yours really, the studio.'

Sacha turned. She had yellow paint on her cheek. 'I prefer the kitchen,' she said. 'It's warmer. It's more at the heart of things.' Sacha seemed to live it more and more completely, her painting. If no one else cooked she'd do it but irregularly, painting while the potatoes boiled to mush or the pie crust hardened, looking through narrowed eyes at her canvas as she chewed her food.

'I feel . . . ' Connie said and stopped.

Sacha put down her brush. 'Want to put the kettle on?'

'I feel . . .'

'What about Red?' Connie flinched. Sacha waited and then filled the kettle herself. Connie watched her broad back, wide shoulders under brown wool. 'What are you going to say to him?'

Connie shrugged miserably. 'He already dislikes Patrick,' Sacha said. 'Imagine his reaction to . . . well, just be gentle with him, Connie.' *Reaction to . . .* Connie found that she wanted it spoken out loud, wanted Sacha to say it, put it into words this odd condoned secret that hung between them like some sort of sticky web. Sacha put the teapot on the table, eased the tea-cosy over it, crocheted wool, tea-coloured from all the splashes. She looked directly at Connie for the first time.

'His reaction to you and Patrick together,' she said. Connie made her eyes stay on Sacha's. 'Hungry?' Sacha said after a moment, removing her gaze.

'I like the way you've done the grass against the . . .' Connie nodded at the painting.

'I wonder if the smell of paint suppresses the appetite?'

'Oh Sacha . . . I feel . . . I've taken over the studio and now I seem to have taken over . . .'

'Do you want to pour the tea?' Sacha went to her easel and added a touch of yellow, the smallest touch to the surface of a cup. The brilliance in that dab made Connie bite her lip. It reflected light in a way that made a sudden pattern, a sense that held the whole together.

She didn't remotely want a cup of tea but she poured two cups anyway, forgetting the strainer so that dark leaves floated on the surface.

'It's all right,' Sacha said, sitting down, blowing over the surface of her tea. 'For myself I don't mind about Patrick.'

'You don't mind. You don't miss . . .'

'We haven't had it off for years,' Sacha said and laughed at Connie's face. 'Don't look so stricken! There's Betty.'

'But . . .' Connie stopped. Like a leaf settling on the water realisation came. It had been hinted that Sacha had other lovers but Connie had never seen any sign, thought they must be theoretical rather than actual. But Betty. Betty with the long legs and loud laugh who cycled up from Bakewell, who sat and chatted in the kitchen, joined them for meals, sometimes stayed the night. Of course, Betty was the lover. The thought of another woman had never occurred to Connie. Betty. Ah. It was a gentle shock and a relief. An explanation and a freedom. Connie gazed at Sacha, solid, not glamorous or romantic but lovely. Yes. Of course.

Connie sipped her tea, thirsty now and even hungry. 'I'll make some toast, shall I?'

'But Red,' Sacha said, 'I mind for Red. He'll be angry, hurt, disappointed. He'll *really* hate . . .'

'Yes.' Connie sat down again. 'But he'll get over it, won't he? Won't he? We hardly know each other really.'

'So you have decided.'

'I suppose . . . it seems I have.'

'You're going to stay and be with Patrick.'

Connie nodded, surprised to find that decision made.

'One thing,' Sacha said after a long moment, 'there won't be any babies.'

'Oh?'

'Patrick is unable . . . hard to believe, isn't it? Very ill as a child, that probably did it. So he goes round firing blanks in all directions.'

Connie sucked her breath in, Sacha sounded suddenly so unlike herself.

'Well, anyway, I don't care,' she said. 'I don't think I want children anyway.'

Sacha laughed and began, quite viciously, to saw slices from a loaf of bread.

And there were no children and they were happy, weren't they? Weren't they? Though sometimes a little voice will whisper *What if?* Sometimes the memory of Red comes to her, his kind of innocence. If his fingers were not quite so skilful as Patrick's it was only because they didn't trace the memory of a hundred other women's bodies on hers. If she had kept true to Red, if she had married him, then what? What kind of life would she have had? Children maybe, a very different kind of life. She would not be taped up like this, that's for sure, prisoner in her own room, with that young lunatic downstairs ransacking the place again by the sound of it. Not that he could ever find what he is looking for.

Regret is there, yes, regret not for that life so much as because she doesn't know what that life might have been. And sometimes her heart flinches with the memory of Red's face when he realised the truth. She did not tell him, not in words. He only had to see the way things had changed. It was almost a year before he came back again. He only had to be in the house to read the currents that passed between

Patrick and Connie and Sacha, the subtle way the triangle had shifted. He only had to look her in the eyes. What he read there she is not quite sure but she read hurt in his, hurt and hatred. And that was that. He left and that was one life discarded in favour of another.

Well, what of it? It happens all the time. No regrets, no, no, no, no. Regrets are rats that gnaw at the edges of your heart. Oh it hurts. Mouth dry and the tape makes it hard to swallow. She tries to pull her lips apart, feels the thin skin strain as if it would rip. The tape has a sickening smell. She tries to speak. Of course her voice is still there, makes a kind of ape sound, shapeless. She listens – gone quiet down there now. It is almost dark.

Patrick was her life. Maybe this is the end of it and he *was* it. You can't see the shape of a life till it ends. You can't let yourself mourn for what might have been. All quiet. He's probably gone out, probably he's walking on the beach, stretching the muscles in his legs, swinging his arms, the rain in his long blue hair. Only soft rain and the wind getting up. She presses her palms together, feels the muscles contract in the top of her arms and chest, oh it *hurts*, lifts up her feet to stretch her legs, wiggles her toes to keep the blood flowing.

The tape stinks and pinches and pulls. When he rips it off it will rip this thin skin to rags. If. Patrick all dark. Maybe she can sleep, dark and warm and swimming back and forward in her mind, like her mind is a big warm lake. Yes. She lets her head nod, feels the ache in her neck but feels it far away as if the thick padding of the sleeping bag is between the pain and herself. Between herself and tomorrow.

TEN

Voices. What? A woman's voice calling? But it's quiet. Must have been a dream. Was that the sound of a car? Connie screws up her eyes trying to hear, to remember hearing. There is a memory of sound but it's fading like a wisp of smoke in her head. Her voice batters uselessly against her sealed lips, a stupid reflex. Stop, listen. *Think*. When is it? How long has gone? The door? Did you hear the door? Oh the wooziness like a ginger fog. Something metallic rising in her throat. Stop, breathe, listen, think.

She can't think straight with the whisky and pills and pain and stiffness. Though it's not as uncomfortable as you might think because the fog has a kind of warmth in it, almost a sort of cradling comfort. Or call it a numbing. The skylight is still lighter than the rest of the room, pale angles of paper on the floor. No light on down there. No one there then, the voice just a dream. Where is he? The trap-door is possibly visible as a square of deeper darkness. Might just as well close her eyes for all the good they do peering into the gloom.

What is this? This voice?

There *was* a voice, a female voice. But whose? No one anticipated. But still they do sometimes come, visitors or people lost on hot afternoons wanting directions or a glass of water. But *now*? And someone might have come, that biographer or someone, someone who might help. Should make a noise in case. Only wouldn't the light be on if there was someone there?

She bangs her heels against the floor but it hurts, jarring and sparkling all up her spine to her neck. She gasps, but can't gasp because of her stuck mouth so a panicky vacuum forms in her chest against which her heart scrabbles weakly. Stop this, breathe, think.

Would it be murder if he left her to die, or would it be manslaughter? Man's laughter. A hollow laugh. A hollow man. Patrick. No he was not hollow, he was her love, was her life. He was not hollow. A hollow man whose voice was loud. You could laugh at his ideas, men laughed, mostly women didn't laugh. Not if he chose to look at them so. The way they fell under his spell and she watched that, felt proud because whatever he did with them, he needed *her*. He could fuck them, wonderfully, amazingly but impersonally as pollen falling on the stigma of a flower. But with her he cried and said his fears out loud and clung. Why on earth would you like that, Connie, why would anybody like that?

Voices outside. Yes. Heart beating up in her throat. She forces her tongue between her lips, just the point of it, pressing against the tape. Listen. Moisten the tape with your tongue and listen. There *are* voices. His voice and . . . yes, a young woman's voice. She moans again and bangs her heels but it hurts too much, you can see stars if the nerves in your stiff heels bang on the floor, see stars right up to your tight taped head.

Door opening, light coming on, throwing a trapezoid of light through the trap-door on to the ceiling and the wall. Giving Patrick back his eyes.

'I don't understand . . .' This the female voice.

'I don't fucking well appreciate being followed.'

'. . . not like that, I thought it would be a nice surprise.'

'Yeah.'

'You said you'd ring. I was up seeing my mum, I just thought.'

'Christ.'

'You said where you were going.'

'Keep your fucking voice down.'

Quiet. After a pause the girl's voice subdued. 'Sorry. I just thought it would be nice to see you again.'

Quiet again. Connie groans as loud as she can but there is no effect. She lifts her heels but the pain in her back is too much, she can't bear to crash them down again. It's all right, Con. Help is here. Just listen and wait. Wait.

'Now what?' his voice belligerent, making her feel foolish, no doubt, whoever she is, down in Connie's kitchen.

'I won't stay if you don't want . . .' something else muttered. Speak up, girl. Something familiar about that voice. Someone she met in London, or just one of those well-bred types? 'Brought wine and brought flowers for . . . where is she?'

'Asleep.'

Whatever does he think she's thinking up here? Doesn't he know she can hear, that she will make a noise, attract attention? Her tongue wriggles a space between her lips and the tape. Forcing air out between her lips she makes a guttural sound, loud, loud enough, surely, for the girl to hear.

'Can't we just have a glass . . . in water . . . a vase?' Sounds of movement, the plop of bottle being uncorked. The judder of the pipes, water, the rustle of paper and a faint greenish chrysanthemum smell. Thirst in her throat and right through to her bowels. The pills and the whisky and this fog seem to suck her dry.

Awful thought. Push it away. He said he killed a girl. But that was surely bluff.

She is talking down there, her voice too quiet to hear properly. But she's asking him something about writing, something about a book. So he *is* a journalist then, or writer, and she believed that he wasn't. Getting dull, Con. Maybe his madness is a pose? To see if he could get the elixirs for his newspaper – what do they call that, a scoop. But too well done – and if it's a pretence why tie her up? She sucks air in through her nose and groans again. She wants to shout, *Run*.

'See I'm not . . . ring a cab . . . maybe I'll just . . . ' The sound of a chair grating. The door.

'NO!' A shout but then his voice warms, changes colour. 'No, stay. Sorry, Lisa. It's nice to see you. Not good at surprises is all. All right?' Long pause. 'All right?'

She gives a shrug of a laugh. 'Mobile's not working, anyway. Shit. No phone here, is there?'

'No, looks like you're stuck.' The door closes again.

'Oh dear.'

'What *shall* we do?'

'Better make the most of it, I guess. I feel a bit bad about being here uninvited – and when she's asleep.'

'It's cool.'

The sound of heels on the lino. 'I like it here, don't you? I do like all these shells! The way she's stuck them on the walls. Kitsch or what?'

'Yeah, well.'

'Let's have more wine then? Tell me about . . . but mustn't wake . . .' her voice quietening. The scrape of a match on a matchbox and the whiff of a freshly lit fag.

Another moan. Why can't they hear her? Fog closing again but browner and not so warm, still it muffles the pain which is coming everywhere now, back, neck, shoulders, wrists, heels, ankle bones. No, don't dwell and itemize your every pain. Light coming up and Patrick not in his portrait now, it's just canvas and he's hanging a little way away beside it. The light shining up makes a bright streaming navy-blue of the skylight under rain. On the floor is its reflection like a pool, dark shadow drops trickling across the blue.

They murmur on down there and only some words can she hear, sometimes a laugh, female, nervous. Listen, there's the girl's name. *Lisa*, heard that before. Tony's voice louder than hers but saying nothing of any significance. Connie tries to concentrate but her mind buckles under the weight of . . . everything, the shock, yes, the phrase *in shock* comes to her, surely that's what she must be in. Shock. This odd indiscipline of mind, inability to concentrate even though it might make the difference between life and death. But she swings dizzily between lucid and not, lucid is pain and the other is not and which is worse? Helpless, helpless. Go back then, go back to memory. She tries, a moment of Patrick with his arms around her, face against his living chest, warm, warm and beating but then it's cold and then it's gone.

Quiet now downstairs. She moans again, the damp space on the tape loosening against her breath, the stick giving, soon, soon, she will have a voice. The girl, Lisa, says, 'What was that?'

'What?'

'I heard something.'

'Nothing.'

'It wasn't nothing.'

'Must've been Benson then, dreaming, snoring. I don't know.'

'Funny kind of snoring.'

'Come here.'

'Tony!' A giggle, delighted. What are they doing? Connie hums loudly, this is the way to make a noise, loud hum, the tape vibrates, unbearable tickle against her lips, she tries to bring her wrists up to free her mouth but they are swaddled in the sleeping bag. Patiently, patiently, if she works with her tongue and blows and hums against the tape she will free her mouth.

'That's never snoring.'

'Hey, let me . . .'

'No, just a minute. Is it her? What's up?'

'You want it?'

'No.'

'What you here for then?'

'Tony, stop it, no.'

Connie bangs her heels feeling her mind shatter into stars of pain that brighten up the attic for a flash, tries to pull herself up from the chair but falls back, moans loud as she can against the horror of hearing this, heart banging in time with the explosions in her heels.

'No. *Please.*' Sounds of scuffling, a chair falling. 'Tony, no, please.'

'Shut the fuck up.'

'Aaah!' Surprised pain. NO. Constance fights against the tape on her mouth, nothing will give, she can make a noise now but what good is a noise? Something smashes down there, plate or glass all sharp on the floor. She winces at the thought of soft flesh on the shards of it.

'All right, all right, there's no need . . . I won't fight . . .' the girl's voice gone high like a child's.

'No, you won't fight, fucking tart.'

'*Please.*' Now she's crying. The sound of something tearing. '*Mummy,*' she sobs, '*oh God.*' Tears come into Connie's eyes, useless, useless. A grunt from him, oh no please no he's raping her, raping her and there's nothing Connie can do. Patrick is hovering over the trap-door, clear navy-blue with the raindrops streaming through him. Connie looks at the empty canvas but there is no help there, empty face of a dead man, long, long gone. Nothing Connie can do and if he is raping the girl maybe he will kill her, too. Kill them both. The fog no longer warm but icy. The girl's sobs and the voice of the man, grunting, grunting, like some animal. If Connie could put her hands over her ears she would but there is no escape from what will follow. She lowers her wrists against her lap and lets them lie on the soft pillow of hair, all she's kept, that and the portrait of Patrick shorn.

A crash, a slam. It is finished. Connie shudders, fear and cold combined, and shock yes, *in shock*, tremors that shake her bone against raw bone. Are they gone, both? Or only him? The girl, is she still there?

How long can you sit in the quiet and dark without sleeping? Despite the horror and the pain, Connie does sleep. Even dreams something vague about fish. How can she sleep after all that . . . She wakes, feeling immediately guilty. How long? Some bird crying despite the night – only the sky has lightened. So considerable time gone. Giddiness. No fog. Pain. The memory of the dreadful night plain now the fog has gone, like sunshine on a bomb site, the rising stench of ruin. Long, long quiet.

Then Connie hears the sound of the door, footsteps, the floor vibrating as Tony sets foot on the ladder. The shadow of a gull over the skylight seems to take a long long time. She huddles down smaller and smaller, her insides screwing tight.

And his face is there, face white, eyes red. He does not look her in the eye but looks her over, checking for life, perhaps. His eyes are like those of a child woken from a nightmare to find it real and of his own making. He says nothing, goes down again. She can hear a lumping about down there and then he comes back up the ladder with the body of the young woman, head lolling, hair fair on his shoulder against the black of his own. For a second she is struck by the contrast and shocked at herself for noticing. He lugs her up, struggles her body in through the trap-door, shoves her away from the edge. Her short black dress is ripped at the hem, the skin white on one bare leg, the other still clad in black nylon, the loose leg of a pair of tights trails from between her legs like some awful limp birth. Her cheek slides along the floor over the dust and the dead wasps.

Tony stands over the prone girl. 'Help,' Connie says, manages to say almost audibly. Her heart beats very fast and small like dripping water. He turns and she looks into his eyes but it's like looking through the windows of a burnt-out house, there's nothing there but ash. His lips open as if he'd say a word then close again. She feels almost, almost sorry for him. He suddenly reaches his hands towards Connie who cowers, screws up her eyes, retreats into and into herself for surely this is it. But all he does is pull away the sleeping bag, spread it on the floor and tip the girl on to it. Then he's gone, the door banging, really gone this time.

But Connie is bound up and Lisa may or may not be dead and Connie can do nothing but make useless sounds against the tape. It is all so bright as the sun comes out. It glints on the taut wires of pain threaded through her bones. Each speck on the floor, each insect casts a shadow larger than itself, the thin shadows of wings like cellophane, dust motes glitter in the air. Another perfect morning. The girl lies still, blood clotted in the fair fluffy hair, and there is nothing *nothing* Connie can do.

ELEVEN

Tony trudges along, eyes screwed up against sharp spears of light. His eyes water from such brightness, sun puddled on the rippled sand. Waves wash up and down, up and down, like nothing's happened. The rucksack is heavy on his back. He turns to look back at the trail of footprints that lead from between the dunes and along the beach. Now what?

Starched sheets. That's it. Hold on, Tony, don't lose it now. You didn't kill. She wasn't dead. Breath on your neck when you lifted her. Warmth. You can smell life and she smelled of it. She got what she came for is all. Bitch. So shut up. Cold and clean this morning. It seems to be a lovely day. What next, though? What?

Starched sheets and clean clothes and go back. Not good to go backwards but . . . there was security there. It *was* a life. And Donna next door with her candy soft bed. No harm there. A girly bed with her harmless books beside it, Bible, all the things in her bathroom: perfumes, creams to dip your finger in and sniff, the stuff in her drawers, underwear, white slippers with bunny ears.

He bends down, the rucksack nearly overbalancing him, to pick up a shell. Walks along fingering it, rough and dry on the outside, spiralled: a whelk? Very pointed at the tip, presses his finger on it till it hurts. Almost trips over a sand-castle. He stands amazed. Someone with a bucket and spade has built a castle. When? Too good for a child's castle, it's huge and complicated. Many buckets of sand turned out neatly, some of them crenellated – one of those fancy buckets they must have had. He has a sudden memory of banging a spade on the bottom of a bucket to turn out the sand. This is perfect. No messy broken edges. Someone took their time over this. Someone cared about it, decorated it with shells, those little pink-and-white ones and strips of bright green weed. When was a person here building a sand-castle? He lifts his foot to smash it. But stops. Instead, he presses his shell on to the top to make a little peak and walks away, quick.

Sails out there, lots of sails, some race? Like wings, pink, yellow, green, the sun on them. Gulls on the water, the air fresh as . . . as milk cold from the doorstep with those beads of moisture on the bottle that tell you it's really cold. That's what he needs, to drink something pure and cold and white to fill his hot dark insides. Those wings out there, so childish bright. School milk kept by the radiator, all clotted warm through paper straws. Who was it used to blow in his till it frothed up from the bottle, slimy white? The sour smell of old milk on his jumper. No.

He needs something cold and absolutely clean. His hands stink of woman. Did wash them under the tap but still that smell, can't stand it, dark private stink. Squatting, he rinses them in the sea but the ripples come up to his trainers. Mustn't get them wet. Can't take them off what with his cut foot. Could swim like yesterday, was it only yesterday? Yesterday someone else built a castle on the beach. And that makes him gasp with loneliness.

Is it over then? No elixirs. No saving, is there to be no saving? No Seven Steps to Bliss. Did he ever believe that, really? Worse now than ever. There's nothing. But it's all right. They won't die and no one will ever find him, not stupid, didn't give them his address, not stupid you could never say that.

But Patrick has let him down. Led him to this. To this . . . to this fiasco, this end of a . . . quest. And now what?

He looks back at the castle which casts a long fancy shadow in the early morning sun. All he can do is go forward. Make a plan. Walk to the village, bus to King's Lynn, train to London, tube to Brixton. Home. Safe.

Then? The whole point of that life was the waiting. What now? Oh what *has* he gone and done? Just walk on. Walk.

TWELVE

Connie doesn't take her eyes off the girl but she works against the wiry pain and the weakness in her arms at the tape on her mouth, loosening with her tongue, scraping with the tape on her wrists until at last there is flap loose enough to let her suck in air, to speak audibly.

'Hello,' she says. Her voice sounds strange and creaky to her own ears after even so short a time. By poking with her tongue she frees the other edge.

'Lisa.' No answer. She tries again, louder. 'Hello, Lisa.'

A moan. Oh thank God, the girl's alive. With a renewal of vigour she brings her wrists up again and frees her mouth a bit more. 'Hello, Lisa.' She doesn't know what else to say. The girl groans and blinks, rolls over a bit so that Connie can see her face. Oh yes, recognises her, the rosy girl who came with the photographer. Yes, Lisa, that's right. Not so rosy now. Lisa opens her eyes and blinks, looks up at Connie, dazed.

'It's Constance,' Connie says. 'Remember? Constance Benson. Know where you are?'

The girl says nothing, lies there, blinking, her eyes very pale blue in the sun, dust on her cheek. Eventually her lips move. The voice when it comes is flimsy and dry as tissue paper. 'Yes. I know.' With obvious difficulty she moves, pushes herself into a sitting position. 'Ow.' Her hand goes to

246

her head, fingers probing the thickness of dried blood in her hair, the slight oozing. She brings down her fingers to look at them, thin wet streak of red.

'He brought you upstairs.'

'My head . . .'

'It's stopped bleeding, nearly.'

'But it hurts.' She starts to cry, looks down at her legs, one black nylon, one blue mottled flesh, remembers. 'Oh God . . . the bastard . . .' Her hands go back to her head, 'Oh it hurts. The bastard, the bastard . . . and *you* . . .' She suddenly registers Connie's plight. 'Oh you . . . he . . . ?' She gets to her knees and crawls to Connie. 'I'll get it off.' She reaches for the tape that remains stuck to Connie's top lip.

'Do it quick,' Connie says and shuts her eyes.

'OK. Wait . . .' The tape is off and Connie's lips sting as if someone has swiped her with a nettle.

'Thank you,' she says, tears rising in her eyes. 'Oh you poor child.'

'I feel sick.' Lisa sits back on her heels.

'Could you just . . .' Connie holds out her wrists, the girl looks at her blankly. '*Lisa*.' Lisa picks weakly at the edge of the tape.

'Just help me get free and I'll help you.'

'I'm trying.'

'That's right.'

'Why did he do this? The bastard. I thought . . .' Fresh tears fill Lisa's eyes.

'It's all right,' Connie says, aware that it's anything but. 'It's all right now.' She wants to touch the girl to comfort her, remembering suddenly the incredible comfort in Sacha's hands reaching to her through the chaos of her grief, that hand the only real, the only solid, thing.

Lisa finds the end of the tape and picks at it but she has to stop every minute or so to press the heel of her hand against her mouth as if to hold the horror in. 'It's all right,' Connie says again, 'just keep calm, we're all right,' speaking as much to herself as Lisa. The last bit of tape is the hardest, painful, the skin feels almost melded to the tape, it's like being skinned, she half expects to see raw sinew where the tape has been instead of a white ridge, slightly swollen, edged with angry red.

'Thank you.' The feeling of freedom is amazing. To be able to move her hands. She flexes them backwards and forwards, feeling a sharp fizzing as the blood returns. She rubs at the sticky ridges which are both sore and numb, then extends a hand to stroke Lisa's head. 'There,' she says, 'there, there.' Lisa flops her head against Connie's knee and sobs, choking out words. 'It hurts, oh it hurts to cry, the bastard, bastard.' Connie waits a while, lets the girl cry on, watching the thin trickle of blood that is still leaking from the wound.

'Lisa,' she says after who knows how long, 'Lisa, we must get down from here. You need some hot sweet tea, we both do, we need to . . . to *do* something.'

Lisa raises her head and winces, gives a gulping shudder. Her blue eyes are sore from the crying, smudged about with something blue. Her tears have soaked right through Connie's skirt and tights.

'If you could just . . .' Connie indicates her ankles taped together, and, her shoulders still convulsing, her hands trembling, Lisa tries to undo the tape, but can't get it all off. 'Take my tights off,' Connie suggests. Lisa half laughs, looking wild now, face mottled white from shock and pain, red from weeping. 'It *is* rather undignified,' Connie says, as Lisa puts her hands up Connie's skirt to pull down her tights, and as Connie raises her hips from the chair to help her, the two of them do laugh, high and hysterical, Connie is horrified by her own wild cackle and it *hurts* her poor stiff shoulder, back, all of her, jarring with the stupid convulsions.

'Oh I'm going to wet myself,' Lisa says. 'Oh no . . .' and as she says it Connie can feel her own full bladder on which she has not allowed herself to dwell. And the two of them laugh, wiping away tears and groaning with pain, shuddering with horror and yet unable to stop. Connie can't tell if she's laughing or crying but tears keep coming anyway. Until Lisa manages to get Connie's tights down to her ankles, eases them over her feet and pulls them off. Then the laughter dies.

Connie watches Lisa get shakily to her feet and balance herself to put her foot into the empty leg of her elaborately laddered tights. Then changes her mind and takes them off altogether. She looks round at Connie, eyes open wide, scared. She looks so young and even through the stains of tears and smudged eye make-up she has a baby peachy look, her eyes the palest blue they could be and still be blue. She goes to the trap-door, sways, Connie sucks in her breath, watching her intently, willing her not to faint or slip.

Lisa stops. 'You don't suppose he's . . .' her voice a whisper.

'No, he's not there. He's gone. Don't you see? He's gone and left us.' For dead, she doesn't add.

Lisa goes down, her eyes staying on Connie's until her head disappears through the trap-door. 'Oh the flowers,' she says. Connie looks round the room, at Patrick whose eyes are warm, yes they are, *concerned*, at the floor, the mess of it, the sleeping bag, smeared now with blood, curly whorls of tape, Lisa's tights and her own tights like two shucked skins and the sketches of Tony . . . crumpled now and trampled . . . sketches she almost enjoyed doing. Ha.

It's hard to stand. She has to force herself through the

pain of it. Each movement sends a searing jar right through her. But she has to do it, has to go down. Each rung of the ladder feels like a blade to her poor footsoles. Down in the kitchen she stands amongst the ruins of a bouquet of white chrysanthemums, shakes her head at the stupid waste. Then she fills the kettle. Although it hurts so much even to lift her arm there is pleasure in the freedom to do such a simple thing.

Lisa comes in from the toilet, shivering. 'I'm all sore,' she says. 'How could he have done this to me? How could he? And the flowers . . . I bought them for you.'

'Tea first,' Connie says, 'then a wash. It's a shame about the flowers. But thank you anyway.' She can't bend down to pick them up. The air is filled with the chilly sharpness of their sap.

'I'm cold.' Lisa sits down and lays her head on the table, her arms cradling it. Connie turns the gas heater up as high as it will go. 'I'll get you a shawl,' she says. Goes into the dark hateful room, the floor going now, a hole where maybe Tony's foot went through. Oh the dank stench. If she could bring out the chest of drawers she need never go in there again, seal up the door. Forget it. She shudders. She brings out a pair of long woollen bloomers and an old red shawl, drapes the shawl over Lisa's shoulders. 'Put these pants on to keep your legs warm.'

'You shouldn't wash,' Lisa says, her voice pale and muffled, 'if you're raped. It destroys the evidence. But I don't know . . . he didn't quite . . .'

'What?'

'Didn't quite . . . get in. But still, I shouldn't wash, should I?'

Connie pauses. 'I don't know. I suppose not. I'm glad,' she adds. 'That he didn't . . . quite.' Is that the right thing to say, the tactful thing?

'But I have to wash, it's horrible and sticky.' She starts to cry again, 'Oh, oh, it hurts.'

Connie doesn't know what to do, stands there helpless till the kettle begins to yell and she can turn to the task of the tea.

'I'll put the kettle back on so you *can* wash if you want.'

'Should go straight to the police.'

'Lots of sugar in, for shock.'

'Horrible sticky, how could he? I *liked* him. Why?'

'Because he's not right in the head, dear,' Connie says tartly.

'But I shouldn't have . . .'

'Here's your tea. None of that. Not your fault. I was listening, remember.'

Lisa looks up, forgetting herself for a moment, meets Connie's eyes. 'God, that must have been horrible,' she says.

Connie shakes her head. Oh the pain in the neck when it turns. 'Worse for you,' she says.

'Yes.' Lisa's mouth turns down again.

'Get some of that tea in you. Should have brandy,' Connie says, 'that's for shock. Got whisky, same sort of thing. Here, get that down you.' She pours a drop into Lisa's tea and then into her own. Notices her remaining wine glass is smashed on the floor. Everything smashing and crumbling all about her. All falling apart.

She finds her bottle of painkillers on the draining board. Only two left. That means the doctor's because there's no way she can live like this, if she had to live like this then she wouldn't live and that's for definite because it will get worse, get its claws in, make every slightest movement a misery. There is something else, another idea, but no . . . 'Here,' she says, opening the jar and holding out a pill to Lisa. 'One for you and one for me.'

'What is it?'

'Painkiller. Strong, take it.'

Lisa takes it in the palm of her hand and stares at it. 'I feel sick,' she says.

'Get it in you and some tea, go on. That'll perk you up, you'll be surprised.'

'Perk me up,' Lisa repeats dully.

'Go *on*.'

Lisa puts the pill in her mouth and takes a swallow of the tea, she chokes a bit, and puts her head back on the table.

Connie swallows her own pill. 'See,' she says, 'that's better, isn't it?'

'I need to sleep.'

'No,' Connie says, 'don't do that.' She's got a vague idea that you don't let head injuries sleep.

Lisa gives a weak giggle. 'God, this is like some weird dream.'

'Nightmare more like.' Connie scoops a tea-bag out of the sink in readiness for Lisa's wash. Questions are boiling up in her. She should not quiz the girl now, should not. They must think properly about what to do. *She* must, the girl's in no fit state. She might have concussion. What is right and what is fair and what is prudent? Good that she wasn't properly raped. That at least is good. 'Why did you come?' she says, bites her tongue.

Lisa talks with her cheek still pressed against the table. 'I keep having to remind myself that you're actually Constance Benson.'

'Connie, please. Do sit up, dear, you might drop off.' What would she do then? She's never known first aid, always thought she'd learn, but didn't. Now, she doesn't know what to do for the best. Maybe she should offer something to eat?

Lisa sits up, one side of her face is pink from the pressure of the table, one side ashen. The blood has stopped trickling, drying in a long streak across her forehead. 'You've been a sort of . . . a kind of hero of mine.'

'Me!' Connie sits down opposite, takes a swig of the tea, good with whisky, fortifying. 'Me? Well . . . fancy that.'

'When I was, I don't know, twelve or thirteen my dad took me to an exhibition in Hastings, or somewhere . . .'

'Brighton could it have been?'

'That's it, the Royal Pavilion? And I saw some of your portraits there . . . so *brilliant* they made me want to be a painter.'

'So, you paint?'

'No. No talent,' Lisa gives a weak smile. 'Absolutely zilch. But I love art, especially twentieth-century art . . . especially portraits . . . and especially yours. I don't suppose you remember . . . no.'

'What?'

'I did my dissertation on you. I wrote a letter . . . questions . . .'

'And did I reply?'

Lisa shakes her head then winces with the pain.

'Hush. You shouldn't talk so much. I'm sorry I didn't reply.'

'That's all right. God. I do feel weird, the pill? Kind of floaty. What shall we do?'

'I never was good at being organised. Always meant to answer letters but . . . and some of them asked the most impertinent questions. I'm sure *yours* didn't.'

'Don't be so sure.' Lisa drops her head into her hands. She's shivering.

'Get those pants on,' Connie says, 'go on. Or are you going to wash first?'

'Depends if I'm going to the police.'

'And are you?'

'I should.'

'He shouldn't get away with it.'

'No. He shouldn't. But . . . the thought of all the questions, all that, they look into your sexual history . . .'

'Still.'

'No, you're right.'

'But we're stuck here.'

'We'll have to get into the village.'

'We could try my phone, but I don't think . . . It's in my bag.' Lisa nods at the handbag hanging over the back of Connie's chair. Connie takes out a small pink phone and hands it to Lisa. She pulls out an aerial, presses something, listens, shakes it, shakes her head again. 'No. Bloody useless thing.' She takes the pants and pulls them up over her bluish legs.

'They look quite chic,' Connie says, 'let me get you some socks.' She goes back to the room and picks her way across the collapsing floor to find a pair of socks. Will bring the chest of drawers out and simply seal up this room. Not go in it ever again.

The kettle boils again and she switches off the gas. 'Well, it's hot if you want it,' she says. 'Of course you're not an artist, you're a journalist. How's . . . whatisname? The photographer.'

'Jason. Fine.'

'And you came for more . . . you wanted more – from me.'

'Not really.'

'I kept asking *him* that, why are you here, are you a journalist . . .'

'I don't know about him, he *said* he was a writer but I'm not so sure.'

'But you know him, obviously you must know him.'

'I've been out with him once.' Lisa looks down at herself. 'I don't care,' she says, 'I *must* wash, wash that bastard off me . . . and my hair . . . head . . . what shall I do?' She wrings her hands together, looks at Connie and grimaces. 'I met him at your exhibition, actually, thought he was so *nice*.'

'Well. Look, hot water, soap's there, towel.' Connie pauses, noticing suddenly how limp and grubby the towel appears. 'I'll leave you in peace for a few minutes. Wash or not. You might feel better if you wash your face at least.'

Connie opens the door and steps out into the sunshine. These glorious mornings. She goes round to the toilet, treading softly, holding her breath because he could be, *could* be crouched round here somewhere, hiding. But there is no one. She goes out through the gate drawn by the peaceful heave and flop of the sea. The air is sweet, salty, delectable. She struggles up between the dunes, the sand running into the sides of her slippers, humping cool under her arches. She looks around, strains her eyes in every direction for a sight of him, a sight of anyone for that matter. But there is no one visible. Sand-dunes make good hiding places, she's aware of that as she stands high up, plainly visible herself. She will not be bullied, will not be. She stands and looks at the sea, low tide – and far out, by the look of it, there are sails. A yacht race. But where is he then? Gone, properly gone?

She should cycle to the village, the girl's in no condition, get to the shop and use the telephone, police, a doctor. Help for them both. Tony will have to be caught and locked up again. He is a danger, a most terrible danger, and she has sketches of him from every angle so it should be easy for the police. There must be fingerprints galore. But she can't cycle to the village. She can't go and leave Lisa alone because what if he comes back? And, really, she doesn't want the police in her house. There's never been any call. She doesn't want them snooping around now, not after all this time. Better to get Lisa to the village, but not yet, she's not up to it yet.

No more painkillers, no more booze. Something else then? Is that idea good or terrible? A risk, of course. But worth it?

Connie comes down from the dunes, leans against the gate post to tip the sand from her slippers which are stuck on their tops with white petals. She does not let herself look back at the sand-dunes with all their invisible scoops and hollows.

THIRTEEN

Look between the posters and the postcards in the window: Autumn Fayre, Adorable kittens, Firewood, Baby-sitter, and there's the fuckwit, mouth hanging open, firing sticky labels at tins of something. No one else about. Sharp ping of the door opening, Brand's Hatch roar of tension in the ears, door crashing against rattling crate of Tizer bottles. The tosser looks up, smiles loosely. 'Good morning,' he says. He has a home-made badge on his sweater, 'Barry. Can I help you?' it says in black felt-tip.

'Good morning, *Barry*.'

Tony walks round, locates milk in a glass-fronted fridge, takes a carton, opens and glugs it, most of it, in one go. Barry's lips keep their blubber smile but the eyes swing round, looking for help.

'Must be thirsty,' he says slowly like he's learning to read.

'Was,' Tony says, 'was thirsty.' Prowls about a bit. 'Golden Virginia,' he says. 'Rizlas, matches.' Watches Barry's fat arse in its turquoise track-suit bottoms as he turns to get them. Waits, takes them from the counter and stuffs them in his pocket.

'Did you find her?' Barry says.

'Who?'

'Miss Benson. You were looking for her, weren't you?' Tony takes a Mars Bar.

'Why?'

'That were you, weren't it?' The eyes are little, pale and not quite so stupid as Tony thought.

'Me? Never been this way before.'

Barry blinks. Then giggles. 'Oh, you're having me on. I seen you before.'

He walks round the shop again, filthy place for food, what is it round here, cobwebs mandatory or what? Rips the paper and takes a bite of Mars, chocolate mush round his teeth makes them ache.

'When's the bus?' he says.

Barry rolls back his sleeve and looks at his watch. Thinks for a moment. 'Twenty-five to eleven,' he says. 'You missed that bus, that go at twenty-past ten.'

'When's the next bus.'

'That'll be the afternoon bus you'll want then. That go at four O five.' He looks proud of himself. Tony has to look away. Clean-shaved cheeks. A niff of Brut after-shave. Tragic.

'Remember, Barry,' Tony touches the side of his nose, 'you've never seen me.'

Barry grins and does the same. 'Rightio,' he says, then as Tony opens the door, wincing at the sharp ping, the rattle of Tizer bottles, 'that'll be £3.90p . . .'

'I'll owe you,' Tony calls and shuts the door, carrying with him a last glimpse of flabby puzzled face. Carries it with him down the road. Like a little boy learning there's no such thing as Father Christmas. Fuck it. Fuck. What is it with him? Goes back, door jangling like a heart attack, slams money on the counter before the poor tosser can utter a word and he's out of there again.

Walks fast, head down, away from all that . . . that rubbish back there, mess, dirt, mistakes, confusion, women old and young with their smells and their smiles and their cradling arms. Sand-castles. If he could get in bed, face between his laundered sheets, yes, shower first in his own shower, scrub the smell off him, that greasy clinging feel on his fingers that makes him want to scream, even the sensation of one finger rubbing against the skin of another finger is unbearable. Walks with his fingers splayed, clean air in between. Berries in the hedges and a bird chirrups from behind a hedge of thorns. Just get back, and away and safe. Get back to where you can be clean and you can know yourself again. Where you can take account.

Walks, walks, walks along the road ready to stick out his thumb only nothing comes, does it? Some cretin on a bike, fishing rod on his back, saying, 'Morning,' that's all. Walks, walks, was it this far before? Hot, too, shouldn't be so hot this time of year. Hot stinking hands and armpits, crutch itchy with dried . . . stuff. Stops for a smoke, leaning on a gate, stares across a field of pale stubble.

Rucksack on his shoulders weighing heavy. Sky on head hot and pressing. Blue as . . . fuck knows. She wasn't fucking dead. Neither of them were. So now what? A curdle of soured milk rises in his throat.

He'll have to go back. What *was* he thinking of? Served his time, once, wiped his slate clean, but now he's mucked it up again. He must go back and sort it. Yes. Must go back and silence them. No one knows. No one knows that he was here – only the fuckwit in the shop and no one would listen to him. Must stop it. This will be the end.

Tony leaves his rucksack in the field so he can walk faster. Goes back towards them in the house. Goes back towards the sea, clouds gathering like scum at the clean rim of it. Pale this morning, pale as . . . not as eyes, oh no. He fits his feet in his own backward foot-prints till he comes to the edge of the sea. It is climbing the beach and rinsing away his traces. The dissolving prints are filling with water, foot-shaped, fish-shaped. The ripples wash in, clean and tatty-edged. They wash over softened mounds and a scatter of shells, the remains of the perfect castle. The sun on the water strikes up into his eyes till his vision trembles. It all dazzles. He turns and even the sand dazzles, light trapped inside millions of crystal grains. He trudges up the beach, back towards Connie's, which is the last place on earth.

FOURTEEN

'I like the shells,' Lisa says. 'Liked them the first time I was here.'

'Never mind the shells, we must get organised.'

'From the beach?'

'The little ones, not those big ones.' Connie points at a row of big cockle shells and conch shells. 'Patrick gave me those – and they're not purely decorative.'

'Hmm?'

'They have a function.'

'What?'

'I keep things in them.'

'Like what?'

'Look, we can't sit here all day. We must do something.'

'Yes.'

'Let me just wash your head, put a bit of ointment on.' Connie pours water into a little bowl, fetches toilet paper from outside. She puts a bit of salt in the water, because that's antiseptic, isn't it? She dabs with the lukewarm brine at the place on Lisa's head. The pale hair is stained brown, but the cut is not as bad as all that, won't need stitching. She squeezes a bit of the ointment from the old tube, ugly colour but it smells reassuring.

'Do what?'

'I'll cycle to the village and make those calls, then we'll be all right.'

'No.' Lisa reaches up and grabs Connie's hand.

'What?'

'Don't leave me. What if . . .'

'He won't come back.'

'You don't know that.' Lisa lets go and Connie picks up the comb and starts to comb the fine hair, different texture altogether to his, Tony's. Like baby hair. No, she doesn't know that he won't come back. But what else can they do? If Lisa was up to the walk, head not too bad, a bit of strength back in her voice, even a touch of colour in her cheeks. One thing might help, might make Lisa feel up to the walk. But . . .

'Connie,' Lisa says.

'Is this hurting?'

'Not . . . no, it's nice.'

'What then?'

'No . . . it doesn't matter.'

Connie frowns, lifts a pale skein of hair in her hand, notices that a black hair from the comb has fallen on to Lisa's. She picks it off, drops it on the floor. 'What?' she says again, can't stand it when people do that, leave her dangling.

'It's not the time.'

'Go on.' But Lisa says nothing. Drip, drip, drip. Must get a washer for that tap. So much needs doing, so much.

'Did you always love him?'

Connie pauses.

'I just wondered, always, *always* love him?'

Connie lets the hair fall, sits down. 'I . . . think so, yes.'

'Think?'

'At first I . . . I didn't know, sort of . . . besotted . . . I was so young. It was so surprising, so *flattering*. Then it's hard, he was such a lover, you know, *such* a lover.' She goes dreamy for a moment, then remembers what's happened. 'I'm sorry,' she says.

'That's all right.'

'Not that that's everything, that kind of skill. It can be tiresome.'

'Tiresome?'

'Yes. A performance, you know, sometimes clumsy love . . .' She blinks away the memory of Red's eyes, when he turned away that last time, when he looked from her to Patrick and back again and turned away.

'But it wasn't?'

'No it wasn't just that. I adored him – and I understood him, I understood that a lot of how . . . idiotic he seemed was a sort of pose and . . . oh I just understood him. We understood each other.'

'Nice word adore,' Lisa muses. 'Just another word for love, though.'

'No, it's simpler. Not more, nor less, but simpler.'

'Always?'

'No.' Connie is taken aback at the sudden snap in her own voice.

'No?' There's a noise outside, they both start and look at the door simultaneously, and then each other. But then it's quiet. Connie looks at the big conch shell by the cooker. Maybe that is the only thing to do. That bloody tap will drip.

'He was often with other women,' Connie says, 'well, I'm sure you know that. He was famous for it.'

'And you minded?'

'Of course I minded, wouldn't you? But . . . all under the bridge now. What's the use of minding now? Oh Patrick. People laughed, you know, he was a laughing stock . . . I thought . . . for some of the time I *didn't* adore him. I loved him, yes, I loved him sometimes like a mother loves a child. Wanting to protect, wanting to hide his eyes and stop his ears against the . . . you know.' It's like frail sheets of ice cracking as she talks, she almost forgets Lisa, just a pale shape across the table. 'I started to see him like that myself, as a sham, a fake, an idiot eccentric. Well, he was eccentric but . . . but listen, he was *not* a sham.' She lowers her voice which had risen almost to a shout. Shakes her head at her own foolishness. 'He believed in what he believed in and judging by . . .' She looks over at the big pink conch shell. 'He was right.'

Lisa follows her eyes. 'Judging by?'

The sun has gone behind the thickening clouds. In a moment Connie will switch on the light. She'll prise the conch shell off the wall and remove the little bottle from it. And she and Lisa will each take a drip, surely safe, to take a drip, the merest smear of the stuff each to give them the lift they need to walk to the village.

Connie focuses again on Lisa. Yes, she'll suggest that because they have to do *something*. They can't just sit here and wait for it to get dark. 'What were you going to ask?' she says.

'Nothing.'

'Please.'

'I can't. It just seems such a cheek.'

'Go on.'

'I just wondered if . . . if I could, if you would give me permission to write your life.'

'Ah.' Connie moves to the draining board and picks up a knife. She goes to the conch shell, sticks the point under it and twists.

'What are you doing?'

'You'll see. A biography, eh?'

'Yes. It would be . . . I can't think of anything I'd rather do.'

From outside comes the sudden harsh and gloomy cry of a

bird. They both start. 'Only a crow,' Connie says. She switches on the light and brings the big shell to the table. 'We *could* talk about a book,' she says, 'you'll have to let me think.'

FIFTEEN

Tony crouches, back against the wall, to get his breath back. To get up his nerve. Scrubby place, weeds, crap everywhere, carcass of a sea-bird, red ribs exposed. So this is your chance, Tony. Get in there and wipe the slate clean, two weak women, wipe it clean with whatever, knife or axe or the stretchy nylon leg of a pair of tights. With your own hands alone. Almost anything can be used to kill with. Slate could be wet and shiny clean in a few moments if you only have the balls. Then leg it back to London and start again. Start. Afresh. What though, oh what?

A sudden harsh cry. Christ. Crow, black wings heavy, black wings, curtains, hair. Fuck. Cool it, only a bird.

He stands, a fierce fizz running down his legs as blood returns to cramped muscles. Everything edged with white, a kind of light like sun but everywhere. Dazzle like salt. All that is needed is the walk round, the step through the door, surprise on his side, acts of violence that are necessary. Then off. Could torch the place. His mind flicks contents, take Patrick, yes. Patrick's portrait and Patrick's stuff, but torch the rest. The women's bodies and the wreck of a place. But Patrick let him down, torch fucking Patrick, too then. No. Take the portrait? How? Too big to run with, conspicuous. He almost grins imagining himself on the bus, the train with the painting. Conspicuous or what? But canvas can be cut and folded.

He leaves his stuff on the ground and walks silently up the side of the house, every foot placed with care. No sound from within. Passes the toilet door with its foul smell, passes the spare gas canisters, the old bicycle with cobwebs in its basket. The crow follows, hopping heavily, making more sound with its claws than Tony with his feet.

It's cold. Sun gone now so why the white fuzz, like haloes everywhere? A sharp slant of rain stings his face. He stands back against the wall looking sideways into the kitchen window. Sees nothing, moves round, face pressed against the salt- and sand-powdered glass. As he peers through the light is switched on. Dull swing of bulb. Benson sits down. Lisa has something wrapped round her, some old rag of a blanket. Blonde hair against it, looks for a moment like white hair, old hair, someday she'd be old like Benson anyway. Old wrinkled bitch. They all go that way if they live.

A chink like a spoon stirring brings moisture to his mouth. A sensation, weird, like a hooked finger creeping between his ribs. Some good woman somewhere in another life than this, hot tea and a sugar biscuit. Banish, it cannot be. The fucking crow, fluttering its filthy feathers about him, bouncing round his feet. Fuck off. He aims a kick and catches it as it lifts, a feather falls, it cries out like some old gears grinding. Lisa raises her head from whatever it is she's looking at and looks straight at the window. Tony falls to his knees. Did she see? Guts sudden hot liquid like he'll shit himself. But no. You don't, hear me? You don't do that. Don't lose it now. Hold it, hold it. OK. Waits. Waits. Slowly rises, looks through window and they're still there, same attitudes. Didn't see. Pretty hair in the light. That soft flop of her limp neck. But it is *OK*, just look at her. Those open eyes that let you in. She's OK.

Lisa lifts a cup to her lips. Dark on her hair where the

blood is. Christ. Things on the table. A shell? Benson lifting something, talking, Lisa head on one side, listening, a little frown. What's stopping you, Tony? Clean slate, clean shiny wet slate. And begin again. Haven't got the balls to get in there, is that it? See yourself banged up again? See that and you're lost. Stomach growls, thinks of that cassoulet, warm and brown and rich. Thinks of queuing for grey scoops of mash, orange beans, tomatoes leaking their watery juice. The belching, farting, stinking racket, assault on the ears, the guts, the . . . heart. Can't hack it? Not that – it's the light and heat and two women drinking tea. Can't smash that. Just go. Let them be.

You disappoint me, Tony.

He starts to turn away – but – what are they looking at? Leaning forward. Lisa taking something from Benson, holding it between her finger and thumb, squinting. It's not. Can't be. Cannot be unless she's a fucking liar, Benson, well, why not? Lisa holding what his life had been heading for, between her white finger and thumb. Can that be?

No.

But what else. What?

Tony bursts into the room. There. Two gasps, slow motion. Smell of dead flowers, food, Calor gas. He doesn't look at the pale-blue eyes.

'What's that?'

Nothing. Benson seems to be about to speak but nothing comes. Lisa crosses her hands across her chest. One hand grasping the little bottle.

'What's that?' Still nothing. Tony crunches to the table over the flowers. 'It's the elixirs, isn't it, isn't it? Where was it?'

But they don't need to say. His eyes fall on the big shell, its pink shiny lips curled back like a sneer. He grasps Benson's thin shoulder. Christ, she's got bones like a fucking bird. Red all round her mouth where the tape was. Grabs Lisa's wrist, bitch won't let go, prises the fingers back, snap then, snap, he doesn't care.

'Let him have it.' Benson's voice.

'I'll let *you* have it.' He cringes at that, pathetic, he could kill not to have said that, for no one to know he said that with such . . . pathetic menace. But they are menaced. Not so pathetic then. No. Benson is actually shuddering. 'This is the elixirs. You fucking lied.'

'Yes. I fucking lied.'

'Don't take the piss.' But he backs away. It's dawning like a big soft sunrise that this is it. This is what he came for. He has what he wants. Patrick didn't fail him after all. He has the elixirs, or one anyway. He has it. He fucking has it.

'I'll take this,' he says. 'Is this all? Where's the rest?'

'It's all that he left. Believe it or don't believe it, that's the truth.'

'So I'll have it.'

'It's the Seventh Step,' she says.

The bottle feels faintly warm in his hand. Dares to look at Lisa, her light eyes flaring dark. *The Seventh Step*.

'Nothing *we* can do to stop you, a big strong man like you.' Benson getting it back now, Christ she's got guts. Looking at him with those bright dare-you eyes. Well, sod her, sod the pair of them. Can't wait for this, won't wait. Take this and know what next. That question answered. This is for you, Tony, from Patrick. You made it, you *made* it. Got here, found it. Christ, it's true, it's real, it's *here*. Can hardly believe the feel of the real bottle in his hand as he goes up that ladder. Rain lashing now, won't go out in that. Rain against the skylight streaming, but so fucking what.

Listen – but they're not following, saying nothing. Maybe

a murmur. Darkish so he switches on the lamp. Tries to unscrew the top of the bottle, kind of stuck up with something, wax, flakes of it stick under his nail. Fucking mess here, tape and women's tights and the sketches which he's hardly even glanced at. And look, Patrick there, smiling, *winking*, is he? At last. Strange light coming from him, like a kind of glow. Halo. Haloes are common. Let's see.

Tony unscrews the lid. He squeezes his hips into Benson's chair and strains his eyes to read the faded writing on the label. *Elixir 7*, it says. *Bliss. Bliss* – and in Patrick's own handwriting too. Can hardly believe it. He grins, shakes his head, grins again. This is it then. At last, at long long last. The seventh step. Bliss.

'Cheers, mate,' he says, raising the bottle to Patrick, pausing with it by his lips, how much to take? Oh Christ after all this doesn't give a flying fuck just swig it, just . . . swallow . . . all . . .

SIXTEEN

Connie presses her knuckles against her mouth. Still sore from the tape, still a stickiness in the little hairs. But a sort of smile stretches her lips. Lisa widens her eyes. But they say nothing, just listen, hear the click of the lamp being switched on, the creak of the floor. 'Cheers, mate,' Tony says and then . . . a long quiet. Then a moan. Connie nods, remembering. Lisa opens her mouth but Connie holds up a finger. 'Wait,' she whispers. 'It's all right, just wait.' They listen to Tony moaning softly and continuously for a few moments, like someone experiencing the utmost pleasure, someone far beyond the restraints of self-consciousness, someone in a private heaven. And then his voice rises. 'Oh Christ, so beautiful, oh Christ, oh Patrick, so fucking beautiful . . . fuck . . . ing . . . hell . . . fuck . . . ing . . . bliss.'

And then quiet. Connie's heart is stuttering in her chest, she's feeling what? Relief/release? Lisa's face so *quizzical* it's almost funny. Another inappropriate urge to laugh. And a rush of memory taking her breath away because it was just like, just exactly like. Oh the words differed slightly. Patrick not so profane of course, but . . . and with Patrick she was there to see his face transfigured before her eyes, from old to young, from ravaged to smooth and beautiful.

They had made love in the hot slick of syrup sun that fell through the skylight on a July afternoon. And then Patrick had said that it was time. Connie had refused to take the elixir first. She had not liked to say that she was frightened, not liked to spoil the mood, the glow of love that still radiated from their skins so that you could almost see it tremble in the air between them. 'It will be even more extraordinary than that was,' he had promised, stroking her hip. 'There is some risk,' he'd admitted. She said she'd watch him for the effect and then take hers. But, seeing that effect, immediate, overwhelming, bliss-ful, *final*, she had not. Not ready then to die, not even with her love. Guilty ever since that day for her failure of nerve, not constant guilt but darts and gleams of it, catching her unaware. Though surely, clearly, she did right.

'Last time,' she says to Lisa, recovering her breath, 'I couldn't believe the beauty.'

'What?'

'Patrick's final experiment.'

'What?'

'Patrick blended this and . . .'

'What is happening up there?'

'He will be dead.' Lisa stares across the table at her. 'This was the end of the experiment. I was telling you it was dangerous but I thought one smear on our lips might . . . but now he has gone.'

'Connie.' The irises of Lisa's eyes have been eclipsed by the black.

'He looked so beautiful when he died. Patrick. So young. I shaved him.'

'What?'

'All our time together I wanted him to shave. I wanted him to cut that hair. And when he was sitting there, so beautiful in his chair, I couldn't resist doing it, just to see how he would look.'

'The portrait,' Lisa says.

'Yes, I painted the portrait.'

'Why he looked so strange and young . . . and . . . and . . .
smooth.'

'That's it, dear.'

'Oh my God.' Lisa half chokes, half laughs. 'This is so . . .
this is crazy. I hardly believe . . .'

'And now, I think, *he* will be dead.' They both look up at
the trap-door.

'And you were going to let us take that?'

'I was saving it till I wanted to go. A fine way to go. But I
thought after your . . . ordeal . . . and mine that just a smear
on our lips might buck us up. I didn't want to kill *us*.'

Lisa sits and stares at Connie, taking it in, her teeth
gnawing at her lip until Connie's scared she'll make it bleed.

'So that's what happened to Patrick. He poisoned himself?'

Connie considers. 'That seems a crude way of putting it.'

'But he took something and it made him die.'

'He knew the risk. Thought it worth taking.'

Lisa frowns, twisting a strand of hair around her finger.
'But *why*, Connie, why doesn't anybody know what happened to him? Why did you say he'd disappeared?'

Connie pauses. Her hand scrunches the little cushion on
her lap, the one she made from Patrick's shirt and stuffed
with Patrick's beard and hair. 'He would have been a
laughing stock. He already was, but . . . can you imagine
. . . his, his *vision* gone so wrong.'

Lisa frowns. 'I suppose.'

'The joke is, the joke of it really is that that stuff is . . . the
elixirs were . . . *amazing*, transforming . . . they were what
he said they were, they did what he said they did, but who,
who, would believe? If even I had doubted . . .'

'But it wasn't meant to kill.'

'No, of course not. He just got the dosage wrong. Needed
more experiments.'

'Couldn't someone else have carried it on? Worked it out properly?'

Connie shakes her head. 'No, dear, no. He was a one off. Believe me when I say that no one else could ever have followed his logic. Besides he hardly wrote anything down. Kept it all up here.' She taps her temple. 'I took the bits left over, in the days after his death, to help me, you know, to pull me through it . . . that loss . . . and it was, was what he said it was . . . Joy, Peace, Euphoria, all the seven except Bliss. I didn't take the Bliss, for obvious reasons.' She looks at the ceiling.

Another long pause. Connie is suddenly desperate for another cup of tea. She could drink gallons of tea. It is safe, all right, all safe. The madman has died a blissful death. No need for the police now. She gets up to put on the kettle.

'You could wash,' she says.

Lisa shakes herself as if from a trance. 'Sorry?'

'Well, we don't need the police, do we?'

'Shouldn't we . . .'

'What?' The gas lights with a cheerful whoosh.

'Well, report the . . . the death . . . to them. If he is dead. Shouldn't we check?'

'He's dead all right. Don't see the point of involving the police.'

'But.'

'People disappear all the time.' Connie puts tea-bags in the pot. 'Are you hungry, there's a bit of nice stew left.' She turns to catch Lisa staring at her in a most peculiar way. 'What is it?'

'Constance, what did you do with Patrick?'

'I'll put the stew on to warm anyway.'

'After you'd shaved him and painted his portrait. What did you do?'

Connie brings the teapot to the table and fills her pipe.

'What?'

Connie pours two cups of tea and lights her pipe. 'Sugar?' she asks and stirs three spoonfuls into each cup. They need it, blood sugar, what with all the stress and shock.

'There are things you'd put in a biography and things you wouldn't.'

'Absolutely. Now *what*?'

'Is that a promise, dear?'

Lisa sighs. 'Yes.'

'When I'm dead, you can say what you like but I'm far from dead.'

'You can say that again.'

'Well. I put him under the floorboards.'

'What?' Lisa half rises from her chair.

'Not here. In there.' Connie nods at the bedroom door.

'Oh my God.'

'Buried, you understand, under the sand under the floorboards, oh several feet down.' Connie sucks on her pipe, a lovely deep gurgling sound, sweet pungent smoke in her mouth. There are still these small pleasures. Lisa sits and gawps.

'Drink your tea.'

Lisa takes an absent-minded sip. 'Oh,' she says, 'so you've lived, practically on top of him, for all these years?'

'I haven't *slept* in there, except once.' She shudders, remembering the dreadful night, lying on the damp and mouldering bed like a prisoner with that poor lunatic out here.

Lisa cups her palms round her tea and sips. Her white forehead is furrowed as she thinks. 'So . . . assuming he, Tony, is . . . well, *dead*, what do we do with him? If we're not informing the police I mean.'

Connie looks at the bedroom door.

'No! We can't.'

'I don't see why not.'

'Constance, this is *mad*.'

Connie shrugs. Her neck hurts. But it's all falling into place, as things tend to if you're patient. Later, the village, phone from shop, appointment at doctor's, taxi for Lisa and she can get off home. End of an incident and then she can think. Nice as Lisa is, Connie can't think straight with her in the house. And so much to think about, so much to take stock of now. So much changed. Can't live with anyone, think with anybody else alive in the house. Solitude has become habitual and it's not a bad habit. There are worse.

'Wouldn't we be . . . isn't it illegal, we might get done for something. Murder?'

'Oh come on, dear, be sensible. We both know it wasn't murder. If you want to write, what do they call it, an authorized biography, then you, we, keep quiet about the whole . . . sorry mess.'

'But . . .'

'And after what he did to you . . .'

'They'd find the body and ask why didn't we . . .'

'How?'

'How what?'

'Would they find the body? Why look here?'

'I looked for him here.'

'I don't somehow think he'll have told many people.'

'Maybe not, but . . .'

'We'll have some stew to give us strength. And then we'll go up and fetch him. And then we'll bring him down and you can help me bury him. If I can do it, you can do it. And then I'll cycle to the shops and phone for a taxi for you. And you can go home and write your book.'

'You make it sound so simple.'

'Don't make difficulties where there aren't any.'

Lisa opens her mouth and shuts it again.

'And at least it's only sand we have to dig,' Connie says. 'We can do it, dear.' She pats Lisa's hand.

The casserole lid lifts as the stew inside bubbles, and releases a waft of warm fragrance. Connie gets up to turn down the flame.

Tony is sitting upright in the chair. His eyes are wide open and staring straight at Patrick's portrait. On his face is the most beatific smile. It *is* a beautiful face. Connie approaches and presses on his eyelids to hide the terrible blissful black shine. Behind her Lisa puts her hand over her mouth and gags.

'It's all right,' Connie says. 'He's gone.'

'But . . . I've never seen . . .'

'A corpse?'

Lisa shakes her head, face white, both hands clamped over her mouth. She's trembling.

'Think what he did to you,' Connie says. 'Think about it. He won't do that again.'

Lisa kneels down on the sleeping bag, her fair hair covering her face. Connie looks back at Tony. It is sad of course, a young man dead, all that health, strength, grace, those beautiful bones, that wonderful hair. But you have to keep your head on these occasions. Stiffly she bends to remove the little brown bottle from his still-warm grasp, looks at Patrick's spidery writing just legible on the label. *Elixir 7*, it says. *Bliss*. Connie closes her eyes, remembering. Her lips against his smile, trying to breathe life into him, hand on the stilled heart. How she did love him. Yes, yes, she did.

She looks at Lisa. 'When you're ready, dear,' she says, 'we'll move him down.'

SEVENTEEN

December sunshine slants through the window and makes thistledown of Lisa's hair. 'Are you ready to go then?' she says. 'Is this really all?' She nods towards the small suitcase, two boxes that wait by the door.

'What would I want with any of this lot?' Connie gestures at the room, the squint table, chipped crockery, the gas-heater.

'I suppose.'

'It's furnished, my new flat. It's heated. I won't know myself. Tea before we go?'

'If we've got time.' Lisa looks at her watch. 'Won't it be funny having Christmas somewhere else?'

Connie fills the kettle, listening for the last time for the judder in the pipes, the fierce spurt of water. Funny's putting it mildly. She feels a pang but she *will* not be sad to be leaving. Last night she didn't sleep, afraid to sleep in case she dreamt. If Lisa asks if she is sad she will say no.

'So what's it like?'

'Sea-front, top of a house, stairs, but I can still manage *stairs*, I hope.' A prickle in her voice. Moving somewhere more convenient is not the end, nor the beginning of the end. Don't let anyone think *that*. She's not *that* old.

'But do you like it?'

'Sea view. Near the shops. There's a laburnum out the

back window. Love that in spring, that *savage* yellow. Light. Warm. What more could I want?' She asks the question ironically but actually it's true. There's nothing much more she could want for since it's impossible to travel back and take another track, or to breathe life into the dead. The gas is nearly gone, it putters weakly, pale-blue petals, but maybe enough to boil just one more kettle on.

Lisa sits, sinks rather, on to a chair. 'You all right, dear?' Connie notices how pale she's gone, those apple cheeks faded.

'Fine. No, I guess it just brings it back to me. You know. Being here.' Her eyes dart to the bedroom door and away again. 'I'm still having counselling and all that. It's just . . . being here. It just came over me.'

Connie says nothing but of course she agrees and that is why she has to leave, now. The doctor said she needed warmth, proper facilities, but it is memory that is driving her away. The knowledge of what's in there under the sand, one body on top of the other's bones. One little brown bottle thrown in, too. It was all right when it was only Patrick but now she has nightmares, she keeps this quiet, silly, *silly* nightmares about bones embracing and the worst of it is the noise of the bones, the faint almost chink, the intimate rub of them. Does Lisa have nightmares, too? She studies her face, but there is no sign. The roses already coming back in her cheeks, face familiar now as a friend's. She has become, Connie supposes, a friend. Visited once, a month after the . . . ordeal . . . with a publisher's contract for the biography and a bottle of champagne. And a present for Connie, a working mobile phone. On which she has kept in regular contact, and now she's here with a hired car to drive Connie to her new home.

The gas pops and goes out.

'Blast,' Connie says. 'Damn it. What say a drink then? Just a farewell drop. There is only a drop.'

'You've been here *so* long . . .'

'How it has to be.' Connie sets her jaw. She pours the dregs of a bottle of Grouse into two cups. 'Cheers.'

Lisa lifts the cup to her lips. 'Cheers.'

They are quiet. Connie looks round at the place, the cold sun is merciless in its exposure of the rot and grime. Funny how you can live with that so long and never notice and then suddenly . . . suddenly it is all too much. The tap drip, drips. Don't need a new washer now. That's one thing.

'Been painting?' Lisa asks.

Connie just smiles.

'That's *great*, Connie.'

'Yes.' Connie runs her thumbnail along a deep groove in the grain of the table. She will miss this table. 'Funny, now I've started I can't understand why I ever stopped. It's so . . . it feels so *right*. I've so much missed the colours. Tell you the truth I'm cross with myself for wasting all that time. Thirty bloody *years*. In a *trance*.'

'God. It's so so strange.' Lisa flattens her hands out on the table top. 'Life. I mean that . . . that awful . . . but it's left you *painting* again, odd, amazing, I don't know what to say.'

'Please, nothing about silver . . .'

'I *wouldn't*.'

The sound of the sea is soft, sucking and sighing. And it will be all right because in Connie's new flat, if she opens the windows and strains her ears, she'll still be able to hear and see it, same old North Sea, same rhythm. And there's a telly, too. She really will not know herself.

'Well, anyway.' Lisa gets up, the chair grating and toppling behind her. She picks it up. 'Let's get your stuff out to the car.'

'Patrick's still upstairs, and . . .'

'Of course. I'll fetch it down.' Lisa goes to the ladder.

'No, no let me,' Connie says, cursing herself. Her hands are slippery as she grasps the ladder. She hadn't known what to do but this is surely wrong. She should have wrapped it, hidden it from Lisa, especially now. It will upset her, shock her. Whatever was she thinking? 'You stay down,' she says but Lisa comes up right behind her.

Connie steps up into the bright space. The light is cold and icy sharp on the two faces. Patrick and now Tony. Lisa gasps as she steps up. The face fills the canvas, the hair blue, the finely modelled face stark, kind of hungry, the mouth open as if it would speak. But the eyes, it is the eyes that Connie is proud of, that terrify her, that did so even as she painted. They yearn, they almost burn. Black eyes pierced with light, a cold hungry burning.

'Sit down,' Connie says. 'I should have warned you. Sorry.' *Stupid old woman, stupid stupid tactless old bitch.*

'No.' Lisa walks towards the painting as if she is walking through a dream. She puts out a finger to touch the painted cheek.

Connie's nails dig into her palms. The girl could wreck it, take a knife to it, rip the canvas to shreds and she would be perfectly justified. She might just faint away and then what would Connie do?

But, 'It's amazing,' she breathes at last.

'Oh.' Connie lowers herself down in her armchair, her own legs gone weak as string.

'It's so . . . brilliant. You've got him so . . . I'm no judge really but I think . . .'

Connie looks from Tony's terrible eyes to Patrick's and then to Lisa standing so close, gazing so intently at her work. She still feels like the girl awaiting the verdict that first time,

Sacha and Patrick inspecting her work the first time ever. That girl still there trembling inside.

'I'm so glad you're not upset. I should have warned . . .'

'No, no.' Lisa runs her finger slowly over the painted face. 'Funny,' she says, her voice full of discovery, 'if he wasn't dead I'd hate him but, well, maybe it's just because he's dead I *don't*, not like you'd think.'

'No.'

She shakes her head slowly. 'It's like he's got a sort of gap in him, the way you've painted him. You can see it here,' she touches the eyes, 'a sort of gap. I couldn't see it with him in the . . . well, face to face but . . .'

It is so much what Connie wants to hear that for a moment she's speechless. It still works. She can still do it. Nothing in the world could give her more pleasure than that. 'Yes,' she says at last, 'that's *it*, that's what I saw in his eyes. Poor boy.' She darts a look at Lisa. 'Not that what he did . . .'

'It's all right. And I'm glad he's dead but . . .' She waits a long time before continuing and Connie knows just what she's going to say. 'I'm glad he died the way he did.'

'Blissfully,' Connie snorts. 'Yes, dear, yes.'

The brightness in the room is suddenly quenched as a cloud covers the sun. They stand before Tony's portrait gazing at the blue of the hair, the terrible shine of the eyes, black splintered with blue, those frost needles of light a genius touch.

Lisa puts the tip of a finger on each eye. 'It is amazing,' she says again. She reaches up to lift the paintings off the wall, first Tony, then Patrick, and she carries them down.

Connie stands alone in the room. She puts her arms around herself and shivers. She can't believe now the moment has come that she is really going. She looks at the filthy yellow chair, at the floor scattered with the crisp little bodies of moths, bees and wasps, at the two empty nails on the wall.

'I'll start loading the car,' Lisa calls up. 'All right?'

'Yes, dear, yes.'

Connie goes through the trap-door and down the ladder, rung by rung by rung. Halfway down she stops, closes her eyes to see Patrick's smile.

'Goodbye, my lover,' she says.

ABOUT THE AUTHOR

Lesley Glaister was born in Wellingborough in 1956.
She teaches a Master's Degree in Writing at Sheffield
Hallam University and she is the author of
Honour Thy Father, which won the Somerset
Maugham and a Betty Trask award, *Trick or Treat*,
Digging to Australia, *Partial Eclipse*, *The Private
Parts of Women*, *Easy Peasy*, *Sheer Blue Bliss* and
Now You See Me. She lives in Sheffield.

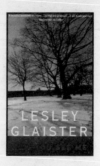

Now You See Me Lesley Glaister
£6.99 0 7475 5771 3

'A beautiful bombshell of a story ... painful and gorgeous ... it will break your heart'
Independent on Sunday

Since walking out on her life at sixteen, Lamb has lived alone in the gaps between other people's lives. Secretly inhabiting the cellar of an elderly man for whom she cleans, she keeps to herself, her life a precarious balancing act – until she meets Doggo, a young criminal on the run. Both strangers to the concept of the truth, Doggo and Lamb are drawn together, glimpsing in one another the possibility of finding solace and maybe even love. But with secrets too dark to admit to even themselves, let alone someone else, first they must learn just to trust in each other ...

'*Now You See Me* boasts a protagonist so heartbreakingly well-realised that you are forced to live through her eyes, in her head, her heart, her skull ... if only all fiction made us worry and care so hard, posed us such dreadfully different questions' *Guardian*

'A beautifully articulated and tender love story ... it possesses an unsettling resonance' *Daily Mail*

'Exceptionally good ... an edgy, occasionally disturbing, beautifully written and emotionally engaging love story that moves with the pace of a thriller ... wonderfully atmospheric, rich and deeply satisfying' *Yorkshire Post*

'A strong and beguiling novel, Glaister's steady, unobtrusive prose building to reveal layer upon layer of long-buried tragedy' *Sunday Times*

To order from Bookpost PO Box 29 Douglas Isle of Man IM99 1BQ www.bookpost.co.uk
email: bookshop@enterprise.net fax: 01624 837033 tel: 01624 836000

bloomsburypbks

www.bloomsbury.com